Every Witch Way but Fiend

Magical Misfits Mysteries - book 7

K.E. O'Connor

K.E. O'Connor Books

EVERY WITCH WAY BUT FIEND

ISBN: 978-1-915378-53-8

Written by: K.E. O'Connor

Chapter 1

Angel surprise

My paws barely touched the ground as I flew along, the scent of the weeping wind belter fresh in the air.

"Juno! You're going the wrong way. Dumb, stubborn cat."

I ignored Oleander Yockley's harsh whisper. He didn't have my finely attuned booping snooter, and I knew what I smelled. Sweaty fur and a splash of fear. The weeping wind belter we were chasing had dashed along this alleyway behind the stores in Crimson Cove less than a minute ago.

Weeping wind belters looked like adorable cats with overly large eyes, but if anyone attempted to pet a wild one, they'd soon discover the tears were toxic, and the small fluffy critters howled gales when angered.

Zandra Crypt, the most wonderful witch who'd ever walked this planet, appeared at the end of the alley and raced to join me.

"You got something?" Her face was pale in the moonlight and her dark hair tucked messily under a gray baseball cap with a witch's cauldron logo on the front.

"It's been here, recently."

"Oleander reckons he saw it head toward the beach." Zandra glanced along the alley, half-crouched and ever watchful for trouble.

"Then he needs his eyes tested. It's the last place the creature would go." Oleander wasn't known for his sharp intellect or amenable nature. Although he knew his critters, which was why he was kept on at animal control.

"We've got to catch this creature tonight. Angel Force has been on Barney's case all day because of reports of it causing damage to people's gardens. They're worried someone will get hurt if they confront it."

I slowed, lifted my booping snooter and inhaled deeply. "Weeping wind belters never hurt out of malice. Fear triggers their attacks. And if some fool stumbles on a den or attempts to pick one up because they think they're cute, it's no wonder they strike back. It's the correct behavior to deploy."

"Let's not have them strike back tonight, shall we? If we catch this one and no one gets injured, I'll call it a win," Zandra said. "And the sooner we get Angel Force off our backs, the better. Cythera has been in a massive grump for days."

"Follow me. I'm certain we're close." I trotted along the alleyway then stopped. It split off at the end, going left to right. "How's Randal doing?"

"He's nervous. I left him with Glenda, checking the streets. She can keep an eye on him and make sure he doesn't blow himself up."

Randal Nix was an adorably geeky tech mage who had an enormous crush on Zandra. The feeling was mutual. Unfortunately, my efforts to get them together had ended in failure. Which was why I'd persuaded Randal to come on this mission tonight. Spending quality time with the witch he adored would make him see he had to ask her out again.

Zandra was in the prime of her witchy prowess, and she wouldn't stay single forever. And I was certain Randal didn't want to miss the opportunity to make Zandra his life partner.

"Which way?" She looked along the dark alley. "I came from the left, and I didn't see the weeping wind belter go that way. Although I may have missed it sneak past while checking under piles of trash."

"The smell suggests this way." I headed along the alley, Zandra by my side.

Sometimes, working at animal control could be more admin than adorable critters, so I welcomed the opportunity to get out with the team and have a mini adventure. I understood the importance of checking licenses and ensuring everyone treated their animals well, but being on the streets, protecting an endangered magical creature from the idiots who may harm it, felt worthier.

There was a yelp and a loud thud as if someone had been thrown against a wall.

"That was Oleander." Zandra looked over her shoulder.

"He probably slipped. He's remarkably un-dexterous. Anyone would think he was crossed with an *ailuropoda melanoleuca*."

"And that's…"

"A Giant Panda. One of the clumsiest animals on the planet. Clumsy and lazy. They barely remember they need to breed. All they do is eat and sleep."

"That does sound like Oleander. Although I have no interest in his breeding activities."

I wrinkled my booping snooter. "Giant Pandas often trip over their own paws and end up tumbling around in a big fluffy ball. Humiliating when you consider it."

"Get it off me! Get it off me!" Oleander yelped.

"Uh-oh. That sounds bad," Zandra said. "Let's go see what's up with him."

We raced to the end of the alleyway, and a chaotic scene revealed itself. Oleander was flat on his back, and the weeping wind belter was attached to his face. Randal hovered by Oleander's feet, a metal spike in one hand. Knowing Randal, it was much more than a simple spike meant to stab.

"It burns," Oleander howled. "My skin!"

"It must be crying on him," Zandra muttered.

"Only because he angered the poor creature," I said.

The metal spike Randal held emitted a pink bolt of light. The weeping wind belter leaped away, and the light slammed into Oleander's head. He howled again and then went silent.

"Sorry! Sorry! It wasn't meant to hit you. And I only set it to stun." Randal stared at the spike then dropped it as if it had stung him.

"You think Oleander's dead?" I murmured.

Zandra sighed. "We'd better make sure he isn't. Think of the paperwork we'd have to complete if we returned with a fatality."

Randal lifted a hand when he saw us approach, but his attention was all on Zandra. Too much attention on her, so he missed the weeping wind belter leaping toward him.

As it blasted through the air, it opened its mouth and shrieked. A wind whipped up and slammed into Randal, knocking him to the ground. The critter dashed away, back to the shadows it had sprung from.

"Where the heck is Glenda?" Zandra's head whipped from side to side. "She was supposed to look out for these two and make sure this kind of thing didn't happen to them."

"She's over there. Watching the show." I waved a paw at a nearby bench, concealed in shadow.

Glenda Ridgeback was a powerful werewolf shifter, who'd been assigned to the Crimson Cove branch of animal control temporarily. She had a laid-back approach to her work, and from the looks of things, she'd decided babysitting Randal and Oleander wasn't on her agenda.

"Get over here!" Zandra gestured at her.

Glenda had her left foot propped on her opposite knee and her arms splayed across the back of the bench. "Awww. Must I? It's fun to watch those two fall flat on their faces. And you should have seen what Oleander did. It serves him right that sweetie pie jumped on his head and tried to kill him."

"It looked more like Randal was trying to kill Oleander with the lightning bolt thingy he was waving around," Zandra said.

"I didn't mean to hit Oleander." Randal remained on the ground, rubbing the back of his head. "And it's not a lightning bolt thingy. It's a spell particle enhancer."

While everyone bickered about who tried to kill who, I lowered to my belly and slunk toward the weeping wind belter. I could see its black eyes glinting in the gloom.

I got within three feet of the creature and stopped. "Greetings. I'm Juno. And I'd advise you most strongly not to touch the wonderful witch I arrived with. I'm her protector, and she is mine."

The weeping wind belter tilted its head from side to side in the most adorable fashion. Fluffy menace.

"You've caused a stir since coming to Crimson Cove. All that hard work destroying those gardens must be exhausting. How about you come home with us and have a break?"

"Home? More like prison," the weeping wind belter hissed, its voice a deep nasally grumble.

"Animal control isn't a prison. It's nice there. And we have snacks."

"All you want to do is capture and condemn." The creature's voice became a pale tremble of whisper on the wind.

I didn't let its quiet ways fool me. This little ball of fluff was lethal. "I'll admit, I believed the same until I got hired by them. Barney Hoffman runs this sector of animal control, and he's a decent man. He makes sure all animals in his care are treated fairly. Wouldn't you like a home with someone to take care of you? You wouldn't need to skulk in the shadows or worry about where your next meal was coming from. You'd be warm and loved."

The black eyes grew glossy. "Who would want this? Unlovable."

"Everyone who sees you thinks you're adorable. And you are when you're not whipping up whirlwinds or burning someone's face off with your tears. You just need to adjust your behavior a bit, and you'll find a happy home."

"They need to adjust their behavior! The skinny one who stinks of wet dog grabbed me. Rude!"

"My apologies for that experience. Oleander isn't known for his good manners. He made a mistake. We all do."

"What about the one who blasted me with the lightning? He wants me dead. Not a friend."

I glanced over my shoulder at Randal. "He has a heart of pure gold, but his equipment doesn't always work." I took a step closer. "It's our job to keep animals safe but also to stop them from hurting others. Come back with us, and we'll find you the right place to live. Somewhere where your wind can whirl free."

The creature snarled and lunged at me. Before it could whip me off my feet with a blast of power, a spell wrapped around it and suspended it in the air. It hissed and howled, punched and parried the magic, but the spell held firm, and the weeping wind belter was trapped.

I turned to see Zandra's arms outstretched and magic pouring from her fingertips.

She looked at me and winked.

Her power had changed since I'd gifted her some of my magic. It was stronger with a darker edge and had given her a new confidence.

I was glad I'd assisted my witch and ensured we'd lived to fight another day after dealing with a tricky demon, who enjoyed stealing bodies and wearing their skins, but in doing so, I'd lost a dream I'd held onto for so long. Now it was out of my reach.

Having gifted power to Zandra, I could never get back everything I'd lost. Would that mean I'd never return to my former glory? It was a question I was figuring out.

"Let me at that evil little monster. It owes me a new face!" Oleander was crawling toward the weeping wind belter on his hands and knees, his eyes bloodshot and tiny burn marks marring his cheeks.

I flicked a spell at him, which knocked him back down. "No revenge for you. Let's get this animal back to base and find it something to eat. It must be starving."

Glenda stalked over on her high black heels and slung an arm around Zandra's shoulders. "Good work, partner. The drinks are on me."

Half an hour later, and after we had secured the weeping wind belter in a comfy pen at animal control, we headed to the local bar next to Torrin Conner's garage, and Glenda ordered a round of witches' brews for the team.

"What are you celebrating?" Finn and Acer, Angel Force recruits, and Torrin, wandered over to the table we'd sat around.

"A successful capture." Oleander's face looked less pink after he'd applied a healing balm to his burns. "I had to make sure the ladies could manage a dangerous creature that was on the loose. We don't want them getting scared and screaming the place down."

Finn smirked. "I'm sure you were your usual knight in shining armor."

"He spent most of the time rolling about on the ground and complaining," I said.

"Typical Oleander style." Glenda kicked out a chair. "Join us."

They all grabbed chairs and settled around the table.

"What did you capture?" Acer was a new recruit at Angel Force and still on her probation period, but she was shaping up nicely, and I enjoyed her affable nature.

"A weeping wind belter," I said. "Adorable, but deadly. We'll find it the perfect home after a short period of rehabilitation."

"You can't rehabilitate some creatures," Oleander grumbled. "That thing was half-crazed. It tried to bite off my nose."

"You mishandled it," I said. "You're lucky you only got mild burns on your arms and face."

Oleander rubbed a finger against a pink mark on his skin. "It's not my fault my presence freaked it out. It must have guessed what I'd do to it if it misbehaved."

"Get on your knees and beg to be saved?" Finn said.

"Roll around like a clumsy Giant Panda?" Glenda flashed her eyebrows up at me. Her werewolf hearing was exquisite.

Oleander grabbed his drink off the table. "I'm going to find better company. You all suck." He stalked away.

"That guy can't take a joke." Glenda chuckled.

The group sipped their drinks and chatted about how their days had been.

"Everything okay?" Zandra leaned closer to Acer.

She stopped pulling apart a beer mat and rubbed her palms together slowly. "Sure. I mean, my family is coming for a visit. They're staying a few days and rented that empty mansion over on Fairy Lane. The one with the stone lions out the front."

"Fancy," I said.

"Showy." Acer's bottom lip jutted out.

"They're the reason we're here so soon after our shift ended." Finn joined in the conversation. "Acer needed to unwind before the family reunion."

"You don't get on with your family?" I said.

Acer sighed and picked at the edge of another beer mat. "It's complicated. I love them, but they aren't always great to be around. And they expect a lot from me. Especially my dad."

I nodded wisely. "You can't always pick your family."

"Funnily enough, they did pick me. I'm adopted, along with my four siblings. There's me, Rabdos, Laylah, Micah, and Forfax. They're all coming, too."

"It must be nice to have so many siblings."

"Yeah, it was okay. Sometimes, it was fun. But..."

"I get it," Finn said. "Half-angel children often have a rough time of it. There's a high chance of rejection by our birth parents because we're a mishmash. A lot of half-angels get dumped into care, and few of them get adopted. The stigma that we're unlucky is so dumb, but it sticks."

Acer's lips thinned. "Don't get me wrong, I'm grateful a family wanted me, but I didn't get any choice what kind of family I was going into."

"If you'd had a choice, would you have picked a different family?" Acer was oozing tension. Every family had its problems, but there was usually something to look forward to when you saw them.

"My parents are different. They're..." Acer's gaze went to the door as the bar quietened.

A group of half-angels stood with their wings partially opened as they inspected the bar and everyone in it.

Acer jumped to her feet and gulped. "That's them. My family loves to make an impression."

Chapter 2

Daddy issues

Acer stepped forward and bumped the table with her hip, almost knocking over everyone's drinks.

She grabbed the edge and steadied it. "Sorry. I... I should go say hello."

"You should take a few deep breaths." Zandra caught hold of Acer's hand. "It'll be okay. I always get tense when I see my family, too."

"Which you barely ever do," I muttered.

She slid me a glare. "What I meant was everyone's family is different, and they all have their quirks, which can be annoying, but I'm sure they'll be happy to see you."

"Yeah, doubtful."

"They made the effort to visit you in Crimson Cove," Randal said, still looking pale and shaken from his encounter with the weeping wind belter. "That must mean they're interested in your life."

Acer looked at the floor for a second. "Like I said, it's complicated. I'd better go over before Dad spots me lingering." She tugged down her white tunic, pulled back her shoulders, and strode over to meet her family.

Her father stood at the head of the group. He was angel-tall and brawny, but rather than the usual massive white angel wings, his wings were brown and stunted. There'd be no way he could use them to fly.

"Part angel, part orc?" I said to Zandra.

She nodded as she tugged on her bottom lip. "Could be."

Glenda tipped her seat forward and stared at the family. "He's firebrand hot! But I can never figure out an angel's age. That hunk of burly love could be anything from ninety to two hundred and fifty. Mix in the orc slow-aging genes, and it's anyone's guess how old he is."

"And I don't like to drool, but Acer's mother is also stunning." Finn stared at the sharply beautiful willowy figure standing beside Acer's father. She had long, straight brown hair down to her waist, and her form-fitting jade green catsuit left nothing to the imagination.

"It's what you get when you have such an unusual genetic mix," Randal said. "To ensure the healthiest child, it's best to procreate with someone who's the opposite magical being to you. Orc and angel pairings are rare. Rare equals unique beauty."

Glenda snort laughed. "That's how you plan on wooing your forever mate? Tell her she's got genetic material that's perfect for making beautiful babies with you?"

Randal's cheeks flushed. "I meant, it's a wonderfully diverse genetic stew."

Glenda tipped back her head and roared a laugh. "Even better. Let's talk about genetic stew over a romantic candlelit dinner, shall we, baby?"

"No! It's just that... well, look at them. They're remarkable. It's all to do with the gene pool. It's... well, I find it fascinating how a rare melding of DNA creates such striking results."

I patted Randal's hand with a paw. "Stop digging this particular genetic hole."

He gestured at the family again and then sighed. "I'd love a sample of their blood. Just out of curiosity."

When Randal got an idea in his head, he wouldn't shut up about it, no matter how many odd looks it got him.

I glanced at Zandra, and she appeared amused by Randal's stammerings. We were all used to his curious ways, and I was pleased she found his quirks adorable. She'd have to tolerate them once they became a couple.

I hopped onto her shoulder and leaned against her head.

Acer hadn't hugged any family member. She stood in front of them, shifting from foot to foot as her dad talked to her, one large hand resting on her shoulder.

"What's he done to his face? He's got bruises all down the right side," I said.

Zandra shook her head. "Maybe Acer's dad is into boxing. He's certainly into commanding the room. That kind of energy can draw the wrong attention if there are troublemakers around."

All conversation had died when the family entered, and everyone still watched them.

After talking to Acer for another moment, her father lifted his head and looked around. A satisfied smile spread across his face. He appeared to enjoy being the center of attention.

He strode to the bar, laid money on the counter, and then gestured around the room.

The bartender nodded, leaned back, and clanged a mottled yellow bell that hung on the wall behind the bar. "Drinks are on the house, courtesy of Mr. Morfiel."

The chatter started again as people dashed to the bar to get their free booze.

"There's a guy who knows how to win favor from strangers," I murmured.

"And he's oozing wealth." Glenda's eyes were narrowed as she inspected the family, a faint gleam of werewolf power in her gaze. "Check out the size of his wristwatch. And every item of clothing on that fine body is tailormade. Although, what's with the gold star pinned to his chest? Does Acer's dad think he's the sheriff around here?"

"What line of work is the Morfiel family in?" I said to Finn.

"Acer said something about retrieval work, but she didn't go into detail." He dipped his chin. "It looks like we can ask for ourselves, though. They're coming over."

Acer walked toward us with her family. The father took the lead, the mother one step behind him, and the siblings in a silent row behind them.

So far, I hadn't seen any of Acer's brothers or sister make a sound. They hadn't even greeted Acer when she met them. They even seemed to control their breathing and stride length, so they were in perfect unison with their parents.

Some of the tension lifting Acer's shoulders left her as she reached the table, and her smile grew genuine. There was even a flash of relief in her eyes. "These are some of my colleagues and friends. This is Finn from Angel Force. And I work closely with Randal Nix, Glenda Ridgeback, Zandra Crypt, and her familiar, Juno. This is my father, Erig Morfiel."

Finn stood to shake hands with everyone, an easy smile on his face. "It's a pleasure to meet you all. I enjoy working with Acer. I'm sure you're proud of her. She's an asset to Angel Force."

Erig shook Finn's hand. "I couldn't resist visiting to see what she's doing. We're always so entertained by her stories."

My gaze lasered on a long, silver chain attached to Erig's wrist. The links were thin, but they looked strong. The chain went up his arm, over his shoulder, and out of sight. As I followed the chain, I spotted a feathered head poking over his shoulder. I took a step forward, and the head vanished.

Erig turned to the rest of his family. "This is my wife, Ollia, and my other children, Rabdos, Forfax, Laylah, and Micah."

Rabdos was the largest and appeared to be the oldest, but only by a year or two. He was dressed similarly to his father in a tailored dark suit. His wings were whiter, and he had elf-like ears. He was the first of Acer's siblings to make eye contact with anyone.

Laylah was the smallest, with half-sized wings, a soft glow flickering beneath her skin. She was also beautiful and her hair cut into a cute pixie crop.

Micah and Forfax kept quiet but nodded at everyone. Forfax wore an oversized trench coat as if trying to make himself look bigger. Micah kept his gaze down and his hands clasped, looking like he wanted to be anywhere but here.

Just like Erig, they had star pins on their clothing in different colors. Ollia's was silver, as was Rabdos's. Micah had a bronze star, while Laylah's was gray. The stars must be a tradition handed down through the family, but I had no clue what they signified.

"Welcome to Crimson Cove," Finn said. "Acer's been looking forward to your visit. She's talked about nothing else for days."

"Of course, she has." There was a slight smirk on Erig's face. "It took some persuading before I was convinced this was the right career path for her. Still, that's what probation is for, and I check with her superior for any issues."

Acer jerked her head back. "You've spoken to Cythera about me?"

"Naturally. It's important no member of my family causes us embarrassment."

Acer's mouth dropped open.

Erig made no apology for this intrusion into her life. "And when she's done having her fun, there'll be a role for her in my company."

"This is what I've always wanted to do," Acer said. "You know that."

"She wants to be just like her father," Ollia said, her low voice just loud enough to be heard over the bar chatter. "Her real father, that is."

"I am her real father." Erig's smile froze in place. "We must let our children make their mistakes. Providing they learn from them and grow, it's never a wasted opportunity. And public service has its place, but a decade or two of working for Angel Force, and Acer will beg to come back to the family business. After all, private practice is where fortunes are made."

"And what business are you in?" I said.

"I profit from my secret talent." Amusement glittered in Erig's dark eyes.

"It's hardly a secret talent, my love," Ollia said. "Everyone knows what you can do. You're the best of the best."

"There's no doubting that." He brushed a thumb under Ollia's chin. "Don't you forget it."

She discreetly stepped back. "Never."

"So, what are you the best at?" I was tiring of this blackguard and his posturing.

"Acer, tell your friends how proud you are of me. I'm surprised they don't already know about my business."

"I've been so busy since I got here. I haven't told them much about any of you." Acer picked at a thumbnail until her mother slapped her hand. She sighed. "Dad can find anything lost."

"Like what?" Randal sat straight in his seat, always intrigued by a curiosity.

"You name it, I can find it," Erig said. "A lost person, a missing vehicle, lost documents. Anything."

"There must be limits to what you can find." Glenda arched a painted eyebrow.

"Sometimes, things are well hidden, so it takes money and effort to discover them. And I need something connected to the lost item. So, for example, if a person is missing, I need to make contact with a blood relative, so I have a vibe to search for. But if there's something that links me to the object or person, it can be located."

"That's astonishing," Randal said.

"It is. And I am." Erig rubbed his hands together. "It's one reason we're here. We're celebrating a business win."

"What did you win?" Zandra said.

"I've just opened my five hundredth branch of Morfiel Retrievals."

"Sounds more like a fancy breed of dog," Glenda murmured.

Erig ignored her, even though Glenda's mutter wasn't quiet. "We thought we'd join Acer and have a joint celebration. Her new little job, and my vast new office."

Acer chewed on her bottom lip. "Dad also wants to see if Crimson Cove could be a good place to have another satellite office."

"There's never any harm in mingling pleasure and business," Erig said. "And I've heard interesting things about this town. It could be a lucrative investment to set up a site here. And if I do, I'll have more opportunities to check in on Acer. Make sure she doesn't get bored of the angels."

"There's no need for you to check up on me. I know what I'm doing."

Erig prodded her shoulder. "You're not wearing your star."

Her cheeks flushed. "It didn't seem right, now I'm not—"

"A part of the family?" Erig shook his head. "You will always be my daughter. Don't lose sight of that because I've permitted you a dash of freedom. Wear it tomorrow."

"What's so special about the stars?" I said.

Erig took a second to consider his answer. "They display worthiness." The chain around his wrist tinkled, and the small, feathered head appeared again. Was that a phoenix clinging to Erig's back?

I nudged Zandra with my booping snooter to see if she'd noticed the bird, but the head vanished again before she got a look.

"Where have you arranged for us to eat?" Erig said to Acer.

"Um... I forgot. It's been busy at work, so I didn't have time to book anywhere."

"Acer! Your father is hungry. You know what a big appetite he has. How will we find anywhere decent to eat if you haven't pre-booked?" Ollia brushed something off Acer's shoulder, a disdainful look in her blue eyes.

"Sorry. I meant to. I got distracted."

"You should eat here," Zandra said. "The burgers are great. They do a mean triple stack with cheese, bacon, and curly fries."

Erig's top lip curled a fraction before a fake smile appeared. "This isn't an establishment I'd normally consider dining in."

"If this place is too down market for you, try Remus's bar, The Honeyed Vein." Glenda was no longer smiling. "It's an exclusive place. Once they let you join as a member, your life will change forever."

As tempting as it was to encourage Erig to take his family into a vampire den, it was unfair on Acer to have her family slaughtered on the first night of their arrival.

Zandra nudged Glenda. "This bar is great. They poached the chef from some five-star restaurant in Highland Vale."

"That's right. He used to work at the Tipsy Piglet. That place had a wait list of six months because his food was so incredible," Finn said.

"Why would a chef of such renown come to a place like this?" Erig glanced around.

"For an easier life. He no longer wanted to work eighty plus hours a week and be yelled at by snooty customers. Here, he can relax, do what he loves, get well paid, and not be left staring at the ceiling every night because he's so stressed. Everyone wins."

"The food is great here," Acer said. "We should try it. There's a table big enough for us in the corner."

Erig looked around again, not convinced. "Micah, have you heard of this Tipsy Piglet?"

Micah stepped forward. "I have. The chef's reputation hasn't been oversold."

"Micah knows his food. This is fine. And I'm hungry. Let's eat." Ollia turned on her heels and strutted to the empty table. There were more than a few pairs of eyes on her as she walked away.

Erig glared at his retreating wife then shrugged. "We'll go somewhere for a fine dining experience tomorrow. Burgers all around tonight." He turned and gestured for the rest of the family to follow him.

My eyes widened. Clinging to his back was a magnificent rainbow-striped phoenix. The silver chain was attached to one of its legs, and its head was down.

"You reckon he's got a permit for that bird?" Glenda thumped her chair down, her eyes narrowed on the feathered creature. "They're endangered, so few people can legally keep them. And that bird sure ain't no familiar. What's he playing at by chaining such a beauty?"

"I'll ask him. Be right back." I jumped off Zandra's shoulder and followed Erig to the bar, where he was ordering champagne. I hopped up beside him. "Nice phoenix. How long have you had it?"

Erig kept his gaze forward as he popped a candy from his pocket into his mouth. "He's magnificent. Only a hundred left in the wild."

"No kidding! I have to ask, since I work for animal control, but we'll need to see your permit."

Erig still didn't waste energy looking at me, simply munched another candy. "Smoke, do you hear that? This adorable cat is looking after your welfare."

The phoenix, Smoke, stared at me with unblinking eyes.

"I'm sure you understand why I'm asking." I kept my tone pleasant, although I flexed my murder mittens. "Animals come first in my profession. And I wouldn't be doing my—"

"I'll get Acer to show you a copy of my permit." Erig turned away from the bar.

"One more thing. Is it true you can find anything lost?"

He finally glanced at me. "I didn't lie about my extraordinary skills."

"Then I need you to help me find something. It's not a person or an object; it's magic. Can you do that?" My heart beat fast. If Erig could truly find anything, then he'd help me retrieve my lost magic.

His chest rose as he inhaled deeply. "Magic isn't simple to discover."

"So, you lied?"

"I never said that. But it'll take time and money." He extracted a white paper bag from his pocket and took out another chocolate-coated candy.

"Then I want to do business with you," I said. "When can we meet, so I can tell you what I need and hear your terms?"

Erig's eyebrows lifted slowly, then he nodded. "Midnight in the local park I passed on my way here. Would you like one? My son, Micah, is the family baker." He held out the bag.

I went to sniff the contents, but Smoke swooped down and scratched my booping snooter with a claw.

Erig chuckled. "Fear not. I doubt Juno is greedy like Rabdos. That boy can eat a pound of sugar in one sitting. I've even ordered Smoke to alert me if Rabdos sneaks treats in-between meals. My son has no self-control."

I hissed at Smoke and licked blood off my booping snooter. "I didn't want a candy, anyway."

Erig stroked a finger along Smoke's back. "You can tell me everything I need tonight, and we'll work out a deal."

"Agreed. See you then." I rubbed my stinging booping snooter with a paw then hopped off the bar and trotted back to my witch and my friends, a spring in my paws.

Despite the unwarranted attack, I felt great. Was this really happening? Did I finally have a way to get back my missing magic?

Chapter 3

Let's do business

Erig was late. I paced one way and then the other, glaring into the gloom as I waited for my tardy companion.

And he wasn't just a few minutes late. We were supposed to have met fifteen minutes ago to discuss our business arrangement, but it seemed Erig didn't consider punctuality a trait to cultivate. No doubt, he was used to people being happy he showed up at all.

If this was how he did business, I wasn't sure I wanted to deal with him.

I paced some more, muttering to myself. The problem was, if Erig hadn't over-exaggerated his ability, he had what I needed to solve my problem. If he could retrieve the last pieces of my magic, I'd get everything back.

Perhaps I wouldn't be whole, since I'd gifted a small amount of power to Zandra, but it could be enough.

I paused in my stomping and tilted my head. There was a small shuffling sound close by, but it was nothing like the overly confident strut of a man who assumed he owned the world.

My pacing resumed, accompanied by a fair amount of huffing. This could be the most important deal I'd ever done. I'd hunted for years for my missing magic before finally giving up and resigning myself to a lifetime of fur, a tail, and four legs. But my new future felt within paw touching distance, and when this worked, everything would change.

And not just for me. I'd find an elite role for Zandra, and any of my friends in Crimson Cove would be welcome. Perhaps Finn could become my bodyguard.

But they were details to be finalized once my power returned. First, I needed Erig here so we could strike a deal.

I had to wait another fifteen minutes before Erig favored me with an appearance. He strolled along the path, whistling, not seeming to have a care in the world. It was only my entire magical future he held in his ring-covered hands.

He nodded when he saw me. "Lovely evening."

"Yes, I witnessed midnight and the thirty minutes that followed most attentively."

Erig chuckled. "Some things are worth waiting for. So, tell me what you need."

I glanced around but had little fear anyone would overhear us at such a late hour. "As I mentioned in the bar, I need some magic found."

"Your magic?"

"Yes, it belonged to me. It was taken years ago."

"May I?" He held out a hand and hovered it over my head.

I nodded.

His warm hand settled on my head, and he rested it there for several minutes. He didn't speak, just closed his eyes and deep-breathed.

I wanted to pull away. There was something off with his power. It felt sickly. I glanced up at him but couldn't see any obvious signs of illness. Maybe he'd had too many greasy burgers and was feeling gassy.

"Old magic. Ridiculously old. I've felt nothing like this before." Erig kept his hand on my head.

"Will that be a problem? You said you could find anything, so long as you had a connection to what was missing."

"It won't be a problem, but it'll prove challenging. And this will be a different hunt than the usual tedious search for a missing piece of jewelry or the oh-so-important paperwork someone was dumb enough not to file properly." Erig finally removed his hand from my head and flexed his fingers several times. "Fascinating. Exactly how old are you?"

"Old enough to know better than to answer that question." I gave him a catlike version of a smile. "Does that give you everything you need to find my magic?"

"Not so fast. I require more context. This power that once belonged to you was taken. How was it taken?"

"Will those details help with the search?" It was never enjoyable to rehash the humiliation I faced at the hands of cruel goblin scum.

"If I don't know everything, I may end up searching in the wrong place, and that would waste my time and your money. I'm sure you don't want that." He tucked his hand back into his pocket and rocked back and forth on his feet.

I took a moment to settle myself. Full disclosure was a price I was willing to pay to get my magic back. "I used to have a different form."

"I sensed that. You haven't always been a cat familiar?"

"No. For many years, I had great power, and I ruled over an impressive number of realms. People worshipped me. I was adored."

"Now, you're a witch's familiar. That's some downfall."

"Until I met Zandra Crypt, I would have agreed with you. I made the mistake of pairing with the wrong magic users to get back what I'd lost. It resulted in what little power I had becoming corrupted."

"I sensed a darkness in you. Has dark power always threaded through your magic?"

"No! I ruled fairly and never lowered myself to using twisted forms of magic to get what I wanted. The darkness seeped into me when I was bonded with a succubus, who had dark witch leanings. I lost myself in that power. But I found a way back with Zandra. She made me see my new form and role in life had value."

His eyebrows slowly rose. "Not valuable enough that you're content to remain as a witch's familiar, though?"

"I had so much, and it was unfairly ripped away, leaving me with unfinished business. I must get back what was taken."

"Who took it?"

I hesitated. "Is that important?"

"I may need to visit the person who stole your magic. Or find sources who know them. Don't hold out on me, Juno, or you won't get what you most desire."

I couldn't decide if Erig really needed this information, or if he was just being nosy. "In my previous form, I had many enemies. People who were jealous of my success and the adoration I received from my subjects."

"You were some kind of goddess?"

I inclined my head. "And a powerful one. I should have known better than to let my guard down. I was ambushed when asleep, the power ripped from me, and then I was trapped in a cage in this fluffy form."

"Sounds humiliating."

"I try not to dwell, but it was."

He grinned. "I'm still waiting for a name."

I sighed. "Nalak. A goblin leader."

"Nalak the Nasty? Nalak the Notorious?"

"Yes, yes. He came up with those nicknames himself. It's pathetic."

"He's not pathetic! He won the last twenty battles he was involved in. Although that's going back some time. I haven't heard of any recent victories."

I hissed at Erig. "You're friends?"

"No. I keep watch on the powerful in case they need my services. I know I can charge them double."

"How benevolent of you."

Erig smirked. "You pay top prices, and you get top service. What made him take your power?"

"Nalak had been eyeing the Gedi Realm, which belonged to me. We'd attempted a peaceful negotiation, but I wasn't interested in releasing it at any price."

"And all its gold. Goblins. Always obsessed with amassing more glitter." Erig shook his head as if money didn't motivate him. "But what do they do with all that gold? They hide it. They don't spend it or show it off. Such a waste."

I nodded, although I couldn't care less what the goblins did with their shiny bars. "The negotiations broke down, and Nalak promised revenge. I assumed it was sour grapes because he'd lost to me, but he must have bribed somebody to get inside my rooms. Whoever it was led him into my chamber, and Nalak struck me with a spell so powerful it should have killed me. When I didn't die, he turned me into this." I gestured at my stunning white fluff.

"It must humble you to lose everything to a goblin. The ones I've met aren't known for being smart."

"Nalak had resources." I sniffed. "And I was too trusting of the people I surrounded myself with."

"I've not heard any news about Nalak recently. He's still alive?" Erig said.

"As far as I know. I kept tabs on him for a while, but he slipped under the radar. I'm certain, if he knew I was alive in this form, he'd attempt to finish what he started."

Erig tapped his fingers together and looked up at the sky for a second. "Dealing with goblins is never pleasant. This won't be an easy job."

My whiskers stiffened. "But you can do it? You can find my magic?"

"Don't doubt my word. I can find anything that's lost. Although magic has a more nebulous quality to it. It can drift and move. Do you know where your magic was stored?"

"I've recovered some of it. Nalak hid it in objects. Rocks or stones. Most recently, I discovered some in a bracelet."

"Interesting. Around here?"

"Yes. All close by. A goblin in disguise carried the bracelet."

Erig stroked his chin. "Magic recognizes its source. From the sounds of it, your power is seeking you, just as you seek it. Nalak wouldn't have been foolish enough to pick one location to store something so precious. He'd have scattered it."

My heart pitter-pattered. "Do you think my magic wants to come home? Come back to me?"

"It's doing just that. I'd suggest you wait for it, but I hate turning down such a lucrative business opportunity."

"I've been searching for a long time. It's difficult to locate."

"And it won't be easy for me. But your energy is strong, and I'll be able to pick up any vibrations of a similar magical signature. It can be done." Erig nodded. "I'm willing to take the job."

I resisted the urge to skip. It was time to talk money. "What are your terms?"

Erig regarded me in silence for several seconds, his eyes narrowing. "Ten percent of your combined realm wealth."

My mouth dropped open. "That's a ridiculous price."

"It's a high price, but think what you'll get. Your former worshippers, all the power, all the magic. Everyone adoring you. When you look at it like that, it's a tiny price to pay."

"One percent. I ruled over eight prosperous realms."

"Did you, now? This gets more interesting. Ten percent is my fee. This isn't a negotiation. I'm the best, and I demand the best for my services." Erig tugged on the silver chain attached to his wrist.

Smoke shuffled into view, and Erig stroked him. The bird cowered against his touch and closed his eyes.

"Three percent," I said. "You'd never have to work again with that amount of money."

"You're not serious about doing a deal. Good luck finding your own magic." Erig turned and walked away.

I gritted my teeth. I couldn't lose this chance. It would take me decades to find my missing magic. "Wait! We have a deal. Ten percent of the wealth of all my realms will be yours once I have my magic returned to me."

He turned slowly on his heel and smiled. "There you go. That wasn't so difficult, was it? I knew you were a smart creature."

I repressed a hiss. "When can you have it for me? How long will this take? If I'm paying so much, I expect fast results."

"Steady now. There's no need to make demands. Wire me a down payment. I'm feeling benevolent, so let's say a token gesture of ten thousand."

"What do you need it for?"

"To show you're committed. And to pay my researchers. I have teams scattered across the world, and they need money to begin their investigations. Then I'll give you a timescale."

I wrinkled my booping snooter. I had assets stored away. "Will gold do?"

"All currency is accepted. Here are my account details." He passed me a small square card. "Send it tonight, and my team will get to work first thing."

"Then what?"

"Meet me here, same time tomorrow night, and I'll have something for you."

"So fast?"

"I always deliver. Have a good evening, Juno." Erig turned and strolled away.

The price I'd pay to get my magic back was steep, but it would be worth it.

I bounced home, practically floating. Everything was about to change for the better, and I couldn't wait for better to arrive.

"What's got you in such a good mood?" Zandra finished unloading the work van.

"Oh, it's nothing." It was everything. I'd spent all day at animal control, replaying the conversation I'd had with Erig in my head. Every time I thought about it, I got more excited.

"Well, whatever it is, I'm glad you're happy." Zandra locked the van. "You've been down ever since Sorcha left."

"I miss her food," I said. "Sorcha does the best smoked salmon."

"You can have all the smoked salmon you desire tomorrow. She's back then."

I jumped off the front of the van and trotted along beside Zandra. "I can't wait. Everything's good. Isn't life good?"

She grinned down at me. "It has its moments. Let's go eat. Vorana made lasagna."

We returned home, but I was so excited, I barely tasted the delicious food or took part in the dinner table conversation. My whole magical future lay ahead of me.

After trying, and failing, to relax for the evening with Zandra, I was glad when she finally fell asleep. I waited until the clock hands got close to midnight then snuck out of our basement apartment and headed back to the park to meet Erig.

I expected him to be late, so I wasn't surprised when he hadn't arrived by twelve-thirty. But as it edged closer to one in the morning, I was done waiting. I recalled where Acer said the family stayed—there were few mansions with stone lions guarding the entrance in Crimson Cove—so I marched to Fairy Lane, past the crumbling lions, and up to the impressive front door.

I thumped my paws against the door and didn't stop thumping until it was opened.

Erig stared down at me. "What do you think you're doing?"

He was in his pajamas. "Did you forget our meeting? I've been waiting at the park for over an hour."

"Go home. I have nothing for you." He tried to shut the door, but I forced my way into the cold tiled hallway. "You got my down payment?"

His nostrils flared. "I did."

"So? You said your team would start researching. Has there been a delay?"

Erig sighed. "I changed my mind. There's no deal to be done."

My heart froze. "You said you could find anything."

"I spent the down payment on researching your power. I can't get you what you need."

"You said you could."

"There's always an exception. Now, if you don't mind, I was in bed."

"I mind very much. If you can't retrieve my magic, then give me back my down payment."

"It's gone."

"How? You can't have spent it in a day."

Erig lifted his hands. "My researchers aren't cheap."

I bared my teeth at him. "You cheated me! Did you have any intention of finding my magic?"

"Of course. And I never cheat people. I have an outstanding reputation."

"You're a cheat and a liar. You said you could find anything."

"I can. But I can also change my mind about taking on more work." He opened the door and pointed outside.

I ignored his gesture. "Give me back my gold." I was so angry, my toe beans were sweating and sticking to the tiles.

"I can't give you what I don't have. I had to ensure your magic was available for retrieval. It wasn't."

"Is this how you make your money? You promise people the world, take a down payment, and then ignore them." Magic sparked off the end of my tail. "What would you have done if I hadn't sought you out? Snuck out of Crimson Cove with my gold tucked in your designer back pocket?"

"That's enough! You're not smearing my reputation by making wild accusations."

"And you're not stealing from me." More sparks of magic shot from my fur and scattered across the tiles.

"Don't make threats you can't keep, little cat."

My claws extended. "No one cheats me and gets away with it. Apologize and return my gold."

Four loud thumps sounded outside the house. I turned to find Erig's adult children standing outside, their wings outstretched.

"You won't win this fight, Juno," Erig said. "Accept you've lost and move on."

I glowered at the four half-angels. Their expressions were blank, and they stood frozen, as if waiting for instruction from their father.

I turned back to Erig. "You may chase me from this house, but I will get my gold, and I'll tell everyone you're a con artist. I'll ruin your business."

He flashed his white teeth at me. "Do that, and you'll regret it. Maybe I'll even seek out Nalak. Let him know where you are and what form you're hiding in. There'll be nothing left of you by the time he's wreaked his revenge."

I snarled and lifted a murder mitten.

"Smoke! Attack!"

Smoke flew over Erig's shoulder and poured flames at me, his claws extended as he swooped past my head.

I leaped out of the way of his flames, but the end of my tail lit up in a fiery inferno. I howled and whipped around, batting out the magical flames before they did too much damage.

Smoke swooped over my head again, and a whisper of an apology hit my ears, along with the word *go*.

"That was a taste of what you'll get if you disrespect me," Erig said. "Leave while you have a shred of dignity left."

I glared at Erig, then Smoke, who hovered by Erig's ear, and then the blank-faced angel children. I wasn't done with this cheat, but this was the wrong time to fight when the odds were so strongly against me.

Furious, humiliated, and with a desire for the deepest, darkest form of revenge burning in my chest, I ran. But I'd be back. And when I returned, Erig wouldn't know what had hit him.

Chapter 4

A rude awakening

Thud, thud, thud!

The annoying noise continued for several minutes before I was fully awake.

"What's going on?" Zandra murmured from underneath her duvet. "Is that someone at the front door?"

"Ignore them. They'll go away." It had taken me hours to get to sleep after my humiliating confrontation with Erig. I'd stewed over his theft and lies, and I was convinced this was how he did business. He sold people impossible dreams then ripped them away when he'd gotten money from them.

I'd plotted terrible revenge on him while lying awake before finally drifting off into an unsettled slumber.

Thud, thud, thud.

"Ugh! I should go see who that is," Zandra said. "They'll wake the dead with all that racket."

"They've stopped." Although I was awake, I kept my eyes closed. "Told you they'd go away."

"You can't go down there!" Vorana's voice was muffled outside the basement door at the top of the stairs. "They're sleeping. So was I."

I sat and shook out my fur. "Vorana's let them in." I inhaled deeply and got a whiff of cinnamon. There were angels in the house.

"And whoever it is, it sounds like they want to see us." Zandra grabbed her robe and tugged it on.

"Stop! I said you can't go down there," Vorana said. "Can't this wait until the morning?"

"You want me to deal with them?" Sage's sharp tone rattled down the stairs.

"No one is dealing with us. We're here on official business."

My toe beans tingled. That was Cythera. A very irate-sounding Cythera. What had gotten her pristine angel undies in such a twist that she needed to show up here so early?

The door opened, and she appeared on the stairs and marched down. Vorana and Sage were right behind her.

"Sorry. She wouldn't listen to me." Vorana gestured at the angry angel.

"You're good." Zandra stood and ran her fingers through her bed-messy hair. "Is there a problem at animal control? Have the animals escaped? That weeping wind belter was feisty."

"This visit has nothing to do with animal control." Cythera was glaring at me. "Juno, you're under arrest."

"Whoa! What do you think Juno's done?" Zandra rested a hand on my head. "Is this to do with all the rodent killings? Or the squirrel hunts? I keep telling her to quit, but she can't resist."

Finn dashed down the stairs a second later. "Sorry for barging in. I'm sure this is a big misunderstanding."

"More like a confused misunderstanding." Zandra cocked her head. "Someone better explain this to us. Fast. I hate being disturbed when I'm sleeping."

Cythera's furious glare remained fixed on me. "Do you know Erig Morfiel?"

"Unfortunately. What does this have to do with Erig?" I shifted on the bed.

"Unfortunately? You're not a fan of his?"

"I don't really know him. Why? What's going on?"

"Erig's been murdered," Finn said. "And we have witnesses who reported they saw you arguing in the early hours of this morning."

"Then your witnesses are full of hot air and fairytales," Zandra said. "Juno's been here all night with me."

I looked at my wonderful witch, forever grateful she defended me. "Um... not exactly here all night."

She stared down at me. "You were, weren't you? I didn't hear you go out."

"I stepped out for a short time to conduct some business."

"You mean to kill Erig," Cythera said.

"Stop saying that." Magic simmered on Zandra's fingers. "Juno wouldn't kill a guy she doesn't know."

"Or any guys I do know. And I can confirm I didn't kill Erig Morfiel." I was convinced by that statement, so why was Cythera looking so certain she was right about this accusation?

"Witnesses claim otherwise," she said. "You're coming with us."

"Juno is going nowhere." Zandra stood in front of me. "As usual, you're making a mistake. And you picked the wrong witch to go up against. Juno stays with me."

Finn lifted a hand. "Sorry to say this, but the witnesses were convincing. The argument between Juno and Erig got heated. Magic was thrown." His gaze went to my still-singed tail.

I tucked the burned end underneath me. "There's an explanation. And it doesn't involve a murder."

"You said you'd make Erig pay," Cythera said.

"Is that true, Juno?" Finn said.

"I... I don't recall what I said. I was angry." I'd certainly thought about making him pay.

"Angry about what?" Zandra said. "You barely knew the guy. How could he make you mad in such a short amount of time?"

"Juno knew Erig well enough to arrange a meeting with him," Cythera said. "We're taking this to Angel Force, so we can officially question you."

"Now?" Zandra said.

"Yes, now. I won't have a killer loose in my town."

"If you take me in, you'll still have a killer on the loose," I said.

No one spoke. Finn looked worried. Cythera kept glaring.

"Let's make this easy on everyone," Finn said. "Come in now in an unofficial capacity, answer our questions, and you'll be back in bed within a couple of hours."

"Getting no sleep, because I'm worried Angel Force is about to make the biggest mistake of their life and charge my innocent familiar with murder," Zandra said.

"It won't come to that." I leaped onto her shoulder and curled my tail around her neck. "I did meet with Erig. I thought he could help me."

"With what?" Zandra said. "None of this makes sense."

"Let's move," Cythera said. "The sooner this murder is cleared up, the better for everyone."

"Then you need to get looking for different suspects if you want this resolved," I said. "You'll find no answers from me to solve this crime."

"That's for me to decide," Cythera said. "Hurry up."

"I'm coming, too," Zandra said.

Cythera shook her head. "You can't sit in on the interview."

"I'll be in there," Finn said.

"No, you won't," Cythera said. "You're too close to Juno and Zandra to be a neutral observer in this investigation."

"You're kicking me off the case?" Finn looked horrified.

Cythera's spine straightened. "I'm aware of your close friendship, so it would be inappropriate for you to be involved."

"What are you saying? You don't trust me? I won't tamper with evidence or hide anything," Finn said. "And if I find evidence that proves Juno killed Erig, you'd know about it."

"It's easier this way," Cythera said. "Juno, you're with me. If you continue to resist, I'll take you out in shackles."

My hackles lifted at her spiky tone. Cythera meant business. "I'm not resisting. I'm processing. You've just accused me of killing someone. That takes time to sink in."

"No shackles! Cythera, you're overreacting as usual," Zandra said. "And if I can't sit in on the interview, I'm still coming with you."

"If you must. I'm flying Juno to the station, though, so you'll have to catch up."

I balanced on Zandra's shoulder and rested my forehead against hers. "Everything will be fine. I'll make the angels see sense. You know I'm not a murderer, right?"

"Of course I know that. But I wish you'd told me what you were up to. I could have helped."

"I'm waiting," Cythera said.

"Wait longer!" Zandra snapped back at her.

"I'd better go before she gets out the chains. See you at the station." I pressed my damp booping snooter against her cheek then climbed down and walked up the stairs with Cythera lurking behind me like a sulky white shadow.

Vorana and Sage were waiting at the top of the stairs, looking concerned.

"Is there anything we can do to help?" Vorana said.

"Just have a delicious snack waiting for me when I get back."

"I can be a character witness for you," Sage said. "Whatever you need. You can be up yourself, but you're no killer."

I appreciated my friend's support. "Thank you. But it won't come to that. The angels are making a huge mistake. It won't be the first time."

"Let's keep moving." Cythera stood by the front door.

Once I was outside, she scooped me up and blasted into the air before I'd taken a breath and told her to watch where she was putting her hand.

We thumped down outside the Angel Force building a few minutes later, and she marched inside, still holding me.

I slid her a glare. "I have legs. They work very well."

"I don't want you running off anywhere."

"I don't have to run. I have magic. If I wanted, I could translocate to the other side of the world. Good luck with finding me then."

"Which would only prove your guilt, so I'm sure you won't do that. Do I need to place you in a cell?"

"You need to place some trust in me." I wriggled until she let me go. I turned and stood in front of her. "Cythera, you know me well enough to understand I wouldn't do this. And if I planned on killing anyone, I wouldn't have a public argument with them hours before doing it. That's insanity."

"No more talking until the interview begins." Cythera massaged her forehead. "Bertoli, are we ready?"

He hurried over and nodded. "Whenever you are."

"Let's get this over with." Cythera escorted me into a plain interview room. She settled into a seat with a file in front of her. Bertoli joined us a few seconds later. He fretted with a pen and pad before mumbling an apology when Cythera glared at him.

She ran through the formalities of the interview, getting my details. "Talk to me about your relationship with Erig Morfiel."

"I didn't have a relationship with him," I said.

"You met him several times since he arrived in Crimson Cove," Cythera said. "I have witness statements to confirm that."

"I met him briefly in the bar when he arrived. Acer introduced us. Oh! How's she doing? She must know what happened to her dad."

"She's been informed. The whole family is aware of the situation."

I looked at the door. "I didn't see her here when we arrived."

"Acer's also not involved in this investigation because of her closeness to the victim."

"I'm assuming she's with her family. How are they holding up?"

"Focus on clearing your own name," Cythera said.

I stared at Cythera and then Bertoli. Their expressions gave nothing away. "What does that mean? Is Acer a suspect?"

Bertoli discreetly nodded then froze when Cythera shot him another glare.

"Tell us about your meetings with Erig," Cythera said. "Was your meeting in the bar the first time you'd met?"

I'd just been given a glimmer of hope. If there were other suspects Angel Force was investigating, I could clear my name. But Acer was a suspect? Why would she want to kill her father?

"Juno! We're waiting."

I nodded. "Acer introduced us. Then the family went to have a celebratory dinner. I'd never met Erig until then."

"That was the only time you spoke in the bar that night?"

"Well, no. I approached Erig when he was on his own. He'd bragged that he had a unique ability to find anything lost." I twitched my whiskers. "I had something that needed retrieving, so I asked if he could help."

Cythera raised one eyebrow. "What have you lost?"

I needed to tell them the truth but would keep the details minimal, so it didn't encourage them to probe too deeply into my history. "Some magic."

"Did Erig agree to do business with you?"

"He was interested. We arranged to meet later that evening and discuss the details."

"That was the second time you met?"

"Correct. We met at midnight in the local park. I told him what I wanted, and he explained how he operated. We came to a deal."

"What went wrong?" Cythera said.

I shifted in the seat. "We arranged to meet the next night. Tonight. Erig didn't show, so after waiting for an hour, I visited him."

"Which is where we have the witnesses who saw you arguing," Cythera said.

"I'm not denying the argument happened. I provided Erig with a down payment for the work, but he went back on the deal. He spent the down payment and then told me he didn't want to do the job."

"You fought over money?"

"Technically, it was gold. He promised he'd find the missing magic. When he couldn't deliver, I asked for the gold back."

"What did he say?"

"Erig basically told me to go away. He kept the gold but refused to help."

"That must have made you angry," Cythera said.

"Of course it did. When I wouldn't leave, he summoned his family as backup and then got his phoenix to burn me." I inspected the sad looking ends of my frazzled tail. "What happened to Erig?"

Cythera glanced at Bertoli. She gave him a small nod.

Bertoli opened the file Cythera had brought in. "Erig's body was found in the local park."

"That was where we met," I said, "which means he could have used that spot to con other people too. It's a good location. Quiet and out of the way. Perhaps he promised more deals and then failed to deliver. When the others realized he planned on cheating them, they attacked him."

"Or perhaps that person was you," Cythera said.

"It wasn't me." I tutted at her. "How did Erig die?"

"We can't disclose that information. But I will say his attacker was thorough."

"Is there evidence at the scene that I did it? Paw prints in the blood? White fur? Anything that actually puts me there?"

Cythera exhaled slowly, her hands resting flat on the table. "I've never hidden that I don't trust you. You conceal things. You have an agenda that you share with no one. Not even your bonded witch."

"Everyone has an agenda. Having a purpose in life keeps you motivated."

She jabbed a finger at me. "Don't be clever. Your freedom is at stake."

"Then help me by giving me information so I can prove I'm innocent."

Cythera was quiet for several seconds. "What did you do after your argument?"

"I went home to Zandra. I stewed about the row then slept. That's where you found me. Look at me." I lifted a paw. "No signs of a fight that led to murder."

"Your tail suggests otherwise."

"And I told you how that happened. You need to find out who else Erig did business with while he was here. They're your prime suspects. He picked the wrong magic user to go up against and paid the price."

"Like you, you mean?" Cythera said.

I suppressed a sigh. This angel was so stubborn-headed. "We're going in circles. It wasn't me."

Cythera leaned forward in her seat. "You have no alibi, and you have a motive."

"That's not enough to charge me with murder!"

"Not yet. But don't leave town. I'll have more questions for you as the investigation progresses."

"I'm going nowhere. I intend to prove my innocence."

"Good luck with that," Cythera said.

"I don't need luck. I have truth on my side." I glanced at the door. "Are we done? Can I leave?"

"You're free to go. But I'll want to speak to you later once we have the preliminary autopsy results back."

"I don't suppose I could get a look at that report once it's ready?"

"Leave!" Cythera said.

Bertoli stood and opened the door for me. I scampered out of the office as fast as I could, my head a whirl of questions and concerns.

I stepped outside and inhaled deeply, closing my eyes and appreciating my freedom.

Someone cleared their throat.

I opened my eyes and discovered Zandra and Finn in front of me.

Zandra crouched and lifted me into her arms. "We need to talk."

Chapter 5

No more salmon

I snuggled against Zandra, letting the stress slide away, thankful for her comforting embrace.

"So, how did it go?" she whispered into my fur.

"I'll tell you everything. I just need a moment to gather my thoughts." I kept my eyes closed and pressed in close.

"Sorry I didn't give you any warning we were on our way," Finn said. "We got a message about a body in the park. Once we identified who it was and informed the family, your name was mentioned. Cythera insisted on bringing you in immediately. I didn't get a chance to sneak off and message you."

"She's always had it in for me." I opened my eyes and hopped out of Zandra's arms. "She believes I'm hiding something."

Zandra's mouth twisted to the side. "Well, you did hide the meeting with Erig from me. Of course, I know you're innocent, but why do that?"

I let out a gentle sigh, not liking the disappointment in her eyes. "Is Sorcha's café open yet?"

"Should be. There were lights on when I walked past earlier," Finn said.

"I'll feel better after I've eaten. And then I'll reveal all." I trotted ahead of Zandra and Finn before they protested or asked more questions. There must be a fix for this. All of this. Perhaps I shouldn't have hidden my midnight meeting from Zandra, but it would have prompted questions, and I'd yet to reveal my full history to my wonderful witch.

Should I have gone for full disclosure with Cythera? She wouldn't have been able to share the information with anyone, so my past would remain safe. But would that information have led to her trusting me even less than she already did?

Cythera was bound to be more suspicious of an ancient demigoddess trapped inside a cat's body than a sassy familiar who called her out when she made mistakes.

The illuminated Bites and Delights sign cheered me, and the door stood open to welcome customers seeking a hearty breakfast. I'd missed our regular feasts and gossip sessions at the café.

I stepped inside and hesitated. The usual scent of freshly brewed coffee and croissants was in the air, but there was a new vibe. And new people.

"What do we have here?" Finn looked around. "Sorcha must have made new friends while she was away."

In the back righthand corner of the café sat half a dozen leather-clad, caped bikers. There were four guys and two women. Standing behind the counter was another biker. He was tall and muscled, with black hair down to his shoulders. He also wore a cape that stopped at his knees. One of his arms was slung across Sorcha's shoulders.

Before I could investigate the newcomers any further, a menacing grumble came from underneath the table the bikers had taken over. Three lithe gray hounds with wiry fur slid into view, their teeth bared as they stalked toward me. And it was definitely me they had their sights on.

Sorcha looked up at the sound and squeaked. She clapped her hands together and dashed around the counter, flinging her arms around Zandra. "I'm so happy you're here!"

"Welcome home." Zandra grinned as she hugged her back.

Although I was pleased to see Sorcha, my attention was on the menacing creatures stalking me. "Greetings, Sorcha. If you know those hounds, ask them to stop looking at me like I'm a tasty appetizer at an all-you-can-catch fur buffet."

"Oh! Ignore them. They're all bluster and no bite. That's Onyx, Midnight, and—"

"Let me guess, something suitably cliched, like Shadow?"

She giggled. "Close enough. Cole. They belong to Gaian's friends. They're kind of their guard dogs, just cuter. They adore belly rubs once they trust you."

There was nothing cute about the beasts who continued to salivate over my succulent form.

A whistle from one of the guys at the table had the hounds retreating into the shadows from where they came from. He raised a hand in acknowledgement.

I hoped this group was just passing through, or I'd need to watch those hounds didn't track my scent and ambush me when my guard was down.

"You're looking good, Sorcha." Finn kissed her cheek. "I mean, you always look good, but the spa retreat has returned your sparkle. And it's great to have you back. My stomach's been grumbling for weeks since you left."

"I'm open for business, so happy to feed you. I'm behind schedule, though." She leaned closer before glancing at the guy behind the counter and blushing. "Gaian is very distracting."

I inspected Sorcha as she chatted with Zandra and Finn. She looked incredible. Her time away from Crimson Cove had done her a world of good. When she left, she'd been wrung out and exhausted, and I'd been worried about her.

"What treatments did you have at the retreat to make you look so amazing?" Zandra said. "I don't enjoy being pummeled by strangers or having hot stones dropped on my back, but I might be tempted if I come back looking like you."

"I only had a couple of massages and a few meditation sessions. And the food was great, but... well, I quit after a week." She glanced at Gaian again, who watched our conversation.

"You left the spa for a guy?" Finn crossed his arms over his chest.

Sorcha swatted his shoulder. "You sound jealous! The retreat was doing me good, and I was feeling better. Then Gaian's bike broke down outside when I was doing a meditation walk. I heard someone cussing, so I peeked through the hedge, and there he was."

"A biker unable to repair his own bike?" I peered without restraint at the handsome man. "What kind of magic user is he?"

"I'll get to that. I thought the way we met was romantic. Don't you think it was a cute way to meet?"

"A guy cussing is romantic? I'm missing a trick," Finn said.

"Hush! You're spoiling my story. I asked if I could help. We fixed the bike, and as a thank you, Gaian invited me for a drink. We've barely been apart since then." Sorcha sighed.

"Sounds intense." Zandra looked skeptical. "Now he's here? You've moved him in?"

"I'd move in if Sorcha let me." Gaian sauntered over to join us. "I can't get enough of this amazing woman."

Sorcha giggled again. "These are some of my closest friends. Gaian Scythe, this is Finn, Zandra Crypt, and her familiar, Juno."

He nodded at us all. "You've got a nice town here."

"We have. This is your first time visiting?" Finn said.

"Never had a reason to come here until I met Sorcha. But the fates aligned, and that was it."

"Sounds like something out of a romance novel," I said.

"I don't read romances, but whatever you say." Gaian rested an arm around Sorcha's shoulders again and pulled her against him. "All I know is I'm one happy guy whenever Sorcha is around. When she told me she owned a café, it was the icing on the cake. The way to a guy's heart is always through his stomach."

"And Gaian has so many ideas for the café," Sorcha said. "I can't wait to try some of them."

"So long as you keep smoked salmon on the menu, I'll be happy," I said.

"Oh! Well, Gaian and his friends are environmental mages."

"Tree huggers?" Zandra said.

Gaian smirked. "We do more than that. We're activists and ensure magic users aren't mistreating this precious resource we live on." His gaze slid my way. "And that includes exploiting the animals on it."

I repressed a groan. "You're plant-based. So, no salmon?"

"I don't eat anything with a face," Gaian said. "Neither should you."

"I'm a cat! We die if we don't eat faces. Well, flanks, legs, you get the idea."

He grimaced at me and looked away.

"Gaian was telling me about some wonderful plant-based alternatives. I'd be happy to get some in for you," Sorcha said. "You and Elijah can be my guinea pigs. Well, cat pigs. Or is that guinea cats? Anyway, I'm phasing out some of the regular items, so I can be more ecologically friendly."

"So, definitely no smoked salmon?" I couldn't hide my horror. I was all for protecting the animals, but I didn't have sharp teeth and murder mittens for no reason.

"We'll figure something out." Sorcha glanced up at Gaian, who looked at me with less than kindness in his eyes.

"Maybe check with your customers, see what they'd buy," Zandra said. "I'd hate for you to spend money on changing the menu, and then no one show ups to eat."

"Of course! It was just something we were talking about." Sorcha hugged Zandra again. "I'm so glad to see you. I've got so much to tell you and Vorana. And the bookstore has changed since I've been gone. I want to hear all about that."

"We'll arrange a get-together," Zandra said. "You still doing banana pancakes?"

"Of course. So many recipes are easy to make plant-based. Pancakes all around?"

Finn nodded. "And two coffees."

Sorcha patted Gaian's arm. "How about you go see if any of the gang needs a refill?"

He kissed her cheek then sauntered over to his group.

Sorcha crouched until she was almost eye-level with me. "There's salmon in the fridge. You can have that, but you'll have to figure something else out if I go fully plant-based."

I huffed out a grudging thank you. Maybe this wouldn't be my regular place if I couldn't have my smoked salmon and cream cheese.

"Let's grab a table," Zandra said.

"I'll bring your food over as soon as it's ready." Sorcha hurried back around the counter.

"I'm all for change, but I'm not sure about this kind of change." Finn stretched out his legs, his gaze on the newcomers.

"A few more plant-based recipes won't be a bad thing," Zandra said.

I caught Finn's eye, and we grimaced.

Sorcha brought over two mugs of coffee and then left to make the pancakes.

"So, what happened after Cythera flew you to Angel Force?" Zandra said to me. "We got there as soon as we could but were blocked from getting in by an over enthusiastic angel, who has Cythera-like aspirations."

I settled into my seat. "Cythera is suspicious of me. But there's no reason for her to be, since I told her everything."

"Which was what?"

I took a second to order my words. "I'm after a particular type of magic. When I learned Erig had the ability to find missing things, I asked to meet him to see if he could help me locate it."

"What kind of magic are you after?" Zandra said. "It must be something special if you can't buy it from a regular store."

"It's old. I've tried finding it myself, but it's hard to locate. When Erig bragged he could find anything that was missing, I wanted to see if he was as good as his word."

"Then you argued?" Finn said.

"Because he cheated me. He took a down payment, spent it, and then said he wouldn't take the job."

"That was what the argument was about?" Zandra sipped her coffee.

"Yes. I demanded the payment back, but he got mean. He claimed he spent it on research, but he'd had it for only twenty-four hours. I recognized a con and called him on it. Things got tense, and magic was thrown."

"Which was how your tail got burned?" Zandra said.

"I'd have kept fighting, but he set his phoenix, Smoke, on me, and his children were also there. It wouldn't have been a fair fight."

"You'd have held your own," Finn said.

"I'm glad you didn't fight all of them." Zandra kicked Finn's ankle. "You could have been badly injured. And you should have taken me with you. I'd have gotten your money back."

"By now, it's probably tucked in a hidden account, and I'll never see it again," I said. "But it's not so much the money; it's the principle. Erig deceived me."

"Everyone saw the fight?" Zandra tapped her fingers against her mug.

"I hadn't intended to make it public, but he ensured there were witnesses. And if they tell the truth, they'd reveal that, when I left, Erig was still alive."

"You don't think it was a coincidence Erig got his family involved when Juno arrived?" Finn said to Zandra.

I hopped onto Zandra's lap. "Good point. I'm a handy distraction to deflect attention from the actual killer. Have you questioned the family?" I looked at Finn.

"Yeah. How did Erig's family take the news of his murder?" Zandra said.

"Stoically. The mother, Ollia, instantly said she saw Juno at the house not long before Erig died, and we needed to question her."

I flipped my tail. "She's lying. Ollia wasn't there when I spoke to him. He opened the door, then his children arrived, but I never saw her."

"Maybe Ollia heard you arguing."

I huffed out a breath. It was possible, and I'd been busy ensuring I didn't get burned alive by Smoke to see who lurked in the shadows.

"There were no tears?" Zandra said. "Did any of them seem upset?"

Finn shook his head. "They were all creepily composed."

"Just like they were when we met in the bar," I said. "I wondered if they'd been taught to hold their tongues."

Finn shrugged. "They were quick enough to talk about who could have done it."

"Shifting the finger of blame from one of them?" I asked.

"It's possible. I found it strange the way they all moved straight to suggesting you were the killer."

"Like it had been planned," I muttered. "Which suggests one of them must be guilty and they're protecting them."

"We know it wasn't you, so someone in the family must be in the frame for this murder. Do you know how Erig died?" Zandra said.

"Erig was a mess when we found him," Finn said. "He had bruising on his face and arms, but that wasn't recent. The bruises were at least a week old."

"I noticed bruising on his face when we met," I said.

"What was more significant was the discolored veins on his face and around his mouth. They were new. There was also dark staining on one hand."

"Poison?" I said.

"Maybe." Finn glanced at the counter. "My stomach feels like it's eating itself. Where are those pancakes?"

"They probably still need mixing." Zandra's gaze was on the table at the back of the café. Sorcha was perched on Erig's lap, all thoughts of our banana pancakes gone.

"When will the results from the autopsy be back?" I asked Finn.

"They're rushing things through. There should be prelim results in a day or two."

"We're not waiting for Cythera to trump the charges on you." Zandra shoved back her chair. "Let's forget the pancakes. We'll grab something from Vorana, and then figure out our next move."

Finn looked mournfully at the counter. "I really wanted pancakes. Maybe I should nudge Sorcha into action. Remind her she has starving customers waiting."

"Sorcha's love life is dominating her thoughts at the moment. That'll pass," I said. "Let's focus on making sure I'm not a murderer."

"How about we go talk to Acer after we've eaten?" Finn said. "She'll know her family best."

I nodded. "And she can point us toward which family member was most likely to murder her father."

Chapter 6

Not such a happy family

We'd spent longer than we'd planned at Vorana's house, since she'd wanted to hear everything about the surprise arrival of the angels at her front door. She'd made an enormous batch of pancakes for Zandra and Finn, I had salmon, and then she'd grilled us at the dining table in the kitchen.

After that huge breakfast—I'd had three helpings—I'd taken a fortifying nap, and Zandra let Barney know we'd be in late to work.

Two hours later, we were on our way to find Acer.

"You stay out of sight," Zandra said as we approached the Angel Force office. "If Cythera learns you're poking around, it'll only make her think you're guilty."

"Guiltier. I'm happy to stay out of that uptight angel's way," I said.

"Acer should be out soon. She always takes an early lunch," Finn said. "I'll grab her as soon as she appears, and we can go somewhere quiet to talk. She'll help. She'll want to get to the bottom of this as much as everyone else."

"More so. She must be in shock about what happened to her father," Zandra said.

"Maybe. Acer was there when the family was informed about Erig's murder," Finn said. "She reacted the same as everyone else. And she didn't ask many questions about what happened. It was as if she didn't care enough to ask."

"Or she already knew what had happened." I raised a paw to stop the protests. "I wouldn't have considered Acer a suspect, but Cythera is suspicious of her."

Finn pinched the bridge of his nose. "I hate that she's on the suspect list, but it makes sense she needs to be, along with everyone else in the family. We always look at those closest to the victim first."

"Not in Cythera's case," I grumbled.

"Did Acer defend Juno when the rest of the family pointed their fingers at her?" Zandra petted my head.

"Kind of. She started talking about how helpful you both were to Angel Force, but Ollia told her to be quiet. The children seem under the thumb. Almost scared to speak, despite the power they must have."

"Maybe they were taught not to speak back to their parents." Not every family was happy when the front door was closed and their true faces bared.

We waited twenty minutes until a glum Acer loped out of the building.

Finn gave a quiet whistle from our position in an alleyway near Angel Force.

Acer looked around and spotted us. Her expression grew quizzical as she walked over. "What are you doing here?"

"Waiting for you," Finn said. "I'm sorry about your dad. I didn't get a chance to talk to you when we visited the house. How are you doing?"

She shrugged. "Thanks. I'm fine. But disappointed. I just got suspended."

"What happened?" Zandra said.

Acer glanced over her shoulder. "Let's get out of here, and I'll tell you."

We hurried away from the building and waited for Acer to speak.

"Cythera called me into her office ten minutes ago. She said that, after considering the evidence in my dad's murder, she can't rule out any of the family members as suspects. Including me."

Finn grunted. "She is something else. She knows you. Cythera hired you because of your incredible references."

"I'm trying not to take it personally. We all know how murder investigations go. Family and loved ones are the first to be scrutinized. But suspension?" Acer shook her head. "I thought Cythera was about to fire me. Maybe she still will."

"That's unfair," I said. "And no offence to your family, Acer, but I'm pleased to learn I'm not the only suspect. Although I don't think you did it."

"I appreciate that. Sorry about the early morning wake-up call you received," she said. "That must have sucked. I tried to tell Cythera you weren't involved, but she didn't listen to me."

"Cythera is being extra careful with this case," Finn said. "She won't even let me work it because of my friendship with Juno and Zandra."

"I get it. All of it. But Cythera didn't have to be so blunt. And she could have put me on another case or asked me to take paid leave until things got sorted." Acer scuffed her feet as she walked. "She made me feel guilty, and I've got no reason to do so."

"Cythera brings that out of people. She must have had specialist training while at the angel cadet academy," I said.

Acer shrugged again. "Anyway, I'm out of there. And I won't be allowed back until they solve the case."

I stopped outside Vorana's bookstore. "Vorana does the best free cookies. We could sit and talk inside."

"Sure. I've got nowhere else to be," Acer said.

I glanced at the new sign installed above the door. There were two adorable green-winged scarabs sitting at either end. Vorana's new sponsor, Amenia, had been true to her word and had provided regular funding to ensure Vorana could keep the store, despite the rent increases.

And it seemed the sign was magical because business had never been better. Maybe Amenia was being more of an advocate for the store than anyone realized. New customers visited daily, and Vorana had never been so busy. She'd also never been so happy. Now her bookstore was safe, she had nothing to worry about.

Vorana spotted us when we entered the store and waved, but she was with a customer, so didn't join us.

We found empty seats in a quiet corner and settled in with a plate of free chocolate chip cookies.

While Acer ate a cookie, I sniffed some scarab knickknacks that must have been delivered courtesy of Amenia. There were small paperweights, scarab-themed bookmarks, and small metal clips you could put over the pages of a book so you didn't lose your place. All tasteful, and I approved. As did the customers, many of whom carried scarab trinkets along with their book purchases.

Finn sat forward and rested his elbows on his knees. "Does Cythera have any evidence a family member was involved with what happened to your dad?"

Acer finished her cookie and sucked the crumbs off her fingertips. "I'm not sure. She won't discuss the case with me. Any question I asked was met with silence."

"Do you think any of them could be involved?" I asked.

Acer moved her mouth from side to side. "As you know, I was adopted, along with my siblings. And on the outside, everything looked great. There was lots of money, and Erig was always busy building his business and impressing people with our perfect lifestyle. Sometimes, it was fun. We had the best education, great clothes, went to parties, and traveled to expensive vacation resorts."

"But dig below the surface, and things weren't all that rosy?" Zandra said.

"Not so much. Erig had crazy high standards for us. He wasn't easy to be around and was always hard to please."

"It can be tough when you get adopted," Finn said. "Two magic users who were part demon dragged me up. It didn't work out so well. I'd have done better if I'd remained in care."

Sympathy shuffled across Acer's face. "I sometimes wondered that about my situation, too. At first, I was grateful anyone wanted me. And when I was small, there were happy times. Ollia used to dress me up and show me off at her fancy parties. Everyone would coo over me because I was such a cute kid with little pointed ears and sparkly skin."

"I imagine a half-elf, half-angel makes for an adorable infant," I said.

"Oh, sure. I was to die for. That was the only reason they picked us." Bitterness plucked the sharp words out of Acer's mouth. "Ollia, I mean, my mother, she wanted adorable babies. They never had their own."

"They couldn't naturally conceive?" I said.

"You've seen Ollia, right? She's obsessed with keeping her amazing figure. And she wouldn't risk ruining it by having kids the old-fashioned way. So, they adopted. And they wanted beautiful half-angel, half-elf babies."

"Which aren't that hard to find in care," Finn said. "Angels are the worst about keeping their purity promises."

Acer snorted a kind of laugh. "Or they have a shameful secret to hide. I was a dirty little secret that needed to be gotten rid of fast."

"Who knew angels could be so scandalous?" I said.

Finn scowled at the floor. "They're not perfect, no matter what they like to tell you."

I didn't want to poke the bear by reminding Finn he was a half-angel.

Zandra rested a hand on my head. "Go on, Acer."

"My birth parents were far from the dream couple when it came to fidelity. From what I've been told, my dad wanted to keep me, but his wife insisted I vanish. He had an affair with my Elven mother, and when I popped out with adorable wing nubs, all hell broke loose. Especially when my birth mother showed up saying I was his."

I leaned closer to Acer. "So, what happened?"

"I got dumped. My biological dad's wife made a deal with my birth mother. She got paid a huge amount of money, and..."

"You were sent into care?" Zandra said.

"It was partly a shame thing. My birth mother didn't want her reputation ruined, but I imagine the payout she got for giving me up made things easier." Acer reached for another cookie. "I got adopted by the Morfiel family, but a few years in, things got less easy. I wasn't so cute, and I started talking back. Erig and Ollia hated that."

"Which was why you left?" I said.

"I waited until I was old enough then I was out of there. I wanted to distance myself from them, get a fresh start, and be more like my birth father.

That's the reason I joined Angel Force when they relaxed the recruitment rules. He's also in law enforcement."

"They let anyone in these days." Finn's smile was rueful.

"At least you had your brothers and sister as support when things got tough at home," I said.

"Sometimes. But we all had our own battles with our parents. Some fought harder than others. My childhood wasn't terrible, but it was stifling to be forced into a mold you weren't meant to be in." She sniffed the cookie but didn't eat it as the chocolate chips melted on her fingers. "As soon as I could, I moved out and slowly distanced myself from them. And I figured moving to Crimson Cove would mean I rarely saw them. They're not fans of small towns."

"You must have been shocked when your family announced their visit," Finn said.

"Yeah. It wasn't something I looked forward to. And now this." Acer lifted her hands. "All the family drama has followed me and ruined my chance of making a name for myself at Angel Force. This is all Cythera will remember me for."

"Maybe not. She has her moments of abject dumbness, but she can also forgive," I said.

"I hope that's true. I enjoy working at Angel Force."

There was a lull in the conversation, and cookies were consumed.

"Since Cythera gave away nothing about why your family could be involved in this murder," Finn said to Acer, "do you know if Erig had enemies who could have done this?"

"He had a lot of people around him who told him what he wanted to hear, and no one ever stood up to him, but I'm sure there were people whose noses he put out of joint. They won't be sad about his death."

"Because of the way he did business?" I said.

Acer glanced at me, a guilty expression on her face. "Yeah. Something you've experienced."

"It's the reason I'm a murder suspect," I said. "Did your father get rich by cheating people?"

She lowered her head. "Not always, but he rarely followed through on the complicated jobs because they took too much effort. Erig liked to work as little as possible for his money. I'm sorry, Juno. If I'd known you planned on doing business with him, I'd have warned you off."

"That's not your fault," I said. "I shouldn't have believed his over-inflated claims that he could find anything lost."

"Oh, that wasn't over-inflated. I'd never met anyone before who could do that. So long as Erig could link into the signature or vibe, as he called it, of what was lost, he'd find it. It may have taken him six months of tracking, but he could do it. Would he? That's another question. If it looked like it would take time and involve travel to places he didn't like, then he'd make an excuse not to do the job."

"He used his ability to get stinking rich," Zandra said. "That must have made a lot of people resentful."

"As would lying to them, taking their money, and then not delivering on a promise," I said. "Could someone have followed him here? Or maybe a former client recognized him and got revenge?"

"Those are possibilities," Acer said. "I wasn't involved in the business, so I don't know much about it. I remember heated encounters like the one you had with him, though. Clients would be furious when he'd take their money and then do nothing other than tell them he couldn't get them what they needed."

"I'll have to look into those names," Finn said. "Well, Cythera will. I won't be able to get near this case."

"We need access to inside information, though," I said.

"I've got friends on the inside and favors I can call in, so we won't be shut out." Finn looked at Acer. "I know Cythera will have asked, but what's your alibi for when your dad was killed?"

"I'm lucky I have a solid alibi for the time of his death, given how late it happened."

"When did Erig die?" I said. "Cythera shared little when she interviewed me."

"They think he died between two and three in the morning," Acer said.

"So, you were in bed?" Zandra asked.

"Um... no. I was on a stargazing date."

"Then you have a perfect alibi." Zandra grinned. "Who were you with?"

Acer's cheeks flushed bright red. "I was on a date with Bertoli."

Chapter 7

Dating lies

"Well, well, well. Bertoli kept that quiet," I said. "How long have you been seeing each other?"

"It's new. And casual. That was our first official date," Acer said. "We've been flirting for a while, though. He's cute."

"You can't have much better than an angel as your alibi," Zandra said.

"Not that we thought you were ever guilty," Finn said hurriedly.

"I get why you're asking. And given how complicated my family is, I don't object. But I promise I had nothing to do with this." Acer shifted in her seat. "In truth, I want nothing to do with my family. Getting recruited to Angel Force and then getting my placement here were my first big steps to cutting ties. I was done with them. Why tangle myself back in with a murder?"

"It makes no sense to me," Finn said. "As far as I'm concerned, you're not on my suspect list."

Zandra nodded.

"It seems your family isn't ready to let you go," I said.

"I guess not." Acer sagged in her seat. "I should get going. I expect Ollia will want me around, and I need to make sure everyone else is doing okay."

We finished our cookies, and after a quick goodbye, Acer hurried out of the bookstore.

"Let's find Bertoli, just to double-check Acer's alibi," I said.

"You don't trust her?" Finn said.

"We need to be certain we can rule her out."

"Acer seemed nervous, but I didn't get the sense she was hiding anything from us," Zandra said. "I agree with Finn on this."

"So do I. But let's make sure we're missing nothing."

Finn shrugged then nodded. "Fair enough. And I'll talk to Cythera about getting Acer back to work. Since she's got an alibi, there's no way she could have killed Erig."

"It seems harsh of Cythera to suspend Acer." I trotted along beside Finn and Zandra as we left the bookstore and walked along the street. "You can see the effect it's had on her."

"Cythera always thinks about Angel Force's reputation before anything else. She forgets those angels also have feelings." Finn studied his mobile snow globe. "Bertoli is on patrol. Let's follow his route. We should find him doing laps around the eastern side of town."

Since the day was pleasantly warm, I was happy to wander along looking for Bertoli. Finn sent him a message saying he wanted to meet but didn't get a reply.

"Someone's being grumpy today," he murmured.

"Change isn't easy," I said. "At least he's trying to be a nicer angel."

"Bertoli is different since he came back from that extended retreat." Finn gave me a pointed look. "Although he never fully explained what prompted his rapid departure. Cythera still hasn't forgiven him for that. It messed with everyone's schedule. She even had to take a night shift, and Cythera never works nights."

"Perk of being the boss," Zandra muttered. "Although I shouldn't complain. Barney always does his share of late shifts at animal control."

"Yeah, you've got a good one there." Finn tucked away his mobile globe. "I just wish I knew which version of Bertoli was showing up. The friendly one or the surly one. I'd know to bring in treats when he was having a bad day to soften him up."

"There he is!" Zandra said. "I recognize the pink-tinted wings."

Finn chuckled. "They do make him stand out. He complains about them most days. I keep telling him the color is fading, but I'm not sure it is."

"It's odd he was the only angel who got pink wings after taking the sleep reversal potion," I said. "There must be something special about Bertoli."

Zandra chuckled to herself. "I guess he's unique."

"Something you want to share?" Finn arched an eyebrow.

She kept chuckling. "I know I shouldn't have, but I added something special to the potion I gave

Bertoli. I was annoyed with him after he messed up arresting that demon. He almost got me and Juno killed because he wouldn't listen to sense."

"Zandra Crypt! What did you do?" I loved it when my wonderful witch was devious.

"Nothing bad! Well, it was a tiny bit bad. Aurora was always obsessed with changing my hair color when I lived in Willow Tree Falls. She used a rare type of mugwort to get the color to take. So, I added a tiny amount to Bertoli's sleep reversal potion. I didn't expect it to last so long, though."

Finn was laughing and shaking his head. "It's Bertoli's birthday soon. Maybe treat him to the color reversal spell."

"I don't know. The pink suits him," I said.

"I'll consider it." Zandra winked at me.

"Hey, Bertoli! Wait up." Finn raised a hand and waved.

I hopped onto Zandra's shoulder. "Once we clear Acer's name, who should be our next target in this investigation?"

"None of Acer's siblings made much of an impression when we met them at the bar. I didn't get a read on any of them. Let's focus on Ollia next."

I nodded. She was as good a suspect as any, and she'd been the one to point the finger at me following the discovery of Erig's body.

Bertoli had stopped and was waiting for us to catch up with him.

"Anything exciting on patrol?" Finn said.

Bertoli looked mildly suspicious as we arrived. "It's been quiet. I figured I'd do a couple more rounds and then take a break. I didn't think you were out today. And with partners."

"No, I'm not down for patrol duty. I've been helping Acer, though."

"Oh! Of course. It's terrible what happened to her father." Bertoli glanced along the street. "I've not seen her to ask how she is. Is she holding up?"

"I expect you'll want to comfort her later," I said.

Bertoli's forehead furrowed. "Check in on her, you mean? Sure. You never want a colleague to be unhappy."

"Acer's more than that to you, though, isn't she?" Finn said.

Bertoli's wings fluttered. "What's that supposed to mean?"

"You two are dating, aren't you?"

Alarm flashed across his face. "No! What makes you think that?"

"You didn't take Acer on a stargazing date?" Zandra said.

The alarmed expression remained lodged on Bertoli's face. "I've never taken her on any date. We work together. That's all."

"You're sure?" Finn said.

Bertoli planted his feet and crossed his arms over his chest. "It wouldn't be appropriate to date someone I work with."

"I know there are rules about it," Finn said, "but it's not frowned upon, so long as you don't let it interfere with your work and you let Cythera know."

"I wouldn't do anything so unprofessional." Bertoli sniffed and looked away. "Acer is deluded if she thinks we'd ever get involved."

I shared a confused look with Finn and Zandra. Why was Bertoli so certain he'd never go on a date with Acer? She was cute, smart, friendly, and as pretty as they came.

Bertoli's mobile snow globe buzzed, and he pulled it out of his pocket. "I have to go. We keep getting alerts of vandalism around town."

"This is more important than random acts of vandalism by bored teenagers," Finn said.

"Not to me. I have a job to do, and I intend to do it to the best of my ability." Bertoli turned, crouched, and shot into the air.

We stared after him, standing in a swirl of dust and tiny white feathers.

"What just happened?" Zandra said. "Did Acer lie about her alibi, or did Bertoli conceal their date?"

"If it was Acer, she'd know we'd check with Bertoli to ensure she was telling the truth." I batted a feather that floated past my face.

Finn ran a hand through his hair. "Maybe she figured we'd never ask Bertoli because we trusted her."

We were quiet as we digested that unsavory possibility.

"Which means Acer is still a suspect?" Zandra said.

"And a suspect with something to hide," I said. "Sadly, she needs more investigation."

Finn sighed. "I really hope Acer didn't do this. I like her."

"But you'll dig into her background?"

He nodded and sighed. "Of course. Let's get to work."

We were just leaving animal control, after spending the afternoon catching up on overdue paperwork, when a message came in from Finn.

Zandra opened it. "He's got new information on Acer. A contact outside of Angel Force helped him get it."

"Does he say what that information revealed?" I asked.

"No. But we're meeting for pizza in fifteen minutes to find out."

"Then let's go." A deluxe seafood medley with a thin base awaited my salivating mouth.

Ten minutes later, we were settled in seats at Voss Black's amazing artisan pizza parlor. The place was busy with orders coming in regularly, and Voss's familiar, Sid the crow, was perched in one corner, keeping an eye on everyone, as all good familiars should.

Voss strode over, balancing three large plates in his hands. He set them down on the table, making sure I got the seafood medley, and grinned. "Relaxing after work?"

"Sadly, still unofficially on duty." Finn tapped the file he'd set on the table.

"Is this about the vandalism?"

"No. Have you been affected?"

Voss nodded. "All along the alley at the back, someone has daubed weird marks and tags in black spray paint."

"That must have been what Bertoli was investigating earlier today," I said.

"If he did, I've not seen him," Voss said. "And I reported the problem to Angel Force as soon as I saw it. They said they'd send someone, but the rumor goes, they've been getting reports about vandalism all day, so they must be busy."

"It's the first I've heard about it," Finn said. "But then I've barely been in the office."

"We rarely have a problem with graffiti in Crimson Cove," Zandra said. "I've lived here a while now, and I don't think I've ever seen any graffiti."

"I'll get it cleaned off as soon as the report's been filed and pictures taken if the angels need them."

"I'll check in on your report when I'm in the office tomorrow," Finn said. "You should be fine to clean it off, though."

"Thanks. Enjoy your pizza." Voss hurried away to serve another customer.

I'd been nibbling on a delicious slice of seafood medley pizza while they'd been chatting. "What did you find out about Acer from your contact?"

"It's not good." Finn grabbed his own slice and then flipped open the file. "I called in a favor to get this, since it wasn't an official request from Angel Force, but a friend in foster services revealed things were seriously dysfunctional in the Morfiel family. There was a file on several of the children involving reports of neglect."

"Was Acer one of them?" Zandra said.

"Acer, Forfax, and Micah. Apparently, neighbors reported hearing arguments and seeing children being marched out to barns and left inside for days."

"As a punishment?" Zandra asked.

"I'd have to assume so," Finn said. "Erig and Ollia were interviewed whenever the reports came in, but they somehow got out of it, and things went no further."

"Maybe they got the children to lie, so they wouldn't get in trouble," Zandra said.

"Or bribed the officers who came to investigate," I said.

Zandra scowled and picked a slice of mushroom off her pizza. "What about Acer and her siblings? Didn't they back up the reports?"

"No. None of them would confirm what had been done to them."

"Acer didn't mention this when we asked about her family," I said. "Although I can understand her not wanting to talk about it, but she can trust us."

"She's not talking for a good reason." Finn flipped the file shut. "She thinks her past is shameful. She's probably embarrassed, too. We can't all have peachy childhoods and loving families looking out for us. Not every family cares about their kids or encourages them to have a full life. In circumstances like Acer's, you take what you're given. Maybe Acer was scared that, if she told the truth, she'd be dragged back into care. That's hardly a picnic."

"I never assumed it was," Zandra said. "But if she's keeping things from us, it makes me suspicious of her."

"Even if it's not relevant to this case?" Finn said.

"If she suffered at the hands of neglectful parents, it has to be relevant," I said. "It's a motive for murder."

"It's not Acer! She didn't kill her dad." Finn dropped his slice of pizza on the plate. "You wouldn't understand what she's been through. You've always had the Crypt witches watching your back. Any trouble, and they'd be there for you, tearing off heads, blasting enemies, and making sure you had nothing to worry about."

"Hey! Tone down the righteousness," Zandra said. "I get why Acer doesn't want to talk about this, but I also know where you're both coming from. My upbringing was no joy party, either."

Finn glowered at her. "You weren't in care, though. It's different."

"Sure. But my dad fell in with a bad crowd. And you've met my mother. Back then, Adrienne was a mess. Scatty, distracted, and always looking for a good time. She'd sometimes leave me on my own for days. And if my dad wasn't doing dodgy deals with some demon, he was getting drunk because magic had messed his head up. I also didn't always have the Crypt witches by my side. For a long time, they didn't even know I existed."

"And let's not forget the small matter of an age up spell you did on yourself," I said gently. "You missed a number of important formative years by doing that."

"As you're always reminding me." Zandra's tone would have made an angry ogre pause. "I couldn't wait to grow up. I was missing out on too much. And it worked. Nothing bad happened to me by using that spell."

I opened my mouth to suggest otherwise, but her glare silenced me.

Zandra touched Finn's arm. "We all know life can be tough. Everyone goes through trauma."

"It's how we handle the trauma that counts." I had to ignore my food to deal with this tense situation. "You can let it eat you up and dictate your future, or you can stand tall, forgive, and move on. The past can't be changed."

"There are spells..." Zandra's sharp expression softened. "But you're right. Stay locked in a battle with your past that'll ruin you or move on. Try something different."

Finn tipped his seat back then dropped the legs down. "Sorry. That was out of line. People are so quick to assume they know what it's like for kids who don't have a support network when growing up."

"Well, I do know. Although I was glad when I found the Crypt witches and got help with my magic." Zandra glanced at me. "And I have no regrets about using magic so I could stop being a kid and have people take me seriously."

"I mean, I sometimes take you seriously," Finn said. "After all, you're basically a thirteen-year-old in real life, aren't you?"

Zandra glowered at him then grinned. "Exactly. Which means I can be a brat and get away with it."

Finn laughed, and the tension faded.

"So, given this new information, Acer must still be a suspect," I said.

Finn nodded slowly. "As much as I hate that fact, yes. We'll have to talk to her again and find out why she lied."

The vast quantity of dough, cheese, and fish in my gut grew heavy. Poor Acer. I didn't want her to be the killer, and I had sympathy for her reasons, but if she'd done this, we couldn't allow her to get away with it.

Chapter 8

The truth will out

"Another day, another critter saved." I stood by the pens at the back of animal control, sending calming magic to the scared, floppy eared floating moon rat we'd caught. The critter had given us the runaround through a dozen gardens before finally giving in.

"Dinner at the café?" Zandra said.

"Works for me. So long as Sorcha's new friends don't have those hounds with them."

"They were probably passing through." Zandra shrugged on her coat. "Maybe they wanted to check out their buddy's new girlfriend."

I sniffed. I didn't mind hounds, but only when they behaved and knew their place. "I've yet to make a decision about her choice of partner. Although Gaian seems to make Sorcha happy, so he gets a point for that."

"Yeah. I've never seen her like this. It's gonna take some getting used to. Not that she was miserable when single, but I always got the impression Sorcha wanted a companion to do fun things with."

"Let's hope this is the right companion for her." My stomach growled. "Let's eat."

We wandered to the café, but as we approached, I slowed. The lights were off.

Zandra checked the time. "Sorcha must have changed her opening hours. She always opens in the evenings."

We stopped by the door, and Zandra tried it. It was locked.

I peered through the glass, but there were no signs of movement at the back of the café.

"Sorcha hasn't changed the opening details in the window," Zandra said. "I hope she's feeling okay. That weird flu thing she had really messed with her."

"Let's go to the bookstore. Vorana always knows what Sorcha's up to."

We walked over to the store to discover Vorana closing. She raised a hand when she saw us but didn't smile.

"What's up?" Zandra said.

"Sorcha canceled on me at the last minute. We were going for dinner at the café and then catching a movie. I was just tidying the store and getting ready to close when she sent a message saying she was going out with Gaian instead." Vorana thumped down a book. "She's never put a guy before me. Never!"

"And as I keep telling you, Sorcha's in the dumb, goo-goo eyes phase of her relationship." Sage was sprawled on the counter, flat on her stomach, watching Vorana work. "She'll soon come to her senses and realize you're more important than some cape wearing eco warrior."

"She's dated before and never done this. Not once." Another book got thumped on the table.

"Have you met Gaian properly?" I hopped onto the counter next to Sage and gave her a greeting headbutt.

"A couple of times but only for a few minutes. And never on his own."

"What do you think of him?" Zandra snagged a cookie from the tin on the counter.

"He's good-looking and friendly enough. But... I don't know. Maybe I'm jealous. Sorcha always puts our friendship first, but she's known this guy for five minutes, and she's practically moved him in. And he's making changes to her business. And now, she's blowing off girl's night! I don't get it."

"Relax. Sorcha will get bored with him any day now. She'll apologize, and Gaian will be a distant memory," Sage said.

A message buzzed on Zandra's mobile snow globe, and she pulled it out. "It's Finn. He's got Acer with him, and he wants to meet. Is it okay for them to come here?"

Vorana nodded. "Sure. It's not as if I've got anything better to do since my social plans just took a nose dive into an unflushed toilet."

"You could rub my belly," Sage said. "That would keep you occupied."

Vorana walked to the counter, tickled Sage's belly, and then blew a big, wet raspberry on it.

Sage squirmed and grumbled while purring at the same time.

Vorana lifted her head. "You want a raspberry kiss, Juno?"

I politely declined. There was only one witch I let blow raspberries on my belly.

"I heard about Acer's dad." Vorana looked up from her continued belly raspberry blowing mission. "How's she doing?"

"She could be better," Zandra said, "especially since Cythera has her on the suspect list for the murder."

"Not Acer! She's too sweet to do anything so awful."

"We agree," I said. "The trouble is, she lied about her alibi. And there's tangled family business in her past that gives her a motive for wanting Erig dead."

"Like what?"

"It's best if we let Acer share that information," Zandra said. "It's personal."

"Oh! Of course. I didn't mean to pry. I like her. I hope she's not involved in her dad's murder." Vorana walked over and flipped the sign on the door to closed. "Stay as long as you like. I'll brew coffee, shall I?"

"Thanks. That would be great," Zandra said.

"I'm worried about my witch," Sage whispered to me the second Vorana went out the back to make coffee.

"Is it because Sorcha let her down? Like you said, it's a phase. Sorcha will get over this guy and realize he's just like the rest, then she'll be hanging out here all the time, and Vorana will be happy again."

"It's not about Sorcha ditching Vorana. Ever since the sleep reversal fiasco, she's seemed disappointed in me." Sage made a grumbly growl in the back of her throat.

I inched away, in case a furball projectile was imminent, but nothing appeared on the counter. "My friend, we've been over this. Vorana adores you as much as you adore her. She's more than content that you're her familiar."

"On the surface, maybe, but it's more of a pity contentment than a real contentment. But I have a plan to fix that."

"Have you figured out how to capture a squirrel for her?" My ears flicked. I'd love to be in on that hunt. Pesky tree rats.

"No, but I have a solution that's almost as annoying. You'll see. It'll make everything right. Vorana will never be disappointed in me again."

Before I had a chance to question Sage further, Finn and Acer arrived. After a swift round of greetings, we settled into chairs with fresh coffee and some of Vorana's cookies.

She lingered for a second. "Should I stay or go?"

"You're fine to stay," Acer said. "I'm curious what this is about, though. Finn didn't tell me much on the way over."

He touched her arm. "I've been doing some digging into your family. There were reports filed about things your parents did to you and your siblings. Punishments? The barns."

The color drained from Acer's face. "How do you know about that?"

"I needed to know exactly what your family was like. How it was for you growing up with them. From the reports, it didn't sound good."

Acer closed her eyes, and a shaky breath came out of her mouth. "Are you questioning me in an official capacity?"

"I'm off the case. I'm asking because we're friends. We're all here because we want to make sure you're no longer a suspect. And I'd hate for you to get in trouble for something you didn't do."

Acer's hands flexed into fists, and she opened her eyes. "I didn't tell the whole truth. The early years were okay, but I remember difficult situations. I've blanked most of them out, but as I got older, things got grim. Erig, our dad, was a cheating tyrant, who loved to play people against each other."

"Including members of his own family?" I asked.

A tear rolled down Acer's cheek. "He got pleasure out of it. He had this one game, where he'd pick his least favorite child of the month, and the rest of us had to bully them. It was horrible."

"That's awful." Vorana pulled up a chair, sat next to Acer, and caught hold of one of her hands. "Did you tell him you didn't want to be a part of his sick games?"

"We were young and wanted to make him and Ollia happy. There was always this unspoken threat that we'd get sent back into care if we didn't obey. And they drilled it into us that we always had to appear to be this perfect family. Nothing could have been further from the truth."

"Erig picked on all of you in the same way?" Finn said.

"We all had to do the bullying and be bullied. He said it developed character. But all it did was mess us up."

"How did your siblings react?" I asked.

"We were all adopted around the same time, so we got the same indoctrination. With Laylah, she was the embarrassing wild child for a while, but Erig loved destroying that glowing ember of freedom in her." Acer gulped back more tears. "I remember the day she finally broke. She didn't speak for a week. She even went for a stay in the hospital. It was our parents' idea. When she came back, I could tell she was angry, but she kept it inside."

"What about Rabdos?" Zandra said. "Isn't he the eldest?"

"Yeah. He was the first to be adopted. He always claimed he wanted to be just like Erig. And he was being groomed to take over the business, but I was never certain Erig was serious about handing it over. He'd say he saw something lacking in Rabdos. It used to crush him, so he'd work harder to prove himself."

"You have two other brothers. Is that right?" Vorana said.

Acer nodded. "Micah is the introverted one. He coped with our weird family by withdrawing to the kitchen and learning to bake amazing cakes. He was barely around unless Erig insisted on it. And when he was, he kept quiet and put up with whatever happened to him."

"And Forfax?" Finn said.

"He was more open about wanting out, but Erig never wanted him to go and blocked every opportunity."

"He let you go, though," Zandra said. "How did you manage that?"

Acer's mouth settled into a hard line. "Erig saw less value in girls. And I think he was amused by the thought of having a daughter in Angel Force."

"I expect he saw the value of having an insider in law enforcement to exploit in the future," I said.

"That had been mentioned," Acer said. "I pretended it was a joke, but I knew he was serious."

"Was your mother involved in any of this terrible treatment?" Vorana said.

"Ollia is unique. She's part troll and part angel, so she has this odd ability to be coldly indifferent and seethe with anger at the same time. Hand on heart, I can say she doesn't love any of us. She definitely didn't love Erig. The only person she looks out for is herself. Since Erig's games and punishments never affected her, she let it happen."

"You must have all despised him," Finn said. "And her."

"We all disliked him. But I promise you, I didn't kill him. I really was with Bertoli."

Finn's expression grew pained.

"Bertoli claims otherwise. He said there was no stargazing date," I said.

Acer sucked in a breath. "He's lying! I can't understand why he didn't tell you we were together."

"When did the date happen?" Vorana said.

"The night Erig was killed," I said.

Vorana cocked her head. "Did you go to Gallows Mount?"

Acer nodded. "How did you know that?"

"I saw you! I had to come back to the store late because I left some keys behind the counter. I was looking for them when I heard voices. It surprised me that anyone was out so late, so I took a look. It was Acer and Bertoli."

"That's right. We walked past here," Acer said. "We went to Gallows Mount because Bertoli said it's one of the best lookout spots nearby."

"It's also an excellent make out spot," Zandra muttered.

"I'll back Acer on this if she needs a witness," Vorana said. "They were one hundred percent together. She couldn't have killed Erig."

Finn blew out a breath. "Why would Bertoli lie to us about something so important?"

Acer hunched in her seat. "I know exactly why."

I gave her a quizzical look, but she said nothing more.

"Let's get him here and see what he has to say." Finn jabbed at his mobile snow globe for a few seconds. "That message should get him here double quick. I said it was an emergency, and Cythera insisted he come to the bookstore straight away or he was fired."

"Uh-oh. That won't make him happy," Vorana said.

"I couldn't care less if he is unhappy. He's messing with our colleague and friend, and that's out of order," Finn said.

Acer gave Finn a tear-splodged smile. "Thanks for believing in me."

Finn ducked his head. "I'm sorry I doubted you. I should have known better."

A second later, Bertoli landed outside the bookstore and marched to the door.

Vorana hurried over and unlocked it to let him in.

He nodded at her then looked around. "What's the emergency? You said Cythera was here."

"Not exactly, but I knew that tiny white lie would get you here," Finn said.

"What's this about?" Bertoli looked at Acer and then looked away just as quickly.

"You lied to us. You said you weren't on a date with Acer on the night Erig was murdered." Finn stood and glared at Bertoli. "Vorana saw you together."

"I... I... maybe I was with her. But I don't want anyone knowing my private business. It has nothing to do with you."

"It does when Acer is a murder suspect," Finn said. "You must have realized she'd be under suspicion once her dad was killed."

Bertoli's mouth opened and closed several times. "I swear, I didn't. And I've been busy on other cases, so I'm not up to speed with the Morfiel investigation. Acer's not a suspect, is she?"

"She is. And you've made things tougher for her by pretending you weren't together." Tiny flickers of crimson demon light drifted across Finn's wings.

I hopped onto his shoulder and gently bit his ear. "Stay calm. Going rogue demon won't help this situation."

Finn took several deep breaths, and the crimson light faded, although his anger lingered. "Do you even care Acer's been suspended until this is cleared up?"

Bertoli spluttered several nonsense words. "I'm sorry. I had no idea. And I didn't think keeping quiet about our date would cause so many problems for you."

Acer kept her head down and shrugged.

Desperation dug into Bertoli's handsome face. "We were together. We went stargazing. I thought Acer would like Gallows Mount because she has an interest in astronomy. I just kept it to myself because I didn't want our personal business gossiped about at work."

"This has nothing to do with your personal business not being talked about." Acer stood slowly, and her wings extended. "You were embarrassed to be seen with me."

"It's not that," Bertoli spluttered.

"You didn't want to be seen with me because I'm only a half-angel. I expect your parents would be mortified to know you'd asked me out. And to be clear, you did the asking. I never chased you."

His cheeks flushed crimson. "I like you regardless of your heritage."

"Regardless of my mutt heritage, you mean? I get it. I've had this most of my life. I go to job interviews, meet new friends, or go on a date with someone, and they judge me because of my birth parents and their seedy behavior. Something I had no control over."

"I wouldn't do that. I didn't do that. I... I... I'm sorry. I made a mistake."

"I'm the only one who made a mistake by wasting my time on you. If you'll excuse me." Acer stormed out of the store.

"Nice one, Bertoli," I said.

He stared at the open door. "I... I... don't know how to make this up to her."

"You'd better get that girl flowers," Finn said.

"It'll take much more than flowers." Zandra shook her head at Bertoli. "You should be ashamed of yourself."

His shoulders sagged. "I didn't mean to upset Acer. I really am sorry for not being truthful."

Finn sighed. "The damage is done. But at least we know Acer is innocent."

I gently nibbled on one of his wing feathers. "So we can cross one name off the suspect list. But which member of the Morfiel family is the killer?"

Chapter 9

New fluffy recruit

Finn grabbed our empty plates and mugs and carried them into his open-plan kitchen. After clearing Acer's name yesterday, we'd arranged to meet in the morning to review the remaining suspects. It was time to figure out which member of Erig Morfiel's family hated him enough to kill him. Given what we'd discovered about him, they were all sitting on the prime spot.

Finn returned to the living room and settled on the couch next to Zandra.

"You know, this is my weekend off," Zandra said around a yawn. "I'd planned a lie-in, movie in bed, and then dinner at the café. No brain power engaged."

"But then Juno got herself messed up in another murder by becoming a suspect." Finn lifted his hands. "What you gonna do? Let your fluffy sidekick go down because you're feeling lazy?"

I hopped onto Finn's lap and prodded his hard stomach. "Zandra's my sidekick, and a loyal one.

96

Of course, she'd put aside a weekend of sloth to protect me."

"I'd planned on helping you, but if you call me a slothy sidekick again, I might change my mind." Zandra reached over and tickled me under the chin.

Finn laughed. "I had plans, too. But you need rescuing, Juno, so we're not abandoning you in your hour of need."

I dug my claws into his thigh before jumping off. No rescue was needed. I'd just gotten myself into a mildly tricky situation. It would fix itself as soon as Cythera stopped looking at me as if I was a gassy bog toad she'd been trapped in a small windowless room with.

"I found pictures of all the family online. Thought they'd be useful to focus our thoughts." Finn spread the colored pictures across his coffee table.

"I was thinking we should focus on the wife, but given what we've learned, we need to concentrate on the adopted children," Zandra said.

"Agreed. By the sounds of it, they had the same terrible childhood," I said, "which gives all of them an identical motive for wanting Erig dead."

"We're not discounting Ollia, though, right?" Finn tapped the picture he'd printed off, showing her in a tight white catsuit as she posed alluringly for the camera.

"Though the children have a strong motivation for wanting Erig dead, Ollia's cold and calculating," I said.

Zandra nodded. "Quality traits for any killer."

"So, we have Ollia, the mother, and then the four children, Rabdos, the eldest, Laylah, the former wild child, and then Forfax and Micah." I shifted about on the cushion I'd landed on. "Reluctantly, you'd better keep my name on that list, too. It's what Cythera will be doing."

"Although Cythera wouldn't talk to me about developments in the case, I know she's got you at the bottom of her list," Finn said. "She grudgingly acknowledged there's zero evidence at the crime scene that you committed the murder."

"If it's any comfort to her, let her know any murder I commit would be done at a distance and using magic. Blood is difficult to get out of white fur."

"Not helping yourself there, Juno," Zandra muttered. "Stick with the 'I'm innocent' line. Don't talk about murdering with magic or rinsing blood out of your fur." She petted my head.

"I'm pointing out the practicalities. Cythera is all about being practical. And she must know the issues with white, given that's all angels wear."

"Not all of us." Finn pointed at his dark jeans. "And only when we're on duty."

"I've never seen Cythera wear anything but white," I said. "Although it is her color. It suits her."

"Getting back to the murder." Zandra arched an eyebrow at me. "How angry will Cythera be when she realizes we're poking around in this investigation?"

"If she figures out what we're doing, there'll be yelling. I might get suspended," Finn said. "But it'll be worth it."

"It will to clear my name," I said. "What we really need to move things along is access to the autopsy results."

Finn shook his head. "There's no way Cythera will give me that information."

"Could you sneak a copy out?"

"Pictures of suspects I can get, even background information from contacts outside of Angel Force, but autopsy results? Not a chance."

"I'll get them," I said. "I can sneak into Angel Force and read the file. Maybe even make a copy. Or borrow one."

"Um... you sure you want to do that?" Finn said. "Cythera will spit feathers if she catches you snooping, especially since your name is still on her suspect list, even if it is at the bottom."

"It won't be the first time I've done it. And it's the weekend, so Angel Force will be quiet."

"It would be handy to see the autopsy results," Zandra said. "Once we know how Erig was killed, we may be able to eliminate more suspects."

"And I've faced worse than a grumpy angel when on a mission," I said. "Give me two hours, and I'll have the information we need to solve this case."

Finn shrugged. "Then you're up, Juno. Show us what you got."

❦ ❦

"I'm glad you could help on this retrieval mission." I walked next to Sage, looking nonchalant as we approached the Angel Force building. There was nothing to see here. Just two fluffy buddies out for a mid-morning stroll.

We'd timed it so any angels working a shift would be on patrol or dealing with cases, rather than taking a lunch break in the kitchen.

Sage looked around, her expression grumpier than usual. "So long as I don't get slung in a cell, I don't mind helping."

"This mission will assist in clearing my name of a murder charge," I said. "Not that it needs to be cleared, but you know what angels are like when they get an idea in their feathered brains."

She grunted, looked around again, and slowed. "He's late."

"We're waiting for someone else? I only invited you on this kitten impossible mission."

"I invited somebody along. Where is he? Poor timekeeping makes a bad impression."

"Is it Archie? As much as I adore that oversized hellhound floof, he's not the right candidate for a covert stealth mission."

"It's not him we're waiting for. Remus has taken Archie on a familiar cruise to the Antarctic. They'll be gone all month. He's probably moon bathing, eating rare steak, or swimming in the icy sea."

"Sounds enchanting. Elijah?"

"Definitely not Elijah. He's even grumpier than me when he gets dragged on these missions. He complains constantly."

"I blame the lack of fur. He must always be cold. That would make me grumpy."

"There he is! Three minutes late." Sage tutted and planted her front paws on the ground, a sour expression on her fluffy face.

An adorable black-and-white kitten bounded toward us, a sparkle of magic around it.

"This is who we're waiting for?" I asked.

"It is, unfortunately."

The kitten slowed to a trot, its tail up. "Good to see you again, Sage."

She nodded.

"And you are?" I said, since Sage hadn't made the introduction.

"Great to meet you, too. I'm Ember Dreamscape, at your service."

"Greetings, Ember." I glanced at Sage, but she provided no explanation as to why this adorable fluffy baby had joined us. "And you're here because..."

"Ember's my replacement," Sage said. "I figured he needed to see what life was like around here before making a firm commitment."

I stared at her, unblinking. "He's your what?"

Ember nodded enthusiastically. "I can't wait to take on my role. And meet Vorana. She sounds incredible."

"Less talking, more observing." Sage trundled toward Angel Force. "If this works out, Juno will always be asking you on her harebrained kitten impossible missions. It's up to you if you want to be a part of them."

I hurried after her. "They happen a few times a year at the most."

"At least weekly," Sage grumbled.

"They sound exciting. I was honored when you invited me to join you." Ember bounded after Sage. "Can I help with your wheels?"

"Don't touch me!" Sage hissed at him.

I was so stunned by Sage's revelation that I didn't know what to say. I thought I'd talked her out of this ridiculous notion. Sage and Vorana were perfect together. Sure, Sage was grumpy and slightly smelly, but her magic was pure, and she had a strong, protective streak that was devoted to Vorana. It would be cruel to separate them.

"You coming or not?" Sage called over her shoulder.

Ember looked back at me and nodded. He sure was a perky little thing.

I dashed to Sage's side. "You sure about this?" I whispered in her ear.

"Let's focus on getting that file. Around the back?"

"Yes." I glanced over her head at Ember. "Have you discussed this new addition to the family with Vorana?"

"We're not talking about that. If you get distracted on this mission, you'll get in trouble. And that means I'll get in trouble for being persuaded to tag along."

I studied Ember, who was looking around and taking everything in. "You should at least talk to her before any decisions are made. Forging a new familiar bond can be tricky."

"It's a surprise. She'll be happy. Sure, Vorana says she doesn't need anyone else, and I get the usual blah, blah, blah every time I bring it up, but we know the truth. I'm past my prime. A good familiar recognizes when they must step aside and find the perfect replacement for their witch."

"Sage! That's not how this works. We're together forever. Until one of us dies."

"Maybe I'm dying. Have you ever thought about that?"

I touched my friend's side. "Are you unwell?"

"I'm covering all the bases. Do you want this dumb file or not?"

What I wanted was to argue with Sage and make her see how stubborn headed she was being, but I had to focus on the mission. "We will talk about this later."

Sage shrugged, while Ember looked on with interest in his adorable green eyes.

I calmed my hectic thoughts. "The plan is simple. The room where they conduct the autopsies is behind this wall. We get through the back door, into that room, and find the file. If it's not in there, we'll risk going into the office to see if Cythera has a copy on her desk. That's where things could get tricky."

"Will there be a body in the room?" Ember looked less perky and more petrified.

"If it is, it'll be in a cold store, so you won't see it," I said. Most likely, it would. Although the room was chilled, so the bodies were often out on display.

"Will we have to fight any angels? They're kinda big."

"Hey, kid. I picked you because your resume claimed you had all kinds of amazing powers. Translocation. Invisibility. Speed. Super strength. You lie to me?" Sage jabbed a paw at Ember.

"No! I can do all of that and more. I'm just unsure about using my amazing powers on law enforcers. I could get in trouble. I don't want to be cast as an anti-hero. I'm a good kitten."

Sage snorted her disapproval. "This is the gig. Take it or leave it."

"I want in! If this is what you do on a daily basis, I'll get used to it."

"This isn't what we usually do." Sage must be wanting to test how impressive this young cat was to see if he was worthy of joining with Vorana. Although, even if he was worthy enough to be her new familiar, I was certain she'd have a few things to say about this surprise new arrival.

"Let's get this over with," Sage said. "It's almost time for my second breakfast."

"You get a second breakfast?" Ember's eyes grew wide.

"Always. Vorana is an excellent witch. Make sure you appreciate her once you're bonded."

"Of course. I'll always respect my witch." He licked his lips. "You're so lucky. I can't wait to meet her."

"All in good time, kid. You need to prove yourself to me first."

I shook my head at the odd pair then pressed a paw against the back door and used an unlock spell. It opened with no problem, and we slid inside.

"We could use invisibility magic," Ember said. "I'm great at that."

"That's not something I excel in," I said. "It's handy magic to have, though."

"Don't use that power around Vorana," Sage said. "She won't want you sneaking up on her and frightening her."

"I'd never do that to my witch." Ember puffed up his white chest fluff. "But if we have to break into places regularly and steal things, it'll be useful to have me around."

"Like I said, this is an unusual day. Most days, we lounge around, grooming, sleeping, and playing with our witches," I whispered.

"The job is more difficult than that." Sage swatted me on the back of the head. "Don't go putting ideas in his head."

Was Sage trying to put Ember off? She'd been the one to recruit him, but maybe she'd had a change of heart. I hoped that was the case. Ember was an adorable little thing, but I liked having Sage around, even when she was whacking me for not holding my tongue. And I was certain Vorana did.

We crept toward the morgue on our bellies.

"I'll go first and see if the coast is clear," Ember whispered.

"You stay with Sage. I'll look." I crept to the door and edged it open with my booping snooter. There was no one inside. I gestured the others to follow, and we snuck in.

The place was empty. There were no bodies, living or dead.

"You take the desk over there. I'll check over here." I dashed to a table and hopped onto it. There was a pile of folders on one side, which I sorted through.

"Hey! Stop doing that. We're not here to play," Sage snapped.

I looked over to see Ember batting a pen around. He looked so kitten-like that it was hard to believe he was ready to become someone's familiar. I checked the next file but couldn't find the autopsy report.

Something clattered to the floor, and I froze.

"Did you hear something?" a voice said outside the room.

"Hide!" I darted off the table and squeezed behind a filing cabinet. I didn't have time to see where Sage and Ember had hidden.

The door opened, and a few seconds of silence followed. "You sure you heard the noise from in here?"

"Um, not for certain. Maybe it was farther along the corridor."

There was a quiet chuckle. "It's the dead coming back to life."

"Don't even joke about that. It happens more often than it should in this town. Let's get out of here. There are cookies in the kitchen, and we need to grab some before the others get them all."

Two sets of footsteps hurried away.

I waited another minute then wriggled out from behind the filing cabinet. Sage and Ember were nowhere to be seen. "You can come out. The coast is clear."

They materialized before my eyes. Ember had his paw squashed on top of Sage's head.

She shoved him away and growled. "That was your fault! If you hadn't been distracted by those pens, they wouldn't have heard us. You almost ruined this kitten impossible mission."

Ember hung his head. "They looked so shiny, and they needed to be batted onto the floor."

"You two wait outside and be my lookout," I whispered. "I'll finish in here."

"Now look what you've done! You've upset Juno." Sage shoved Ember toward the door. "Out you go. I need to re-check your references if this is the standard you're offering to my witch. Unacceptable."

Poor Ember. He couldn't do anything right as far as Sage was concerned. But I understood her grumpiness. She'd put everything on the line, thinking she was doing it for Vorana's benefit. I hope they found a happy compromise.

I jumped onto the desk and flicked through several more files before I discovered Erig's autopsy results.

I drew in a breath and then exhaled slowly. Someone had really wanted this guy dead.

Chapter 10

Triple dead

I dashed back to Finn's apartment with Ember and Sage, not sparing a second to tell them about the shocking discovery in the autopsy report.

Sage must have been reprimanding Ember while they watched for angels because he hadn't made a peep during the journey.

"Go easy on him," I whispered to Sage. "He's young and still learning. You must remember what that was like."

"I was still a professional, no matter my age. I wouldn't have messed around on an important mission like he just did."

"This is Ember's first try at being bonded with someone. He must be nervous."

"I interviewed over one hundred familiars to find him. He's the best there is. Vorana deserves the best."

I wanted to tell my wonderful fluffy friend she already had the best, but Sage wouldn't listen to me.

Finn appeared in the hallway as we burst through the front door and grinned. "You made it back! I half-expected we'd have to bust you out of the cells when you got caught. And who's this? You found a new friend at Angel Force?"

"This is Sage's friend, Ember," I said.

Finn greeted Ember. "Come through. We've been going around in circles looking at the suspects, and Zandra is getting grumpy."

We followed him into his living room.

"I'm not grumpy. But I am pining for my movie marathon rather than this murder marathon. Did you get a look at the autopsy report?" Zandra patted her lap.

"It made for interesting reading." I hopped onto her lap and nuzzled her.

She scratched her short fingernails through my fur. "Get in any trouble?"

"It was easy. A quick in and out."

Zandra nodded at Ember. "Your kitten friend is cute. Where did he come from?"

"That's Ember." I pressed my booping snooter close to her ear. "And there's a story there. I'll fill you in later."

Sage flopped onto her belly and closed her eyes, while Ember sat alert, looking around with interest.

I turned to face the group, my back to Zandra so she could keep tickling me. "The autopsy showed Erig was an unpopular guy."

"We know about the poison," Finn said. "Was there something else?"

"There was definitely poison in his system. Witch weed juice mixed with mandrake root."

"Nasty stuff," Zandra said.

"Erig also had significant bruising on his torso and head."

"From a fight?" Ember said.

"The bruises were old, so not from a fight that happened since he's been here," I said. "But the marks show he took a hard beating."

"Could that have been a first attempt to kill him?" Finn said.

"I wondered that."

"Anything else?" Zandra said.

"When a ring on his right hand was examined, they found it had left a dark stain on Erig's skin. The residue was tested, and toxic magic was discovered."

"Erig was beaten, poisoned, and polluted with a dark spell." Zandra shook her head. "You were right. Someone really didn't like that guy."

"Or whoever killed him wanted to make sure he wouldn't survive," Finn said. "What was the actual cause of death recorded as?"

"The poison killed him. But Erig must have been weakened from everything else that happened to him," I said. "And the use of his own ring to contaminate him suggests someone had easy access to taint it with the toxic magic."

"A family member," Finn said.

"Someone who shared a room with him and watched him get dressed every day," Zandra said. "Ollia would have known what rings Erig favored."

"It has to be someone in that family," Finn said. "Apart from Acer, they all live together. None of the other children have moved out of the family home."

"Erig probably forbade them from leaving," I said.

"We need Acer's help with this. She can get access to the family without them alerting Angel Force about what we're up to," Finn said.

"Why shouldn't we tell the other angels what we're doing?" Ember said. "Don't you work for them?"

Finn nodded. "I do. It's kind of complicated, though."

"I'm a murder suspect in this investigation," I said. "So, we must be careful."

Ember gasped at me, his large eyes growing even wider. He was such a cutie.

"Before you go making assumptions, I'm innocent. But Finn is a close friend and therefore unable to work on the case in an official capacity. He still wants to make sure my name is cleared and that of his angel friend, Acer."

"We're doing our own investigation?" Ember wrinkled his cute little booping snooter. "Will we get in trouble?"

"Only if we get caught," I said, "which we never do. Well, rarely. It's only happened once or twice, and we've always found a way out."

"And if we solve this case for my boss, she won't stay angry with us for long," Finn said. "If you're worried, you don't have to be involved."

"He does have to be involved. Ember needs to see what life is like living in Crimson Cove," Sage said.

Finn looked puzzled then shrugged. "Suit yourself."

I shot Ember a sympathetic glance. So far, it seemed Sage was intent on only showing him the bad things. She was definitely trying to put him off of bonding with Vorana.

"I'll message Acer," Finn said. "See if she can get us in with the family. We need to give her an update, but then we have to talk to them and see who's the most suspicious."

We waited half an hour, and coffee was consumed along with delicious dried fish treats Finn kept for me, although I was happy to share with Sage and Ember.

Acer arrived at Finn's apartment, and we gave her an update on everything we'd learned from Erig's autopsy.

She sat in silence for a full minute. "The guy had it coming. I wish I could say otherwise, but I'm not surprised someone wanted him dead so badly. Given how he treated everyone, not just his family, it's almost a shock that nothing like this happened before."

"Does anyone in the family have skills in using poison?" Finn said.

Acer hesitated then shook her head.

"You can get poison anywhere," Zandra said. "If you know the right people, it's easy to buy. Or you can mix it yourself."

Acer nodded. "Technically, any of them could have done it. Me included."

"What about the tainted ring?" I asked.

"Erig had his favorite rings, and if it's the one I'm thinking of, he only took it off when he went to bed. It was a gold band with two hands holding a crown," Acer said.

"That was it," I said. "So, any member of the family could have gone into the bedroom while he was sleeping and tainted the ring?"

"It's possible. I wouldn't have risked it. Although Erig was a sound sleeper, and Ollia takes what she calls her happy pills to send her to sleep. Maybe someone took a risk, and it paid off." Acer checked the time. "We should get going. I told Ollia I wanted to talk to her, but I didn't say you'd all be with me. She'll hide it well, but she'll be furious about being ambushed. Ollia loathes surprises."

"You go without us. I'm taking Ember for a walk around town," Sage said.

"Good luck, Ember," I said.

"I'm the one who needs luck on my side," Sage grumbled.

After saying goodbye to them, we headed to the family's rental.

"Juno, you can't come in with us," Finn said. "Ollia is still claiming you killed Erig, so it'll looked suspicious if you're with us."

"I'll listen through a window." I pointed to a lower floor room. "Will that do?"

Acer nodded. "I'll make sure we're in there so you can hear what's going on."

I dashed around the side of the building and hid from view but close enough so I could hear the conversation and peek through a gap in the foliage.

Acer knocked at the front door, and it was opened a few seconds later by Ollia, who wore a red, off-the-shoulder jumpsuit with a flowered print. A perfect outfit for a grieving widow.

Her gaze flicked from Acer to the rest of the party. "If I'd known you were bringing company, I'd have laid out refreshments." She stepped forward and air-kissed her daughter. Zandra was introduced as a consultant. Something that wouldn't have made her comfortable, but she'd play the role to perfection.

"They're here to talk about Erig," Acer said. "Are the others home?"

"I didn't know they were supposed to be." Ollia stepped back and allowed everyone inside.

"I said I needed to talk to the whole family. They need to be here."

"They're independent adults, so they come and go as they choose."

The door was closed, so I was excluded from the rest of the conversation. I dashed to the window and waited impatiently for it to be opened.

The window slid up, and Acer poked her head out and winked at me. "It feels stuffy in here."

"Don't keep that open for long, or it'll get cold," Ollia said.

"Thank you for agreeing to see us at such short notice," Finn said. "This won't take long."

There was silence before Ollia spoke again. "I didn't realize this was what I was agreeing to. What's this meeting about?"

"I'm rechecking alibis for the night of your husband's murder."

"Hasn't that been dealt with? I already told you the angry white cat did it. She argued with my husband then killed him later that night in revenge. She accused him of theft. She was aggressive. Even I feared her."

I grumbled to myself. Ollia was lying through her perfect white teeth.

"We've spoken to the cat in question. She is still a suspect, but we're opening other avenues of investigation to see where the evidence takes us," Finn said.

"It'll take you to that wretched cat. The thing is mean. It should be put to sleep."

I flicked my tail back and forth. I'd been right to be angry that night. Who wouldn't be angry when cheated out of so much gold?

"Could you talk to me about your relationship with Erig?" Finn said.

"I was his wife."

"And was the marriage happy?"

"As I've told another angel who asked the same question, there were turbulent moments. My husband was a successful individual. Sometimes, he let the power go to his head. It made him a little cold."

"Were you unhappy because of that coldness?"

I lifted my paws onto the window ledge and peered through. Ollia stood with her hands on her hips, dominating the room with her incredible curves.

"There were times when it was a struggle, but having my wonderful children helped me get through the tricky days," she said.

"Children can be such a comfort," Zandra murmured.

Ollia didn't miss the sarcasm. "Do you have any?"

"One. Sort of."

I suppressed a chuckle. She meant me. I was Zandra's fur baby. Better than any real baby.

"Then you understand." Ollia made a point of turning away from Zandra. "I was never able to have my own children, but bringing unwanted infants into my life has brought me joy. Even when they choose not to stay with me."

That barbed comment was aimed at Acer, who remained tightlipped and tense in her mother's presence.

"My family means the world to me," Ollia continued. "I work hard to make sure everyone is content. It gives me satisfaction to offer discarded children a position in life they can be proud of. We've taken them around the world to elite social events and shown them things they'd have never been exposed to if they'd remained in care."

Had they shown them love, though? Or sadly used these lonely, scared adoptees as social candy to flaunt to their friends?

"Acer, I know you're grateful for what we've done for you, aren't you?" Ollia said.

"I'd tell you every day how grateful I am if I could."

An icy smile crossed Ollia's face. "Of course you would, my dear. And you'll return to the family now your father has gone. I'll need support while I grieve."

Acer remained silent.

"Could you remind me again where you were when you learned of Erig's death?" Finn said.

"In bed. I was asleep. I have trouble sleeping, so I took some herbal pills to help. I was out for the count when I was roused with the terrible information," Ollia said. "I'd assumed Erig had come to bed after me, so I was devastated when I got the news."

She couldn't have looked any less devastated. Ollia was picture perfect.

"Who woke you?" Finn said.

Ollia drew in a breath.

I leaned closer. Had she forgotten part of her lie? Was she about to expose herself as the deceiver I knew her to be?

"One of the children. Maybe Rabdos. They were all there. It happened so fast, though, and I was in shock. That night is blurry."

"That's understandable." Finn didn't look convinced by her manipulation of the facts.

"Acer, you must come home when this is over." Ollia swept open her arms as if expecting Acer to run into them. "You broke your father's heart when you left. He wanted you to join the family business, just like Rabdos is so keen on doing."

"I'm happy working at Angel Force," Acer said. "The family business isn't for me."

"Reconsider. Your father had such high hopes for you."

"Let Rabdos take over."

Ollia lowered her arms. "Rabdos struggles. He's pushed hard but has yet to achieve your father's high standards. I'm not sure he can manage without your help. You always were the clever one."

"Could we speak to Rabdos?" Finn said.

"I haven't seen him this morning. In fact, I'm not sure when I last saw him. It must have been around the time Erig argued with that murderous cat.

Although…" Ollia tapped a manicured nail against her chin.

"Is there something you want to tell us about Rabdos?" Finn said.

"No, it's nothing. I'm sure. It's just strange that I've barely seen him since his father's death. I expect he's grieving alone. Tears are a sign of weakness. Erig was always telling us that."

"You only tell people that if you're a monster," I muttered.

"Could you ask the rest of your family to get in contact with me directly so I can re-check their whereabouts?" Finn said. "Here are my details."

"I will, but you're looking at the wrong people. Pursue that cat. There was something deeply suspicious about her. I stood beside my poor husband and watched her fight. I sensed a terrifying darkness in that creature." Ollia shuddered. "You shouldn't have dangerous things like that roaming around your town. Look what happens when you do."

Ollia was lying again. She'd been nowhere near Erig when we'd argued.

"As I said, we're looking into all avenues of investigation. But I would like to double-check where everyone was at the time of your husband's death," Finn said.

"Good luck with that. My wayward children are a law unto themselves, as you've no doubt noticed with Acer," Ollia said.

Acer mumbled something I couldn't hear.

"If there's nothing else I can do for you, I'll show you out."

The door to the room they were in was shoved open, and Forfax wandered in. His top lip pulled back in a sneer as he saw Acer. "Oh, look. It's the one who got away."

Chapter 11

Sulky siblings

Forfax strode into the room. He planted a formal kiss on his mother's cheek, having to stand on his tiptoes to do so, then walked over to Acer. "I'm surprised to see you again so soon. You usually avoid us." He didn't greet Acer, simply flicked at something on his dark sweater, his hair dropping over his face.

"You know I'm helping with the investigation into what happened to Dad." Acer's shoulders rose slowly.

Forfax glanced at Finn, taking note of his angel wings. "Is that true?"

"Why would your sister lie about something so important?"

Finn had sidestepped the question by asking another, but there was truth mingled in his response. Acer and Finn worked at Angel Force, and the family didn't need to know Acer had been suspended and Finn kicked off the case.

"Why waste your time with us? You were quick enough to escape the second you got the chance."

Bitterness traced through Forfax's words, and his expression sharpened.

"I never got all the way out, though." Acer glanced at Ollia. "Dad still made demands of me. And you know he only let me join Angel Force because he wanted an insider."

"Like you'd have any influence over what the angels do," Forfax said. "I imagine they've got you pushing papers around the desk and making coffee."

"Sometimes I do that. But we all have to start somewhere."

"Children! That's enough! Acer is our... experiment. We wanted to see how she'd do out in the big bad world without support." Ollia pursed her lips. "How are you financially, my dear? Making ends meet?"

"I'm fine. I need no help from you."

"You wouldn't ask even if you did," Forfax said. "You always were the stubborn one."

"Stop bickering. Your father would have hated it. And we have guests."

Acer rolled her eyes. "Erig encouraged our bickering."

"Show him respect! He's barely cold, and you're already being rude."

"Acer's probably relieved he's dead," Forfax said.

"So are you. You don't have to deal with his judgment and disappointment over your choices in life. Or rather, lack of them."

Forfax shoved his hands into his pockets. "It still feels like he's here, judging us, doesn't it? I expect he'll come back and haunt us."

A small smile crept onto Acer's face. "He'd be mean enough to do just that."

"Your father was never mean. If he took you in hand due to bad behavior, it was for your own good," Ollia snapped.

Acer and Forfax shared a hidden smile that Ollia couldn't see.

Finn cleared his throat. "Forfax, while you're here, I'm rechecking everyone's whereabouts on the night your father died."

He glanced at Finn. "Why bother? We all know who did it."

"We want to make sure we catch the right person," Acer said. "We look at family or partners first, since the victim usually knows their killer."

"What about the cat?" Forfax glanced at Ollia. "We said it was her. Has the story changed?"

My hackles rose. What story? If I didn't need to keep out of the way and silent, I'd give them a piece of my mind. This family was setting me up, which only made me more convinced one of them had done it, and they were covering for the killer.

"We're making sure we missed nothing," Finn said. "Could you tell me where you were?"

"I was here. It was late, and I was in my room. Dad got into an argument with that white cat, and he summoned us to deal with it."

"How did your dad do that?" Zandra said.

Forfax looked down his nose at her. "Who are you? You don't look like you work for the angels."

"Zandra Crypt is our freelance consultant," Finn said smoothly. "We use her for our most important cases, and we take what happened to your father seriously. The investigation has been given our total focus."

I was proud of my witch when she didn't snap back at Forfax and simply nodded.

"Whatever." He glanced at Acer. "She cool?"

"Zandra is the coolest. So is Finn. They want to help."

Forfax nodded, but he kept an eye on Ollia to gauge her reaction. She remained composed yet watchful, like a rattlesnake considering its next move.

"Dad trained us since we were kids, so we'd be alerted when he needed us. It was a psychic connection," he said.

"Psychic messaging is unusual. Few people can create such a powerful summoning bond," Finn said.

"It was because of Smoke," Acer said. "That was why Erig bought the phoenix. The bird was connected to him, and Smoke would send us messages. Dad trained Smoke for a long time until he was good enough."

"Us too," Forfax said. "We had daily training when we were kids. I'd get these raging headaches and nosebleeds, but that never stopped him from pushing us. He insisted on an hour's training a day."

"I remember," Acer said. "That was rough on you."

"On all of us," Forfax muttered.

A look passed between them, and some of the tension faded.

Ollia settled into a seat and picked up a book but flicked through it rather than reading.

"How's the plan going to join the flying squad?" Acer nudged Forfax. "When will you get wings you can actually use?"

He scowled. "The last time I submitted an application, Dad blocked it. He called in a favor with some friend of his, and the paperwork got lost. I resubmitted three times, and the same thing happened. That's when I figured out he was interfering."

"He interfered, as you call it, because he cared for you. A career in the flying squad guarantees a premature death. Surely, you wouldn't want to put that burden on your parents." Ollia didn't look up from the book she was fake reading.

"Can't I be the one to decide what career path to take?"

"Your father wanted the best for you. That kind of career is far from the best."

"Which is why he threatened to cut me off and make me destitute if I strayed from the business," Forfax said.

"He was still threatening you with that?" Acer said. "I'm sorry. I didn't know."

"Why should you? You got out. You no longer had to deal with his twisted sense of right and wrong. I hated it."

"You're so dramatic." Ollia lifted her hard gaze and settled it on Forfax. "You could have left and made your own way in the world. You all know the conditions of leaving the safety of the family."

If I'd been dragged into this family, I'd have run away and not stopped running until my toe beans were bleeding.

Acer touched Forfax's arm. "It's not so bad on your own. Sure, there's the occasional week where I only have enough money for bland pasta and oatmeal, but I finally feel free."

Forfax snorted. "Dad kept tabs on you. He knew what you were doing. You had the illusion of freedom, but that was it. If we weren't blaming that cat for his murder, I'd suggest the angels look at you."

Acer whacked his arm. "Hey! That's a lousy thing to say. Take it back."

"Make me! Maybe you learned Dad was having you watched. You were always the unstable one in the family, always arguing back, no matter the consequences."

"Because I have a backbone."

"No sense, more like."

"Children! We don't need to air our private business in front of strangers," Ollia said. "You speak as if you lived in a prison. We gave you everything."

"Except love and kindness," Acer murmured.

"Those things must be earned." Ollia set down the book. "We provided you with a dream lifestyle. Of course, you had to give something back."

"Even when we did, it was never good enough to make Dad happy," Forfax said.

Acer caught hold of his hand. "He's gone. We really are free. He doesn't get to control us anymore."

The smile on Forfax's face looked strained, as if it rarely made an appearance. "Maybe. I don't know. There feels like so much unfinished business. How will this end?"

I tilted my head. What end did Forfax want? The family broken up? A chance to move on and try life without his parents' oppressive, unhealthy influence looming over him?

"Your father would have hated to see this public display of weakness." Ollia stood and stared down her children until they lowered their gazes. "We're a powerful family, and we have a reputation to maintain. Having outside interference investigating what happened to your father is enough of an embarrassment. I will not have my children fall by the wayside. You know better."

"Tell that to sulky Rabdos," Forfax said. "I've hardly seen him since all this happened."

"Do you know where your brother is?" Finn said. "We'd like to speak to him, too."

"He's hiding." Forfax's eyebrows shot up. "Maybe he did it! He was always the first to break when Dad played his games."

"Stop talking." Rage radiated through Ollia's tone. "Your father did everything to give you an ideal life. How dare you be so ungrateful!"

"Because Forfax is sick of being manipulated, just like I was." Acer's free hand was clenched in a fist behind her back, so only I could see it. "Now Dad's gone, Forfax can have a normal life. He can leave this insanity behind."

"There is nothing insane about being gifted a life of privilege, you ungrateful child."

Acer turned to Forfax. "Get out! Walk away. There's still time. Have a better life than this one."

He grimaced then shook his head. "If it wasn't that cat or you, I reckon it was Rabdos. He pretended he wanted to be just like Dad, but he secretly hated him."

Acer tugged on her brother's arm, a pleading expression in her eyes, but he refused to look at her.

"Do you have evidence to support that claim?" Finn said.

Forfax's bottom lip jutted out. "Rabdos pretended he looked up to our dad, and Dad pretended he was grooming Rabdos to take over."

"And turn him into someone as warped as Erig," Acer said.

"Only pretend?" Zandra said. "Your dad wasn't planning on handing the company to Rabdos?"

"Depended on his mood. Although you could never tell what he really thought."

Ollia strode to the door. "There'll be consequences for this conversation. You've both disrespected the dead. It would serve you right if your father haunted you."

"We're being truthful for once. It feels weird but also amazing," Acer said.

"Perhaps I'll summon his ghost and tell him what you've been saying. He'd be so disappointed." Ollia strutted out of the room.

I was tempted to join the conversation. From the way Forfax spoke, he wasn't convinced of my guilt.

"Forfax, I've got to ask, do you think the cat that visited Erig killed him?" Acer said.

I could have kissed her for asking that question.

Forfax huffed out a breath. "I dunno. Their argument was intense."

"I've told Angel Force how Dad's business really operated." Acer glanced at Finn. "They know he wasn't always honest."

"Wow! You really do want Ollia to summon that creepy old goon back so he haunts you, don't you? She'll go crazy if she learns you dug up the rancid skeletons and aired them in public."

Acer kept her chin up. "I'm exhausted from hiding things. Our family is so full of secrets that I don't know which one I'm supposed to keep from one week to the next."

Forfax's gaze went to the floor. "I'd be surprised if the cat did it. Sure, they argued, but we chased it off. Smoke set fire to its tail, and it ran."

"Why did you say in your original statement you were convinced the cat had done it?" Finn said.

Forfax shrugged. "Ollia. She woke us before Angel Force showed up to give us the news Erig had been found murdered."

"How did she know?" Zandra said.

"I didn't ask. She said to follow her lead. We had no clue what she'd say, but then she pulled out the theory the cat did it. It wasn't a ridiculous idea, so we supported her."

"You think your mother could have killed Erig?" Zandra said.

Forfax tipped back his head and let out a slow exhale. "They'd been together a long time and enjoyed antagonizing each other. They loved being spiteful. Maybe Erig pushed things too far, and Ollia snapped."

"He could have changed his will again," Acer murmured. "Told her he'd cut her out."

Forfax nodded. "He was always doing that. He said it kept us on our toes, so we never knew who'd inherit his fortune."

"We've made a request to see your father's will, so we can check if any recent changes were made," Finn said.

"It's a motive for murder if Erig was threatening to leave Ollia destitute," Zandra said.

"She'd have gotten something, but I'm certain most of the assets would have gone to Rabdos. Even though Erig loved to humiliate him, he was the only one who showed an interest in the business," Acer said. "Erig's first love was money, and he wouldn't have given the business to anyone who'd sell it or run it into the ground, like I would."

"Same here," Forfax said.

"Can anyone confirm you were in your room the night your father was killed?" Finn said to Forfax.

"I was alone. Even in a family of this size, I was always alone."

"You've got me," Acer said.

"I appreciate that. Shame you walked out on us, though."

Acer sighed and shook her head.

"If no one's got any more questions," Finn said, "we'll get out of your way."

"I've got one." I hopped onto the window ledge.

Forfax took a step back. "You're the cat who fought Erig. Have you been there this whole time?"

"Juno's with me." Zandra walked over and lifted me into her arms. "And she's innocent. It's the reason I'm involved. I need to clear my familiar's name."

Forfax winced. "Sorry about making you a suspect. You heard it was Ollia's idea?"

"I don't blame you for supporting your mother. It sounds like she mistreated you over the years. You're afraid of her," I said.

"Not as much as I used to be." Forfax inspected me from a distance. "Did you kill Erig?"

"No, but we'll continue to investigate until we find the real killer."

"You had a question, Juno?" Finn glanced at the closed door. "Ollia could return at any moment, and she won't be happy to see you here."

"I'll be quick. I was thinking about the phoenix your father carried with him. Has anyone retrieved Smoke?"

"No. And I don't know what happened to him. He was always under Erig's control. Maybe, once he died, Smoke got free from his chains and flew off."

"Phoenix are rare creatures. He'll be worth a lot of money. I'm surprised you don't want to find him," I said.

"Why bother? And he'll be long gone by now. He despised Erig almost as much as we did." Forfax looked at Acer. "Can we meet later? It would be good to catch up."

"Sure. Send me a message, and we'll figure something out."

"Anything else, Juno?" Finn said.

"All done here. I was simply curious about the bird."

We said our goodbyes to Forfax, Ollia was nowhere to be seen, and left the house.

"What are we all thinking?" Finn said.

Zandra rolled her shoulders. "That this investigation is far from over."

"I'm thinking Ollia is cold, broken, and hiding something," I said.

"And she has no alibi," Zandra said. "She also lied. And she coached her children into covering for her and pinning the murder on Juno."

"Which makes her guilty?" Finn said.

"Forfax also has no alibi," Acer said.

Zandra glanced over at her. "Do you think he could have done it?"

"He wanted to get away the most, after me. Maybe Erig's threats got to him."

"I'm also wondering about Smoke," I said. "He'd been chained to that monster for a long time and forced to work for him. Maybe he destroyed Erig."

Finn groaned. "Please don't add another suspect to the list. We've already got enough."

I wasn't convinced Smoke had committed the crime, but I still wanted to find him.

Chapter 12

Will he, or won't he?

"It's coming through now." Finn stood in front of the screen on his desk in his apartment. After we'd interviewed Ollia and Forfax, we'd returned to Finn's place and got to work on getting a copy of Erig's will.

Finn had called in another favor, and with Acer's help, they'd convinced the team dealing with the estate to send a copy of Erig's most recent will to her.

"Anything juicy in it?" I hopped onto the desk and peered at the screen.

"The last I knew about the will, Erig was leaving something small to most of us," Acer said. "Ollia was to have an annual allowance and a home, but almost everything else was going to Rabdos."

"He was the favored son?" Zandra said.

"The most obedient son. I never knew whether he followed Erig around like a love-struck puppy because he admired him or because he knew it was the best way to avoid being picked on too badly." Acer dropped into a seat next to the desk. "Not that it always worked. Erig got irritated with Rabdos' groveling and would be spiteful. He'd yell at him and tell him he was useless and he couldn't trust him with the business."

"That must have been hard for Rabdos to hear." Finn was still focused on the screen as the pages slowly came online.

"Rabdos rarely talks about how he feels. He's focused on forging ahead, shaping himself into the next version of Erig. It was disturbing to see such a twisted transformation take place." Acer ran a hand down her face. "When I first met Rabdos, he was sweet. Every day, he'd come to our rooms and wish us good morning and tell us he loved us. He said he'd never been told he'd been loved before, so when he got the chance to tell others, he always did. It just about broke my heart when I heard that story."

"That's tough. To live in a family where you're never told you're loved and wanted," I said.

"It happens." Finn didn't look away from the screen. "The family I was placed with did the bare minimum to keep me alive so they could collect the money at the end of every month. There was no love in that household."

I jumped onto Finn's shoulder and nuzzled his ear. "Well, know this. You're loved by us. You're a true and loyal friend, and our time in Crimson Cove wouldn't be half as much fun if you weren't here. You have a place in our hearts. Isn't that right, Zandra?"

"Absolutely. You're a part of Juno's misfit gang. Once you're in the gang, you never get out."

"Why would anyone want to leave my crew?" I said. "They'd miss all the awesome fun."

Finn chuckled and patted my side. "I appreciate that. It's good to know someone cares."

"You can never tell a person you love them enough," I said. "Those three words are important. Hugs too. You say the word, and I'll get Zandra to hug you as often as you need."

"I didn't agree to do that!" Zandra looked alarmed.

Finn grinned at her. "That's the last page downloaded." He enlarged the document, and we leaned in close to read it. "It's just as you said. Your dad left a small financial settlement on each of you, and an apartment and a stipend for Ollia. Everything else goes to Rabdos."

"How much are we talking?" I said.

Finn scrolled through the pages. "Eighty percent of everything Erig owned goes to Rabdos."

"That's about a hundred and fifty million," Acer said.

Zandra whistled out a note and raised her eyebrows.

"It looks like we've just found an excellent motive for murder," I said.

"We need to find Rabdos to ask him about that," Finn said. "Acer, any idea where he's hiding?"

"No, but it's not out of character for him to go AWOL. Sometimes, when the stress got too much for him, he'd tell Erig he had to do some research for a couple of days. I followed him once, and he booked into a budget hotel. He took in a bag of food, locked the door, closed the curtains, and that was it. He retreated."

"There are a few hotels around Crimson Cove," Zandra said. "We should check those. He could be hiding in one of the rooms."

"You think he's hiding because he's sad about what happened to Erig?" I said to Acer.

"I can't imagine he's unhappy. Erig made his life just as tough as he did for all of us."

"Maybe the added pressure from your father pushed him over the edge," Finn said.

"He could have stepped up the bullying, but I missed it because I wasn't around," Acer said.

"There's a note at the bottom of the will. It says here there's an appendix to this document." Finn clicked onto another screen. "The message from my contact said it's missing. Apparently, it was updated a week before Erig was murdered, yet there's no copy on file."

"It was updated then lost?" Zandra said. "They must keep copies."

"According to this note, Erig sent a message to say he'd made an amendment that would only be disclosed after his death. He stated the will won't be valid until the request in the appendix has been carried out." Finn looked at Acer. "Have you seen this document?"

She chewed on the side of her thumbnail. "That's got nothing to do with me."

"Would Ollia know what was in the appendix?" Zandra said.

"You could ask her, but she won't tell you anything. Ollia was kept out of that side of his affairs, same as all of us."

"This missing document could be the reason Erig was murdered," I said. "He made changes to his will that affected someone, and they weren't happy about it."

"You're thinking Rabdos?" Finn said.

"He was to inherit the bulk of Erig's assets. What if the appendix changed that? Or stipulated certain conditions Rabdos needed to fulfil before he got the money?" I looked at Acer. "Was there something your father wanted Rabdos to do before he could inherit?"

"There was one thing." She closed her eyes for a second. "It's kinda sad. Erig wanted Rabdos to produce heirs who'd inherit the business. He was always nagging Rabdos to settle and, as he called it, breed. He wanted to ensure his business would remain in the family."

"Rabdos never found the right person to... breed with?" Zandra said.

"I don't know. But even if he'd found his soulmate, he wouldn't have had a child with her."

"Acer, what aren't you telling us?" I asked.

She kept chewing on her thumbnail. "When Rabdos turned sixteen, he got us together and made us swear on a pact. He said it would be wrong for any of us to have kids and continue this sick family legacy. It was such a messed-up home to be raised in, and he couldn't stand the thought of his children enduring a moment in Erig and Ollia's company. He made us promise we wouldn't have children until they were dead."

"You agreed to this?" Finn said.

"Sure. I spent most of my childhood being terrified into obedience. There was no way I was having any kid of mine go through that. Besides, I was young when I agreed to it. There seemed no harm."

"It's another motive for murder," I said. "What if Rabdos met someone, and they fell in love? His partner could have fallen pregnant, so he acted to protect his new family."

"I doubt it," Acer said. "Rabdos lived to work and to serve Erig. That's all he did. The only time he stopped working was when he was asleep."

"He could have met someone in the business," I said.

"Erig forbade office romances. If he got a hint people were seeing each other, they were fired. It was written into everyone's contract, so it can't be that."

"You said you've not been around your family much," Zandra said. "You could have missed something. Rabdos might have bumped into someone in the street and they got talking. Romances happen in the most unusual places."

"But as my wonderful witch can testify, they most often happen at work," I said.

She gave me the stink eye. "We have to locate Rabdos and find out what he's up to. What if he knows about the will? Or he's gotten serious about someone and needs to keep an unborn child safe?"

"You do that. But I think it'll be a waste of time." Acer lifted herself off the seat. "I should get going. I've got a few things to do before I meet Forfax."

"Does he want to talk about what happened to your dad?" Finn said. "I could come with you as backup if you're worried about meeting him on your own."

"It's more likely he wants to talk about how he can get out of the family. I'm the only one who's done it, and I know he's still desperate to get away."

"You sure you don't need anyone to come with you?" I said.

"I'm good. Forfax is the least deceitful in the family. We used to be close when we were younger," Acer said. "And I know he wants to change. I'll see you tomorrow."

Finn walked Acer to the door. We said our goodbyes, and she hurried away.

We sat in silence and read through the will again. There was nothing alarming in the contents, apart from the mystery of the missing document.

"Did either of you think Acer's behavior was suspect when we questioned her about the will?" I said.

"A little. You think she's hiding something?" Zandra said.

"What would she keep from us?" Finn said.

"Having seen how sneaky that family is, it could be anything. Maybe Acer overheard something bad but doesn't want to lose a sibling by revealing the information. Although she'd hang Ollia out in a heartbeat if she had the proof that Ollia killed Erig."

"Acer's not sneaky like that," Finn said. "I trust her not to hide anything important."

"She could be concealing family secrets because she's scared of the repercussions if they're revealed," Zandra said.

"Let's not get Acer tangled back into this mystery. We still have Laylah, Rabdos, and Micah to question," Finn said. "Maybe they'll help solve this mystery." He opened a connection on the snow globe on his desk, got the contact number for Ollia, and keyed it in. After waiting a few seconds, she appeared on the globe.

"Yes?"

"Hey, Ollia. It's Finn again. I was hoping to speak to your other children. Are they home yet?"

"As I told you, none of them are here. I'll pass on your contact information, but it's up to them if they wish to speak with you."

"You're home alone?"

"What of it?"

"Nothing. Sorry to bother you." He took a breath to say goodbye, but Ollia disconnected.

"Helpful as ever," I said. "Anyone with a distrustful mind would think that family doesn't want us involved in their business."

"You don't need a distrustful mind to realize that." Zandra stood and shrugged on her jacket.

Finn pinched his chin between his finger and thumb. "That family should be supporting each other in a difficult time like this. Ollia may be stone cold, but she just lost her husband, yet none of her children are around to keep an eye on her."

"Her devious, game playing, cruel husband," I said. "She'll probably dance on his grave when the time comes."

"True enough. Maybe they're all taking a break from each other." Finn patted his stomach. "Let's go grab food and then figure out our next move."

We agreed to try the café again and see if Sorcha was open that evening, and I was keen to ensure the salmon hadn't been banished from the menu.

I'd just wandered past the Gingerbread Bakery, heading toward the café with the others, when a smoky smell filled the air.

I backtracked to the bakery and peered through the glass. It was unlike Tia to burn anything. She was a pro when turning out the perfect loaf.

There was a single customer inside, gesturing at the chalkboard menu, her back to me and a baseball cap pulled low. Tia raised a hand to her, nodded, and turned from the counter.

Then the air vanished, and the bakery exploded.

Chapter 13

Burned buns & breadsticks

Acrid smoke and the stench of burning fur roused me to my senses. I was on my back, my paws in the air, and my tail on fire. Again.

I rolled over, patted out the flames, and looked for Zandra. Where was my witch? She'd been ahead of me with Finn, but I had no clue if the bakery blast had reached them.

Then I spotted my angel friend. Finn was crouched, his wide wings curled around him, flames flickering off his feathers.

I dashed through the smoky air, staggering, my heart pounding and my head a throbbing mess of pain and confusion. I cast a dowsing spell, and a small, grumpy rain cloud appeared over Finn's head and soaked him, putting out the flames within seconds.

Only when the last flame flickered out did he lift his head and lower his wings. Zandra was safely tucked underneath him, just as I'd hoped she would be.

I flung myself into my witch's arms and pressed my face against her forehead. "Are you hurt?"

"All good. Other than ringing in my ears." Her hand went to my charred tail. "You look like you didn't do so well."

"It's nothing that can't be fixed." After taking several deep breaths, sharing the same air as my witch, reassuring myself she was fine, I turned to look at Finn. He was a smoky, soaked mess, but he was a most welcome sight.

I bounced out of Zandra's arms and landed on Finn's shoulder, scraping my tongue across his cheek several times. "You saved my witch's life. I'll be forever in your debt."

He chuckled and gently pushed me away. "Juno! That tongue is like sandpaper. Get it away from me. I know you clean your butt with that thing."

I nipped his ear. "My hygiene habits are none of your concern."

"They are when you're licking my face." He gently lifted me off his shoulder. "I'd have saved you, too, but you weren't close enough to cover when the bakery went up."

By this time, more people had arrived on the scene to see what had happened to the store. We were helped up and dusted down. Several people suggested we go to the hospital, but none of us were badly injured, and I could heal my tail with magic and sleep.

As soon as we were on our feet and steady, we ran back to the flaming bakery. The large glass window at the front of the store had shattered outward, covering the ground in lethal slices of jagged glass. Smoke belched out of the opening, filling the air with a toxic sludge of ash and fumes.

"There were people inside when the explosion happened," I said. "We need to get them out."

"No one would have survived that blast," Finn said.

"We need to check! Tia was inside. Maybe Binky, too. They could be hurt."

"Juno, wait!" Finn tried to grab me. "If they were in there, they won't be alive. There was no warning that the explosion was about to happen."

I ignored him and leaped through an opening in the broken front door. I'd expected nothing but flames and destruction inside, so it surprised me to see not everything had been ruined.

There was a large black mark on the floor, suggesting the explosion was localized to that spot. The spot the customer had been standing in.

"Juno, get out of there!" Finn called from the doorway. "Backup is on its way. They'll deal with this."

"Why bother when I'm already here?" I muttered as I examined the scene, continuing to look for signs of life. "Binky. Tia. If you can hear me, make a noise. Anything."

There was a faint groan from the back of the bakery.

I jumped over broken glass and damaged chairs and ran into a stockinged foot, missing a shoe. "Tia, is that you?"

Even though the smoke messed with my booping snooter, this foot smelled like that of a stranger. Tia usually smelled of delicious baked goods and sugar, not expensive floral perfume.

I scrambled over the body, checking for injuries as I made my way up the torso, and discovered Laylah Morfiel on her back, with blood in her hair. "Stay still. I'll get you out of here."

She groaned again. "My family."

"Of course. They'll soon be by your side. Stay strong. You're not allowed to die on my watch." I pressed my paws gently against her chest so as not to aggravate any injuries and used a translocation spell to get her out of the bakery.

Zandra was instantly by my side. "Is she alive?"

"Just. But she doesn't look good." While I'd been inside the bakery, several angels had arrived on the scene, including Cythera.

"Oh! That's Laylah Morfiel!" Zandra said.

Finn crouched beside Laylah and grabbed her wrist.

"Move out of the way." Cythera strode over. She stared at Laylah's charred, smoky form. "Take her to the hospital," she instructed two waiting angels.

"We should go back into the bakery. Tia was serving Laylah when the explosion happened," I said. "I called for her and Binky, but they didn't reply. They must be stuck somewhere. They could be injured."

"Hey! Up here."

I turned and discovered Tia and Binky poking their heads out of the apartment window above the bakery. Thank the stars, they were alive.

"Are you hurt?" Cythera called out.

"We're good, although trapped. And the floor is getting hot. The fire could get through to us at any time."

"Bring them down," Cythera instructed another angel.

"Wait. My family," Laylah said again.

"We'll let them know you're being taken to the hospital," I said. "Do you know what happened in there?"

"Stop delaying my angels. Laylah needs immediate medical treatment." Cythera glared at me. "Why are you always at the site of every problem in this town?"

"This one's not my fault. We were just walking past the bakery when it exploded. If you let me question Laylah, I could find out why."

"I do the questioning. Why isn't Laylah moving?" Cythera motioned for her angels to hurry.

"Because she's not breathing." Finn looked up from his examination of Laylah's still chest.

"Get her back!" Cythera batted aside a waft of black smoke.

"She was alive in the bakery. She's only just gone," I said. "You have time to resurrect her."

Finn pulsed out some of his angel magic, covering Laylah in a pale pink light. "She's not responding. Her injuries must be serious."

"She was in the direct path of the explosion," I said. "When I walked past the bakery, Laylah was at the counter. She must have been knocked back and hit a wall, so she could have internal bleeding."

Cythera kneeled and attempted to stabilize Laylah, but she remained motionless.

"If Laylah isn't brought back in the next couple of minutes, it'll be too late to save her," I whispered to Zandra. "We must help."

Zandra nodded. She kneeled and caught hold of Laylah's smoke blackened hand, while I rested my front paws on my witch's leg. The second I made the connection, the power I'd gifted Zandra flared to life and flooded out of her in a brilliant rainbow arc, pouring into Laylah's heart.

Zandra looked at me with wide eyes but said nothing as the angels watched. This had never happened to us before, but we wouldn't let on that we didn't know what we were doing. Rainbows were always a good sign.

Laylah gasped and drew in a shuddering breath.

"Well done," Finn said. "I thought we'd lost her. Nothing I did made a difference, and I couldn't find any magic to grab and ignite."

"You see what you can achieve when you have an exceptional cat familiar by your side." I glanced at Cythera. "We come highly recommended by all who use our services."

"Take Laylah to the hospital immediately," Cythera said to the waiting angels. "Make sure she's seen as a priority."

Zandra leaned back and went to drop Laylah's hand. Her brow furrowed. She flexed her fingers, but their hands remained joined.

"Stop messing around," Cythera said. "Laylah is in a critical condition."

Zandra glared at her. "I'm aware of that, having helped bring her back to life. But our hands are stuck together."

I sniffed around Zandra and Laylah's hands. Something magical had bound them, and it didn't want to let them go. Maybe rainbow magic wasn't so special.

"Zandra Crypt! Release your magical hold on her. Draw back whatever it is you used," Cythera said.

"If I draw it back, Laylah might die!"

Cythera's lips puckered. "You sound as if you have no clue what magic you used to return her to the land of the living."

Zandra opened her mouth, but no sound came out.

"We're in full control of our powers. Always have been, always will be." I hopped onto Laylah's chest, which rose and fell in a comforting rhythm. "But sometimes, our magic is so powerfully awesome, it comes with an occasional side effect."

"For the goddess's sake." Cythera sighed. "Take them both to the hospital."

"I'm going too," I said. "Where my witch goes, I go." And I wanted to see exactly what was going on with this wonderful new magic we'd poured into Laylah. And, although the conditions were less than perfect, we'd just gotten direct access to another murder suspect. If we were literally stuck to Laylah, she'd have no choice but to answer our questions about Erig.

Cythera dismissed us with a wave of her hand and strode to the bakery, several angels scurrying behind her as she barked out orders.

"I'll stay here and give you an update when I know more," Finn said.

Zandra nodded then squeaked when an angel scooped her up. I clung to her shoulder as two angels took off in unison, one of them carrying Laylah and the other Zandra.

Our icy, wind-whipped journey was over quickly, and we were hurried into a treatment room, Zandra's hand still melded with Laylah's. We had no choice but to take a seat and keep quiet while the doctors and nurses went to work to make sure Laylah remained stable.

Laylah mumbled several times as they healed her, each mumble relating to her family.

"Maybe she'll settle if she has a family member beside her," I whispered to Zandra. "It sounds like she doesn't want to be surrounded by strangers."

"You're in charge of bringing someone here to comfort her." Zandra gently lifted her hand. "Any idea how long this unwanted hand bonding will last?"

"No clue. No clue why it even happened." I hopped off her lap.

"I felt the power you gifted me fire up. It was intense. I didn't feel like I had control over it. And I honestly didn't know if that arc of power that shot out of me would help Laylah or kill her."

"She was already dead, so there was no risk of that."

Zandra arched an eyebrow. "Anything you need to tell me about this magical gift? Should I not use it?"

"Maybe there was a tiny malfunction," I said. "You need to practice using the power. Get a feel for it." I cleaned my smokey whiskers.

"It'll go on the list of things to do when I'm not rounding up angry critters and solving murders. Go! Find a family member and get them here."

I was glad Zandra sent me off. I didn't know how to explain that jolt in our bond. It shouldn't have happened, and Zandra was plenty powerful enough to use that magic without it causing her any problems.

I bounded out of the hospital and over to the Morfiel's rental property. I didn't bother knocking because I was certain Ollia would fob me off with some excuse about the family not being there. Instead, I went around the back and peered through several windows until I discovered Micah sitting in the corner of a room with a book on his lap.

After giving my singed tail a sniff, I thumped my paws against the glass, causing Micah to jump and look up. He stared at me for a second then set his book to one side and walked to the window, releasing the latch and lifting it.

"You're that cat who fought with my father." Micah was the smallest family member, with shiny, pale skin and a nervous twitch under one startling purple eye.

"Yes. Greetings. I'm Juno. And I'm innocent of all murders present, past, and future. However, I'm not here because of your father's death. Your sister, Laylah, has been in an accident. She needs you."

His eyebrows rose. "How bad? Is she..."

"Alive. But she needed urgent attention at the hospital. They're getting her stable while we speak." I inhaled and caught a whiff of smoke on Micah's clothes. "Have you been to the Gingerbread Bakery?"

"No, but I know the place you mean. I walked past it yesterday. Why do you ask?"

"That's where Laylah was injured. She was at the counter when there was an explosion. She's been asking for her family since it happened. I imagine she needs comforting."

Micah looked away. "I doubt that's true."

"It's all she's been asking for. You should come with me."

Micah sighed. "She won't want me there. Laylah's independent, and she does her own thing. If anyone tries to take care of her, she yells at them. She learned that skill from our charming father."

"Maybe so, but she's still injured." I tilted my head. "You don't seem concerned or surprised. You don't like Laylah?"

"I... I am sorry she's been hurt. Will she recover?"

"You can find that out when you speak to the doctor." I sniffed again. The smoky smell was coming off him. Why did Micah stink of smoke? Had he been at the bakery when the explosion happened? Had he caused it? Was that the reason he was so unsurprised by the news of his sister's injuries?

"Something wrong?" Micah said.

"Do you smoke cigarettes?"

"Never."

"Have you been around any fires today?"

He opened his mouth then hesitated. "Not exactly."

"And you're certain you haven't visited the Gingerbread Bakery today?"

"Wait a second." Micah took a step back. "You think I had something to do with what happened to Laylah?" He lifted his arm and brushed ash off the sleeve of his pale sweater.

"The smell coming off you and the evidence of ash on your clothing suggests that's exactly where you've been." A warning drift of magic sparkled across my fur.

He looked up at me and raised a hand. "It's not what you think. I only smell like this because I'm looking after Smoke."

"Your father's missing phoenix?"

"Yeah. He must have gotten free from Dad when he was killed in the park. Smoke came back to the house in a confused mess. I took the chain off his leg, and he started to smolder."

"Smoke went full phoenix on you?"

"Yes! He ignited. There was nothing left but a pile of ash and an egg. That egg hatched almost immediately." He let out a long sigh. "I have a baby phoenix and no clue how to look after him."

"Congratulations! That's a wonderful addition to your family."

"I don't want him. I'm not ready for that kind of responsibility." Micah's mouth twisted to the side. "But I also don't want the little guy to die."

"What about another family member taking him?"

"I've kept quiet about him to the others. Ollia would mistreat him, and everyone else... I don't know. They've got their own things going on. I was wondering about giving him to a sanctuary."

"I'll have him! Take me to your flaming chick so we can bond."

"You know how to look after a phoenix?"

"I work at animal control. It's what I do!" Technically, I had no idea. But how hard could it be? And Smoke had been there when Erig was killed. It was important to keep him safe and happy.

"Err... okay. Follow me. He's upstairs."

Chapter 14

Mama cat

"You sure you want to do this?" Micah led me up the staircase in the house. "Phoenix chicks are fussy and hard to keep alive. They often ignite, and you have to start all over again before you get a stable one."

I bounded up the cold wooden staircase behind him. "Positive. And an infant phoenix needs tender care and constant companionship. You shouldn't leave him alone at such a delicate time."

"I had to get out of there. Smoke keeps setting me on fire. That's why I stink. And I had to fireproof my bedroom. The whole place would have gone up by now if I hadn't been drifting a containment spell everywhere. It's tiring. I'm really not ready to be a parent."

"Was Smoke due to regenerate? He was old?"

"No. He wasn't that old. But he exploded at unusual times. I always thought he was faulty."

"Those could have been stress-induced regenerations," I said. "And being a witness to what happened to your father must have been too much for Smoke to take. I imagine his mental state was already fragile, given his incarceration by Erig."

"Yeah, Dad didn't treat that bird well." Micah glanced at me, a guilty look on his face. "It's why I kept him after he came back. I felt an obligation to give him a better chance at life." He led me into a tastefully decorated pale blue bedroom with navy accent cushions. Sitting in a large cage on a charred piece of cloth was an adorable tiny crimson and purple phoenix with faint stripes of pale blue on his tiny feathers.

Smoke squawked when he saw us and flapped his stubby wings to get our attention.

"Get him out of that cage," I instructed. "Phoenixes don't thrive by being imprisoned. If you don't give them freedom and plenty of mental stimulation, they perish."

Micah's cheeks flushed as he pulled keys from his pocket and unlocked the cage door. He shoved his hands in and grabbed Smoke, dropping him on the floor, when a tiny fireball shot out of Smoke's beak and burned a hole in Micah's sweater.

"Handle him carefully!" I dashed to the phoenix and gently rested a paw on top of his head. Fear and agitation pulsed out of the tiny bird. "Greetings, little one. We've met before. I'm Juno, and you rather spectacularly burned my tail to protect Erig."

"The bird won't remember that, will he?" Micah examined the burn in his sweater.

"Phoenixes retain all their memories. It's what makes them such magnificent birds. Some have lived thousands of years and have experienced extraordinary things. It's what makes them so valuable." I gently petted Smoke's head.

He gave another squawk then waddled over and leaned against my side.

"He likes you," Micah said. "If you want him, he's yours. I hope you can help him see that life can be decent. It used to make me so angry when Dad mistreated him."

"Did you ever defend Smoke?"

"Once. Never again. I was disciplined." Micah focused on his feet.

"Locked in a barn like your other siblings?"

He lifted his gaze, his eyes wide. "How did you know?"

"I'm involved in your father's murder investigation. We're uncovering interesting things about your family."

Micah lowered his head again. "Yeah, we're one-of-a-kind, I hope. I wouldn't want any other kids to go through what we did."

"It sounds like you all endured a lot."

Micah kept his head down and nodded.

"Help me out. Place Smoke on my back, between my shoulder blades. He should be able to balance there without any trouble. Then we need to get you to the hospital to see your sister."

Micah grimaced. "If I visit, Laylah will only yell at me."

"She's not yelling at anybody. She was almost unconscious when I left."

"That bad? Do you think she'll die?"

"The doctors think they can save her, but it was touch and go when I pulled her from the burning building."

"She is strong-willed. At least, she used to be." He looked at the door. "I'll find someone else to go with you."

"Micah, you're stalling. Your sister needs you, and there's no one else here. What's the problem?"

He ran his foot along the carpet several times. "No problem. Sure, I can go see her."

Micah really didn't look eager to come with me. In fact, he was shaking. "Where is the rest of your family?"

Micah shrugged. "I haven't seen Rabdos for ages, and I don't know where Forfax is. He could be back soon. We could always wait for him."

"Your mother?"

"Ollia went out earlier in the day. She didn't say where she was going or when she'd come back."

"You all lead independent lives from each other." I walked slowly to ensure Smoke remained balanced on my back and was comfortable as I headed back to the stairs.

Micah lagged behind, dragging each foot. "It looks like it from the outside, doesn't it?"

"It's not?" I glanced back at him, and Smoke attempted to nip my booping snooter with his tiny beak.

"Just like Smoke, it feels like I'm living in a giant cage. Sure, it's a beautiful cage, and I get amazing things given to me, but only if I behave the way I'm expected to."

"Having spoken to Acer, I understand how difficult your family is."

We reached the front door, and Micah opened it.

He pulled on his shoes and grabbed a black jacket. "All I want is a quiet life. I keep my head down, which makes things easier, but not always."

I wanted to comfort Micah. This young man was suffering. I rested a paw on his booted foot. "May I ask where you were when you learned what happened to your father?"

"Here. I was asleep in my room on my own. The first I knew about what happened was when Ollia came in."

"Of course. And she told you to say I killed Erig?"

"You heard that rumor?"

"One of your siblings revealed it to me."

"Acer?"

"No."

"Forfax. It's got to be. He's such a snitch. He loves getting people in trouble."

"A truth teller is never a snitch. Forfax saved me from being under suspicion for a crime I didn't commit." I looked up at Micah. "I intend to find out who did kill Erig, though. So, if you know anything about it..."

He shrugged and looked away. "I can't help you with that. Let's go to the hospital so I can get shouted at."

I nodded. Unfortunately for Micah, his alibi was as useless as everyone else's in this family. He couldn't be disqualified as a suspect.

We left the house, and although I asked Micah a few questions about his family, he answered with only one or two words, making it clear he didn't want any conversation. But I'd gotten enough from him to realize how miserable his existence was. And it gave him the same motive as the rest of the Morfiel children. His father repressed and mistreated him, while his mother turned a blind eye. Just like the others, Micah could have lost control and gotten revenge.

We arrived at the hospital and were informed Laylah was stable and had been moved into a private room. When we arrived in the room, I discovered Zandra still stuck to Laylah.

"I swear, if you don't let go of my hand, I'm cutting it off." Laylah was glowering at Zandra and clawing at her hand with her blackened nails.

"Steady yourself, Smoke." I leaped onto the bed and landed on Laylah's chest. "Behave yourself. If it weren't for us, you'd be dead."

"You! You're the cat who—"

"Yes. As everyone keeps telling me, I'm the cat who's alleged to have murdered your father. And as I keep telling everyone, I'm innocent. However, you'll see my truly evil side if you threaten my wonderful witch again."

Laylah's glower didn't get any less severe. "She won't let go of my hand!"

"Because I can't, as I keep telling you." Zandra lifted their joined hands. "See? I'm not holding on. The magic I used to bring you back has connected us. I don't want to be sitting here holding your hand any more than you want me to hold it."

"Can't the doctors sort this?" Laylah looked at the door. "Call them back here. Where are they?"

"They've tried. Nothing will get us apart."

"Give me a chainsaw and five minutes."

I hissed at Laylah and stared at her until she mumbled an apology.

I looked over my shoulder. Micah hadn't come into the room. He was peeping around the edge of the door, so I gestured for him to approach the bed. Maybe seeing a sibling would tame this fiery creature.

Micah reluctantly entered the room. "I heard you ran into some trouble. How's it going?"

Laylah scowled at him. "What are you doing here? I figured you'd be celebrating with the others when you heard the news. Bad luck. I'm still here."

"Um… no. I wouldn't do that. Juno said you wanted family here. I told her you didn't mean it, but she insisted I come to the hospital."

"Why would I want any of you here, gloating at my misfortune?" Laylah tried to cross her arms and almost yanked Zandra over the bed.

I hissed at her again. "Settle! Micah is here to comfort you."

"I'd get more comfort from being in a locked closet with a grumpy puff adder."

"Told you," Micah muttered to me.

I glanced at Zandra, who seemed as confused as me. "When we rescued you from the bakery, you kept talking about your family."

"I hit my head on a wall. Of course, I wouldn't be making any sense. My family won't help me," Laylah said.

"You don't want anyone here?" Zandra said.

"What I want is peace. I want my hand unstuck from yours, and I want you all to leave and never come back."

Smoke squawked in my ear, and a wave of power pulsed from his tiny feet and into my back.

"You think you can help?" I asked him.

He squawked again.

"What you got there?" Zandra leaned closer. "A baby bird?"

"A baby phoenix. Smoke is back from the ashes."

Zandra jerked back when he tried to bite her nose. "He's feisty. Where'd you find him?"

"I'll tell you later. Shall we try getting you unstuck with some baby phoenix power?"

"I'm willing to try anything. Just get me out of here and away from Laylah before I do something I regret."

"The feeling is mutual." Laylah wrinkled her grubby nose. "And you stink of smoke."

Zandra bared her teeth. "You stink of blood, bad attitude, and rudeness."

"Ladies, please. There's no need to trade insults," I murmured.

My wonderful witch and the charred grump in the bed glared at each other.

Smoke remained settled on my shoulder blades and continued to drift out his power.

I checked my bond with Zandra was strong and rested a paw on Zandra and Laylah's joined hands. A hot flash of unfamiliar magic flooded through me.

"What was that?" Laylah stared at her glowing hand.

"Phoenix power," I whispered, in awe of my tiny new friend.

Zandra drew back her hand, and it came away from Laylah's with no resistance.

"At last," Laylah said. "All of you out. No! Micah. You stay."

"You should get some sleep. I'll come back another time." He inched toward the door.

"You're staying. We need to talk. You have some explaining to do."

Micah's shoulders sagged. "Whatever you say."

I was happy to leave Laylah, since she was in no mood to talk about murder or exploding bakeries, her furious focus on her brother. I hurried out of the room with Smoke on my back and Zandra beside me.

She eased the door shut, and before we'd taken a few steps away, muffled yelling started.

"That family is a giant mess of gross nightmares," Zandra said.

"And that family is also a killer's target." Finn approached us from along the corridor. "The bakery explosion was no accident."

"What did you find out?" I asked.

"It's early days in the investigation, but once the fire was out, we looked around. The explosion happened in one spot. Right by the counter, on the customer's side."

"That's what I told Cythera," I said.

"You think Laylah was the target of that explosion?" Zandra looked back at the closed door, where the yelling was still going on.

Finn nodded. "I reckon someone has unfinished business with this family."

"And they're targeting them one by one?" I said.

He looked at me, blinked, and peered closer. "You have a baby bird on your back."

"This is Smoke. After the stress of seeing his master killed, he regenerated. Micah has been taking care of him, but he doesn't want him. So, we're fostering him." I looked up at Zandra.

"We are? I don't know how to raise a phoenix. This is my first ever phoenix encounter."

"Leave him with me. Back to the investigation, Finn." It was best if Zandra didn't dwell on the challenges of having a tiny, untrained, fire belching baby staying in our basement. It would only worry her.

Finn snapped his jaw shut. "Sure. Anyway, it seems likely Laylah was the reason the explosion triggered. We'll know more once we've thoroughly investigated the scene."

"Magic caused the explosion?" I asked.

"Almost certainly."

"Binky and Tia are safe?" Zandra said.

"Other than shaken up, neither of them were harmed. Binky was snoozing on the landing, and Tia had just gone in the freezer to grab some dough when the explosion happened. They got lucky."

"And the bakery..." I said.

"Torched. It won't be open for months."

I grimaced. I so enjoyed Tia's delicious bacon and double sausage baps. They would be missed.

"If there's someone out there who wants all the family dead," Zandra said, "this must be a revenge killing. Maybe Erig ruined one family, so whoever is left is coming after the Morfiels."

"It's the dominant theory Cythera is working on." Finn looked at the closed door. "What's with all the shouting?"

"No idea. I brought Micah here because Laylah needed comforting and was asking for a family member, but the second she saw him, she got angry."

"It's her default setting," Zandra said. "I'm glad you showed up when you did. I reckon she'd have tried to cut my hand off if things had gotten any more heated."

I hissed softly. "She'd have lost her head if she'd done that to you."

Smoke squawked what sounded like a note of agreement. This little phoenix was growing on me.

"I need to catch up on everything I've missed," Finn said. "Did you question Micah when you found him?"

"Briefly. His alibi is identical to everyone else's." I nudged Smoke back between my shoulder blades as he slid to one side.

"That's no help," Finn said. "Why are they all telling us the same thing? It's as if they don't want Erig's murder solved."

"Because they're hiding something," Zandra said.

"All Micah said was that he wanted a quiet life, and he'd kept his head down to stay out of trouble."

"Just like they're all doing," Finn said. "This investigation is stumbling from one crisis to another. Who's next to be taken out if they don't start telling the truth?"

"It feels as if we're spinning our wheels. The suspects have no alibis, and they all have similar motives for wanting Erig dead," I said.

"We're missing something," Zandra said. "Are we looking at this wrong? Does the bakery explosion point to someone outside of the family? Maybe a hired killer?"

"We're widening our options to consider that. Looking into Erig's business contacts and speaking to anyone who had a problem with him. So far, nothing unusual has shown up," Finn said. "Anyone who had a motive to kill Erig has a solid alibi. We're drawing blanks whenever we look outside of the family."

"Which means we're no further along," Zandra said.

Finn sighed. "Let's call this a day. I need rest after almost being blown up and then heroically saving your life."

Zandra smirked. "I never thanked you for that."

"Any time. And I know you'll return the favor." He nodded at us. "Let's try this again tomorrow."

Chapter 15

Circling the suspects

A gentle nip on my booping snooter roused me from my sleep. Smoke stared at me.

"Squawk?"

"Hush. Don't wake Zandra. She gets grumpy if disturbed while asleep."

"Squawk?" The noise was softer this time.

"You hungry?"

Smoke flapped his stubby wings. Overnight, he'd grown several inches. Phoenix regenerated quickly, and he'd be full-sized within a month.

I rolled over so he could hop onto my back then lightly skipped up the basement steps and into the kitchen. I snacked from the dried biscuit bowl always left down by Vorana then gave Smoke a few pieces of brown spotted banana from the fruit bowl on the counter.

Once his stomach was round and full of food, his eyelids drooped.

"Back to bed for you," I said. When we'd returned from the hospital, I'd read up on phoenix care.

When a baby phoenix was in a growth stage, they needed at least twenty hours of sleep a day.

I carried him back down to the basement and settled him on the pillow next to Zandra.

He tried to follow me when I jumped off the bed.

I shook my head. "You have an important job. You need to keep my wonderful witch safe. I only trust her with strong, confident creatures. Can I trust you, Smoke?"

Smoke nodded, his eyes already heavy with sleep. Such a cutie.

I waited another minute until he was snoozing then dashed up the stairs. It was a weekend, and just past dawn, so the streets were quiet. I figured, since I'd been roused so early, I'd make progress in solving this mystery. And I was headed to the hospital.

The corridors were silent as I crept into Laylah's room. She was awake, sitting up in bed, a grumpy expression on her face and her pixie crop clean and free from blood and grime.

"Greetings. How are you feeling?" I said.

Laylah jumped and turned to stare at me. "You again?"

"Still have a murder to solve and a name to clear. Mine, in case you were in any doubt."

She smoothed her hands over the bedsheets. "The doctor told me you got me out of the bakery."

"No one else was prepared to face the flames. But I had to see if anyone had been hurt."

"Well, I guess I owe you thanks."

"You're welcome." I hopped onto the end of the bed and waited for her to continue.

Laylah's gaze went to the window. "My family would never have done that for me. Why did you help a stranger?"

"It was the right thing to do. And I've been hearing about your upbringing from Acer. Not all families are like yours."

She let out a sigh of disgust. "Acer never could keep her mouth shut. It was a good thing she moved out. That mouth of hers was only getting her in deeper trouble with Erig."

"You say his name like it's a bad word."

"I've never hidden the fact I hate my whole family. I'm glad he's dead. He was a warped person. Barely a person." Laylah kept her gaze averted from me. "If he hadn't already been dead, I'd have assumed he set the explosion in the bakery."

I was startled by her revelation. "What makes you say that?"

She shrugged. "We recently argued. It was bad. He was a horrible man. More monster than man."

"What was the argument about?"

"I'm surprised Acer hasn't blabbed to you about it. She was next in line for the same treatment."

"Next in line for what?"

Laylah's mouth turned down. "Erig had to be seen with the right people and get into all the amazing social circles. A few of them proved harder to get into than he thought they would. But he had certain assets at his disposal, and he planned on using them."

"You and Acer were the assets?"

"Got it in one. He wanted to marry us off to his prospects. Less than a month ago, he arranged for us to go for dinner together. He said it would be just the two of us, so he could catch up with what was going on in my life." A smirk distorted Laylah's face. "Not that he didn't already know, since he controlled it. Anyway, we met at the restaurant and were about to order, when this old guy with a double chin and a receding hairline joined us. He was a member of the Dispenza Dynasty."

"The gremlin family?"

"The very same. Erig had been trying to forge links with them for a long time. He figured, if I married this creepy old dude, it would open a door into their family and all the dubious deals they make." She sneered at the wall. "I was disgusted with him. Although Acer's match was even worse. Erig planned to pair her with someone from the Bloodtooth Clan."

"They sound savage. What magical creature are they?"

"Vampires. Not the friendly kind. Mainly feral, but they own valuable property and land. Erig wanted to expand his retrieval business into their areas, but he needed their permission before making a move. If Acer had been married into that nightmare, they'd have drained her or turned her. She'd have vanished. But Erig would have gotten what he wanted, so he considered it a small price to pay."

"No wonder Acer wanted to get away."

"We all did. We still do, but it seems impossible to get away from this weird family." Laylah briskly rubbed her arms. "Once you're in, they never let you go."

"I'm sorry this happened to you, and I'm sorry your father tried to marry you off."

"It's got nothing to do with you. I appreciate that you saved me, but don't waste your time checking to see if I'm okay. I've been on my own and have looked after myself for a long time. That's not changing soon."

"I understand why you feel that way," I said. "But do you really think your father was vengeful enough to kill you because you refused to marry his choice of husband?"

"That was his way. You obeyed him, or you were punished. He wanted me married, and I'd refused. It was the first time in a long time I'd stood up to him. It felt so good, but I knew trouble was coming my way. Then, boom! The spot I was standing on exploded."

If she truly believed that, it gave Laylah a strong motive for wanting Erig dead. Maybe a stronger motive than any of her siblings.

"Is that why you killed him?"

She turned her head slowly then laughed. "I get it. You need to clear your name, so you're pointing the claws at me. Bad luck, kitty. I was at home, along with everyone else."

"In bed? Alone?"

"You got it. I have Ollia and everyone else to back me up." Her gaze went to the door, and her eyes narrowed. "I should get in touch with Angel Force and ask them why they haven't charged you yet."

"They haven't charged me because they know I didn't do it."

"They're thinking one of us did? That's why you're snooping?"

"It's often someone close to the victim who commits the violent act."

"Read that in a cat law enforcement manual?"

"I got it from the TV. But it still stands true."

Laylah glanced away again. "I'm not the family member you should look at for Erig's murder."

"Then who should I look at?"

She went quiet again.

I decided on a change of tact, since the silent treatment would get me nowhere. "Since it couldn't have been your father who planted that explosive magic, can you think of anyone else who could have set it?"

Laylah didn't answer the question, she just kept staring at the wall.

"Do you think you were the target or just unlucky?"

She remained tight lipped.

"You were arguing with Micah yesterday when I brought him to see you," I said. "Was he behind the explosion?"

She played with the bedsheet. "He's always been the quiet one, and he quickly learned that, if he kept his mouth shut, he could fly under the radar and not be Erig's target too often. I always say you need to watch for the quiet ones. They're always thinking and plotting. Always got some scheme going on in the background."

"You argued because you thought he was involved with what happened to you?"

Laylah went quiet again, then she sighed. "It's possible. I reckon he got pushed too far and has lost his senses. Just before Erig died, I saw Micah fighting with him. I was shocked because I've never seen them go at each other before. The only time Micah ever got in serious trouble was when he said he wanted to reconnect with his birth parents. Erig didn't speak to him for a month."

I imagined Erig did far more than that as punishment for daring to look beyond the confines of the Morfiel family, but I kept that thought to myself.

"All I'll say about Micah is don't let his pathetic act fool you," Laylah said. "There's more going on in his head than anyone realizes."

There was a knock on the door, and Acer appeared.

"I am popular today," Laylah said. "What do you want?"

"I figured you might need company, but I see you've already got some." Acer looked at me and raised her eyebrows.

"I was up early and thought I'd check in on Laylah," I said.

"You've done that, so you can both go. I'm tired. Send in the doctor. I want to see when I can get out of here."

"Laylah, you almost died yesterday. You need a few days to recover." Acer stepped into the room.

"You're still here?" Laylah pointedly turned her back on us.

"Feel better soon." I hopped off the bed and nudged a sad-faced Acer out of the room.

She walked along the corridor in silence until we reached the end. "I see almost being blown up has soured Laylah's mood even more. I didn't think that was possible."

"It hasn't helped. Since I didn't get the opportunity to question her about your father's murder, I thought I'd try today."

Acer tilted her head. "Other than cussing you out or ignoring you, did she let anything slip?"

"Laylah pointed the finger at Micah for killing your father and trying to blow her up. Does that make sense to you?"

Acer let out a snort. "No way! Laylah's lying. She has to be. Micah would never do that."

"She saw Micah and your father arguing."

"Micah hasn't argued with anyone in over twenty years. He knows better. I won't say he doesn't have his secrets, but alongside Forfax, I trust him just as much."

"Maybe Laylah lied to divert attention from herself."

"Maybe. Or maybe Micah has been concealing things from me." Acer lifted her hands. "That's what my family does. We're so full of secrets, they make me choke."

I waited to see if Acer would share any of those secrets, but nothing came out other than some disgruntled huffs and mutters.

"I should go. Things to do," she finally said.

"Stick around. You could be useful in this investigation." And maybe let something slip.

Acer tipped back her head. "I guess. If you think I can be useful."

"You're always useful." I gestured, and we turned toward the exit. "Just so you know, Smoke has been found. I'm fostering him for now. Hope that won't be an issue."

Her bottom lip jutted out. "Fine by me. He'll have a fun home with you and Zandra. Glad he's got somewhere nice to live."

I nodded. Unlike my sad angel companion, who'd never experienced the warmth and wonderful feeling of safety in her family. "Let's grab the others. It's time to find out who is behind this, so you and your family can have peace."

Acer shrugged. "Peace and my family don't know how to co-exist."

Two hours later, we were in Finn's apartment with Zandra, who'd not appreciated being woken early to talk about murder. However, she'd dragged herself out of bed, grabbed croissants from Vorana's stash for us to feast on, and we were settled on Finn's comfy couch, Smoke on my back, Acer curled in an armchair, and a sleepy-eyed Finn sipping coffee.

I updated everyone about my brief, spiky interview with Laylah while we stared at pictures of the suspects and ate breakfast.

"Let's run through them all and see if anything clicks into place," Finn said. "Who's first?"

"We'll start with Ollia," I said.

"She's aloof and a liar." Zandra glanced at Acer. "Sorry for disrespecting your family."

Acer sipped from a mug of coffee. "You described her perfectly. Ollia is more mannequin than mother."

"She's also powerful enough to kill Erig," I said. "And there's rage simmering just below the surface whenever we speak to her."

"And Ollia has no alibi," Finn said.

I nudged Smoke back between my shoulder blades. "Then we have angry Laylah. Who's understandably livid, given what she's been through."

"Maybe Erig attempting to get her married off was the final straw," Zandra said.

"It's a solid motive. And again, she's got no alibi." Finn shuffled the photographs around. "Then we have Acer and Juno. Fortunately, Acer has a solid alibi, so we can remove one suspect from the list."

I flicked an ear. "And me?"

"If I didn't know you better, I'd still have you on this list," Finn said. "It's best you don't go doing shady deals with unscrupulous types like Erig Morfiel in the future. You don't want to end up on a second suspect list."

"Technically, this is already the second time I've been a murder suspect since we moved here. You and Bertoli were foolish enough to consider me and my wonderful witch as suspects in Osorin's murder."

"Is that the guy who lost his head?" Acer said. "I read about that case."

"The very same."

Finn laughed. "That was more Bertoli than me, but it was quite a way to introduce yourself to Angel Force and the town."

"That was never the plan," Zandra muttered. "Take me with you the next time you do a shady deal, then at least you'll have backup and a witness if things go south."

Finn crossed a line through both our pictures. "You're off the list. Rabdos is still a mystery, though. His missing-in-action behavior has to be seen as suspicious."

"This is usual behavior for him, though." I looked at Acer. "When things get too much for him, he disappears, right?"

She nodded. "Rabdos will show up in a few days. He must be wondering what's next for him. Does he even want to take over the business? I wouldn't if I were him. I'm certain he only pretended he wanted to run things to keep Erig off his back."

"What about Forfax?" Zandra said. "What did you talk about when you met, Acer?"

"He never showed. I waited for ages. I figured he'd changed his mind."

"Forfax wanted to meet you, though. You didn't force him to meet." I eased my ear out of Smoke's beak and slid him onto a cushion, petting his head to calm his mischievous behavior.

"I don't know what happened to him. I even stopped by the house after I'd been waiting for an hour. He wasn't there."

"So, Rabdos and now Forfax are missing? That's odd," Finn said. "Could they be behind this murder and the attack on Laylah? Could they have made a run for it because they think Angel Force is closing in?"

"I think we double down on our efforts to find Rabdos. Maybe we'll discover Forfax is with him," I said.

Finn's mobile snow globe buzzed, and he pulled it out. He groaned as he read the message. "It's Cythera. She wants me in this afternoon. Apparently, there's been more vandalism. She's giving me the worst jobs."

"Who do you think is doing it?" Zandra said as Finn tidied the photos of the suspects.

"It's bored kids. Walk me out if you like, and I'll show you the latest crime scene."

We left the apartment with Finn and headed into the pleasant morning. There were couples strolling hand in hand, and people taking relaxed walks with their familiars as they enjoyed the day.

"It's over here." Finn pointed to an alleyway that led to the main green space in Crimson Cove.

We wandered past the brickwork and discovered black and red paint daubed along the wall.

"These look like gang tags," Acer said. "I've seen something similar to this. I did a couple of weeks of placement in Sandy Bay when they had issues with the Spinelli gang marking new territory."

"Sorcha's new guy is a biker," I said. "And he brought friends with him. Maybe they're considering setting up base in Crimson Cove."

"If that's true, they need to stop marking territory." Finn tapped the wall. "We don't need gang problems coming to town."

"I can speak to Sorcha if you like," Zandra said, "feel things out. If this is her boyfriend and his friends, she'll be horrified. She'll make him stop."

"And kick him out of town for being so disrespectful," I said.

"Thanks," Finn said. "I don't want to come down heavy on the guy and annoy Sorcha if this isn't him. But this can't continue."

I'd wandered away a few steps with Smoke and was staring at some small marks located lower on the wall. It was a series of lines and splodged dots. I stepped back and inspected them some more, my heart racing.

Smoke squawked in my ear as if sensing my distress.

It wasn't the gang tags we needed to worry about. If I was right about what these marks were, everyone living in Crimson Cove was in trouble.

Chapter 16

Ganged up

We went our separate ways, Finn going to Angel Force to get his orders regarding the graffiti, Acer returning home, since she was still on suspension, despite Bertoli confirming her alibi, and I went to Sorcha's café with Zandra and Smoke.

"You're quiet," Zandra said. "Thinking about the murder?"

"It's on my mind." So were those symbols. I hadn't seen anything like that in hundreds of years. I thought the cult that used them had died out a long time ago. Were they making a comeback? And why choose Crimson Cove to print their dark intentions all over the bricks?

"Don't let your thoughts get too gloomy," Zandra said. "You never know, Sorcha might be trying a new plant-based salmon."

I wrinkled my booping snooter. "Salmon is salmon, end of story. You can't make a carrot into a piece of salmon."

Zandra chuckled. "Let's see what we can get to eat."

The café door was open, the lights on, and rock music blasted out. It was a different vibe from the relaxed, friendly atmosphere we were used to. And it was a vibe I wasn't sure I liked.

There were a few customers inside, but the place had been taken over by Gaian and his gang again. And there were more of them. So much for his friends passing through.

"They've multiplied." I hopped onto Zandra's shoulder, conscious of any grumbling hounds lurking underneath a table ready to snap at me. And, of course, I had to keep Smoke safe.

She petted my side. "Things are changing. But look at Sorcha. She's so happy. And I haven't seen her look this healthy in a long time."

We stood by the counter as Sorcha danced among the tables, laughing and chatting with people. She looked the picture of health. So different from when we said goodbye to her when she left for her retreat.

"Hey! It feels like I haven't seen you in days." Sorcha hugged Zandra and tickled me under the chin. "And you have an adorable baby bird!"

"Sorcha Creer, this is Smoke. My foster," I said.

"Temporary foster," Zandra said quickly.

"He's so cute." Sorcha made kissy noises at Smoke, causing him to flap his wings in excitement and almost fall off my back.

"We stopped by the other evening to get food, but you were closed," Zandra said. "You changing things up around here?"

"Oh! No. Sorry about that. Gaian sprung a surprise on me and took me for a romantic night in a hotel. No one's ever done anything like that for me." She glanced over her shoulder and sighed. "He may look tough on the outside, but he's a squidgy marshmallow on the inside. I adore him."

"Glad he's making you happy."

"He really is. I got so used to being alone that it felt normal. I almost expected no one to pay me any attention ever again."

"You always get attention from guys," Zandra said.

"Not from anyone I clicked with. Gaian's just perfect, though."

I narrowed my eyes and studied Gaian as Sorcha extolled his virtues. He sat at a roundtable with five of his biker friends. He was telling a story and had their complete attention.

He may be a good guy, but no one was perfect. Everyone had flaws, some just kept them better hidden than others. Like the Morfiel family.

I didn't want to burst Sorcha's happy bubble, but maybe this guy was too good to be true.

"What will it be?" Sorcha said.

"Do you have any salmon?" I put on my most pitiful voice.

She pressed a finger to her lips. "Come out the back. We can use the vampire room, since there's no one in there. Gaian hates watching people eat animals, so you'll have to be quick and quiet."

Sorcha grabbed two coffees and a couple of muffins for her and Zandra and then snuck us out the back. She opened the fridge and pulled out a pack of salmon. "This is the last. Enjoy."

I hopped off Zandra's shoulder and gratefully accepted the salmon, but I was already figuring out how to get Sorcha to change her mind. I didn't want to have to go to the beach and catch fish every time I wanted a nibble of something delicious.

"Have you heard about the vandalism happening around town?" Zandra settled on a seat.

"No! I've been so busy here or out with Gaian that I'm out of touch with the gossip. My customers are disgusted with me."

"Someone's been daubing gang tags on walls," I said.

Sorcha's eyebrows rose slowly. "There's a new gang muscling in? You think they want to take over from the Shadow gang?"

Sorcha had been on the receiving end of an unpleasant encounter from a notorious gang that blighted Crimson Cove until Zandra and I sorted them out.

"We hope not," Zandra said. "And Angel Force isn't aware of any gang trying to encroach."

"Although, there is one new gang in town we're eager to learn more about," I said.

Sorcha's gaze went to the door. "Gaian! What are you doing back here?"

"I missed you. Wondered what you were up to." He nodded a greeting to me and Zandra.

I'd managed to grab the last piece of salmon and hide it in my mouth, but I was certain he'd seen what I'd been eating. I gulped it down and washed all traces of salmon off my whiskers.

"And those graffiti tags have nothing to do with us." Gaian pushed away from the door and walked in. "That's not what we do."

"What do you do?" Zandra said. "You've changed things in the café since you arrived."

"That wasn't Gaian's influence. It was time I shook things up," Sorcha said. "Things have been the same for such a long time that it was getting boring. Maybe that was why I was so tired. There was no excitement in my life."

"The café was perfect," I said.

"I know why you're saying that." Sorcha looked at my empty plate. "But there's no harm in trying new things."

"Do you know anything about the graffiti?" Zandra said to Gaian. "The marks look like gang tags, so you must realize why we made a connection."

"And they only started appearing when you and your friends arrived," I said.

Gaian placed an arm around Sorcha's shoulders. "I don't take offense over your incorrect assumptions, but we're not your typical biker gang. We're Protectors. We stop the destruction of magical sites and deal with those who pollute them and disrespect the natural law."

"You're environmental activists?" I said.

"That's another term for what we do."

"How do you deal with these polluters?" Zandra said.

"We take them to one side and have a friendly chat with them. Remind them we've only got one big, beautiful planet, and to thoughtlessly destroy it with damaging magic is an idiot's move. They soon change their ways."

"And if they don't?" I said.

"They do. In fact, we've got a demonstration tomorrow to highlight issues involving a local polluter. If you want to see how we operate, you're welcome to come along. Sorcha's joining us."

Sorcha grinned up at Gaian. "It's my first demonstration! I'm nervous to see what happens."

"You'll have a great time, babe. It's really just walking, chanting, then we go get something to eat and have a laugh."

"Although we'd love to join you, we must stay focused on Erig Morfiel's murder," I said.

Gaian lifted his chin. "Right. Sorcha said you help the angels. Tricky case?"

"The family is proving difficult to pin down, and the graffiti is distracting Angel Force. So, if you know anything that could help us..."

"Gaian would never do anything like that," Sorcha said.

"That's right, babe. We don't destroy anything. Our bikes even run on vegetable oil," Gaian said. "We use waste products to power them. And all this leather you see on me, it's made from recycled plastic. When I'm done with it, there's a company I send it to that uses enzymes to break it down."

"There are so many amazing ways we can help the planet." Sorcha pressed a hand to her chest. "And I want to try them all."

I couldn't get on board with this new version of Sorcha if my regular plates of salmon were gone from the menu. There must be some sustainably farmed salmon around here. I'd have to investigate.

"My mission in life is to leave this place better than I found it," Gaian said. "If everyone had that mindset, we'd live in a completely different world."

It was a charming sentiment, but Gaian sounded preachy. We all did our bit, and I never wasted any food Vorana made me. I always licked my plate clean. Zero food waste from me.

"So, you see, Gaian had nothing to do with this graffiti," Sorcha said. "I'm offended you even had to ask if he could be involved."

"It's fine," Gaian said. "I'd expect your friends to make assumptions based on the way I look. People always do."

"That's no excuse to accuse you of something when there's no proof."

"I made no accusations. I'm just ruling people out," Zandra said calmly. "And I want Angel Force focused on figuring out what happened to Erig Morfiel, not obsessing over gang tags on walls."

"Is that what you do?" Gaian said. "You solve the crimes the angels can't?"

"Only when we have the time," I said.

Smoke let out a belch as he nuzzled into my fur. It was time for this baby to go back to bed. I wouldn't mind a nap, too.

"Gaian!" one of his friends called from the café. "We need to talk about tomorrow's route."

"I'd better get back before they plan a route that starts at the pub and never leaves." Gaian kissed Sorcha. "Don't be too long, babe."

"I'll be right out." She watched him leave the room, a soppy expression on her face.

"A friendly word of advice," Zandra said. "I know this relationship is new and exciting, but how well do you know Gaian?"

Sorcha's happy expression faded. "I haven't known him long, but every moment we spend together is perfect. He listens to me, he understands me, and he asks questions about me. I've never had a guy treat me like that before."

"Which is all good, but what do you really know about him? Is he an environmental activist or a troublemaker?"

I winced at the sharpness in Zandra's tone. She was only looking out for her friend, but she needed to be gentler with her interrogation.

"His gang really does protect this planet. They go after those who misuse magic." Sorcha pursed her lips. "I wish I was brave enough to do the same thing. When I compare my life to his, I've achieved nothing. I've served people sandwiches and coffee and gossiped with them. How dull."

"People need to eat," I said. "And gossip makes life interesting."

"Gaian has opened my eyes to something new, and I want to explore that." She gathered the empty plates and cups. "And if you stand in my way, I'm not sure we can be friends anymore."

"That's dramatic!" Zandra followed Sorcha as she left the room. "I'm just telling you to be careful. It's easy to see a new relationship through rose-tinted glasses. You miss flaws because you're infatuated."

"Better to overlook a few flaws than refuse to see a decent guy who's right in front of you." Sorcha thumped down the dirty crockery.

"Meaning?"

"Randal, of course. That guy would do anything for you, but you're so scared of messing up with him that you gave up after a single date."

Zandra's forehead wrinkled. "That single date went badly."

"That's it? One problem and you throw in the towel?" Sorcha shook her head. "I'm not like you. I'm willing to try, and if I hit bumps with Gaian, we'll work through them. You, on the other hand, are closed off to love. And even though it's staring you in the face, you pretend you don't see it."

"We're done here." Zandra shoved away from the counter. "Juno, let's go."

Sorcha shrugged but made no apology.

I hurried after Zandra as she stomped out of the café, swinging her arms and muttering to herself.

"That guy is no good for Sorcha," she finally said.

"Gentlemen callers can be distracting," I said. "Although Sorcha made an interesting point. Perhaps it's time you tried again with Randal. You're perfect for each other."

Zandra slid her version of the Gorgon stink eye my way. "Randal is a distraction I don't need. I have to keep focused on work."

"Yet every time he speaks to you, you giggle and can't concentrate on anything for at least half an hour."

"You're backing up my argument! I don't need anyone making me lose focus, or I'll end up like Sorcha. She wouldn't even consider the possibility Gaian and his friends were behind the graffiti. She accepted his word for it." Zandra looked down at me. "We don't need guys in our lives. We're happy with what we have, right?"

I leaped onto her shoulder, Smoke now asleep, so it was a juggling act, and let out a gentle sigh. "I couldn't be any happier than when I'm with you."

She leaned her head against my side, and we walked along in silence for a moment. "Still no news on Sammy?"

"There have been a few unconfirmed sightings of him and Tinkerbell, but they're still missing. Finn has been great, though, and gives me an update every time he has news. And I have my ear to the ground, but I'm not hopeful of his return."

"They have been gone a while," Zandra said.

"And with Sammy wounded, and the demon who was supposed to watch out for him out of action, Sammy has no links with anybody. No one to help heal him." My heart thudded its unhappiness. I missed my fluffy snuggle buddy, even after everything we'd gone through.

"You think Tinkerbell is helping him to heal?"

"That cat only ever helps herself. I'm fearful for Sammy's future." Things would never be the same between me and Sammy, but I wanted to know he was safe and healthy. Although, since he was a fugitive, it was unlikely I'd ever see him again.

"Let's go get dessert with Vorana and Sage," Zandra said. "There's leftover peach cobbler from last night we can reheat. And ice cream in the freezer."

"Ice cream and cobbler solves everything," I said.

"Maybe not everything, but it helps. Tomorrow, we'll figure this out, and we'll celebrate with Finn. Then life can return to normal."

As my thoughts returned to those odd symbols I'd seen on the wall, I wondered if there'd even be a tomorrow to wake up to. I truly hoped I was wrong about them.

Chapter 17

Mission status green

I clamped Smoke's beak shut just before he squawked a protest. I shook my head at him. We couldn't risk waking Zandra, or she'd only ask questions about where I was going so late at night.

I lay down and let Smoke clamber onto my back, his claws digging in as he settled. He was already heavier than the first time we'd done this. It wouldn't be long before he'd be able to fly, and that would be a whole other level of learning.

After waiting for Smoke to get comfy, I shuffled across the bed and listened to Zandra's steady breathing. She was in a deep sleep, so I was confident I could leave her. I slid off the bed smoothly with Smoke clinging on and crept up the stairs and into the hallway.

Ever since I'd seen those strange symbols, I hadn't been able to stop thinking about them. I needed more information to know how serious the situation was. If I was lucky, the symbols had simply been discovered in a book by bored, naughty children, and they'd painted them on the wall for fun. But if my luck wasn't holding, those symbols meant trouble would soon twirl through town like a toxic dragon's rear-end toot.

Sage was waiting for us at the bottom of the main stairs in the house. She yawned before thoroughly sniffing Smoke. "Does he have to come with us? Bringing a baby on a kitten impossible mission is irresponsible."

"A baby phoenix can't be left on its own. Loneliness kills."

Sage bared her yellowed teeth. "Leave him with Zandra."

"He's been restless. He'll only wake her with his squawks, and then she'll see I'm not home."

"And ask questions that you don't want to answer." Sage slid me the side eye. "Still keeping secrets from your witch, huh?"

"How are things going with Vorana and Ember? Does she know all about her new familiar yet?"

Sage huffed out a breath. "If we're doing this, let's move."

"Still not made a formal introduction?" I tried not to sound smug. I wasn't the only one keeping secrets.

Sage stomped out of the door, whacking her harness on the frame and onto the street. "I've yet to decide if Ember's the right familiar to replace me. We had a long chat after the disaster in the mortuary."

"You think you've made a mistake by inviting him here?"

"I never make mistakes." She glanced at me as we walked side by side. "You think he's too young?"

"Ember must have extraordinary abilities to have passed all the familiars' exams at such a tender age, so I'm not doubting his powers. But sometimes, life experience is more valuable than what we can learn from books."

Sage grunted. "I figured, the younger the better. Then Vorana won't have to worry about him getting old and past it."

"Like you, you mean?"

She nodded. "I only want the best for my witch."

"Ember could have come on this kitten impossible mission," I said. "Then we could have gotten to know him better."

"Waste of time. We're only going to the bookstore to read. That's hardly dangerous. When you told me this was the mission, I thought you were joking."

"There are still risks. If a hardback book falls on your paw, it'll hurt."

Smoke squawked in agreement, even though he didn't have paws.

"And some of those witch almanacs run to over a thousand pages. In the wrong hands, that's a lethal weapon," I said.

Sage grunted again as she motored along in her harness. "I told Ember to go back to the academy, and I'd be in touch when I've made a final decision."

"You made the right choice to send him back. Vorana doesn't need anyone else."

"She does. If I decide Ember is the wrong familiar, I'll ask for more candidates." Sage looked at the ground. "Sometimes, you have to hold up your paws and admit defeat. I've come close to losing Vorana several times because I'm not good enough."

"Only one time that I know of. And everyone was vulnerable because of that sleeping magic. Even I almost succumbed."

"I could have done more. If I'd been younger and stronger, I wouldn't have needed anyone else's help to keep her alive."

"Untrue. But if you want to go down to a part-time role because you're feeling the strain—"

"It's not that. I'd stay with Vorana forever if I could. I'm doing this because it's best for her."

My misguided friend wouldn't be convinced there was another option. Sage was so focused on doing the best for her witch that she was unable to see she was harming them both.

We arrived at the bookstore, and Sage unlocked the door. We put on one small sidelight so as not to attract attention and then headed to the *Symbols and Signs* section.

I settled Smoke on a chair so he could watch without getting in the way then clambered up the shelves like a fluffy monkey.

Sage remained by the chair with Smoke and watched me clamber. "What's got your fur in a twist about these symbols?"

Before I could answer, there was a tap on the glass at the front of the store. Elijah was peering in at us, his hairless gray face dappled in shadow.

"What does he want?" Sage said.

"Let him in, and he might tell you."

Sage grumbled as she trundled to the door and opened it.

He peered over her head. "What are you doing here so late?"

"Reading. What do you want?" Sage snapped.

"I heard there was a newly dead squirrel in town. I planned on investigating."

I almost fell off the bookcase. A dead tree rat! It was the perfect gift for Zandra. I shook my head. No. I must focus on the mission. The symbols were important.

"Did you find the carcass?" Sage had also perked up at the news of a squirrel up for grabs.

"The rumors I heard were fuzzy. It could be in a few different places. I checked one of them, but no joy. Figured I'd take a break when I saw the light on in here, so I came to look." He stared up at me. "What are you doing hanging off that shelf?"

"Invite Elijah in. If people see the door open, questions will be asked," I said.

"Just don't make a mess," Sage said to him. "We're not supposed to be in here."

"You don't have to worry about me shedding fur." Elijah stepped into the store and froze when he saw Smoke. "Who's this?"

"My new foster," I said. "Smoke, meet Elijah. He's part-ghoul, part-cat, so watch his bite."

Smoke squawked and flapped his growing wings.

"I ain't gonna bite the little dude. Just want to take a look." Elijah sniffed Smoke, rearing back when he almost got his booping snooter nipped. "Feisty little fella."

"And possibly a witness to a murder," I said. "I'm taking care of him for now until he's bigger and can choose his own home. One free from chains and intimidation."

"You're looking for a book on how to take care of a phoenix?" Elijah ambled around the bookstore, poking at various knickknacks and earning some well-deserved warning hisses from Sage.

"No, I'm looking for this one. Watch out below." I pulled out a thin, old book and aimed it at the rug on the floor so it wouldn't get damaged when it dropped.

Elijah and Sage stood around the book after it landed, waiting for me to clamber down and join them.

"*Occult Symbols and Their Mystical Properties.*" Elijah read the book title. "What are you planning on doing with this?"

"In case you hadn't noticed, odd symbols have been appearing around town." I checked the contents page of the book.

"I've seen the graffiti if that's what you mean. Figured it was some dumb gang making a move on the place."

"It's more than that. I believe those larger daubings are a distraction. Everyone's looking at the black and red markings and missing the most important symbols." I flipped to the relevant page and rested my paws on it. "These symbols. And they mean trouble."

Sage read down the page. "They're bad omen signs."

"They're more than that," I said. "They're markers of intent. Someone is going around Crimson Cove and putting up these symbols to establish a link."

"What will they do with this link?" Elijah said.

"It says here, a mischief cult used these symbols," Sage said. "A cauldron of gremlins forged the symbols in the fires of the Grantilly Scythe volcano. They gathered followers, usually magic users with little power, and used them to cause trouble."

"Why were the gremlins meeting in a cauldron?" Elijah said.

"It's the collective name for a group of gremlins. Keep up." Sage attempted to box his ears, but he sidestepped her murder mitten. "It grew into a powerful cult, and these gremlins gained a large, devoted following. The symbols contain power. Make enough of them, and the chaos spreads."

"And this weird cult is in Crimson Cove?" Elijah said.

"Not according to this book. They died out hundreds of years ago." Sage's booping snooter was so close to the page, it was almost touching it. "Says here, the gremlins couldn't agree on the mischief they wanted to make, so they ended up killing each other during a fight. That put an end to the cult."

"Now someone has re-discovered the symbols and wants to use them," I said. "If they know the origin of these symbols, they won't be using them for anything good."

"Or it could just be someone messing around," Elijah said. "This symbol information is in Vorana's bookstore, so everyone has access to it."

I studied the symbols some more. "If they'd been used on their own, I could believe it was mischievous, bored youths looking to get the locals gossiping. But graffiti has been discovered all around the town. Angel Force is getting daily complaints. And these symbols are found with the graffiti."

"At all locations?" Elijah said.

"Only one so far, but we must investigate the other sites to see if there's a connection. That's the plan for the rest of tonight."

"Hold your fluffy pants. You said we were just coming to the bookstore. Nothing was mentioned about trudging around town in the dark and cold, staring at marks on walls," Sage said.

"It won't take long," I said.

"Let me take a look." Elijah turned the book so he could get a better view. "I've seen these somewhere else. Not in town, though."

"On their own or with more graffiti?" I asked.

"Just these. Although there were other markings. Lots of circles, pressed on top of one another."

"Where was this?" I said.

"In a cave on the beach."

"And now we're going to the beach!" Sage huffed out a breath, grumbled for a second, then studied the book. "If it were bored children wanting to cause a scandal, why put them there, where no one would see them?"

"I'm unsure. But we need to investigate." I struggled the book back into place on the shelf and then hopped down. "You want to come with me? I can always take Elijah if this is too much for you."

Sage gently hissed at me. "I'm more than a match for this mission. Let's move."

As much as she loved to complain, she secretly adored these kitten impossible missions.

I settled Smoke on my back, and we dashed toward the beach.

"Wait a second," Elijah said. "We're passing a location the dead squirrel is supposed to be."

"We'll take a look later," I said.

"It'll take thirty seconds. It's the reason I came out, and I'm not missing my chance to nab a tree rat carcass."

"It would be so satisfying to see a dead tree rat," Sage said. "It won't take long. And maybe we can share it. Take a leg back each for our witches."

I couldn't disagree with her and was intrigued to see the body. We turned around and hurried along the alleyway Elijah had disappeared into.

He hunted for several minutes, muttering to himself as he shoved aside bags of recycling. "It smells of squirrel, but there's no sign of the thing. I'm too late. Someone's already gotten to it. Just my rotten luck."

"One day, we'll defeat the tree rats," I said.

"That day isn't today," Elijah grumbled. "Let's go to the beach."

I nudged him with my head as we changed direction. "Why the interest in obtaining such a prize?"

"It's for Sorcha. She barely notices me since that irritating guy showed up. He's always strutting around and making a scene. I get no peace anymore."

"Gaian and his friends are noisy." Sage slowed to sniff a food wrapper then caught up with us. "They rumbled past the bookstore on their bikes. They were loud and stank of greasy hot vegetables."

"They're environmental warriors," I said. "Gaian said they run their bikes on used vegetable oil."

"That explains the stink, although I suppose it's better than gasoline."

"They've messed up the café," Elijah said. "There's barely anything decent to eat now."

"Gaian prefers plants to prawns," I said. "I'm struggling to get my head around that, too."

"Does this guy make Sorcha happy?" Sage said.

I nodded. "I've never seen her so cheerful."

"Yeah, I guess he does. But she's not interested in anything else. Only him. And she's not taken in any new fosters since he turned up. Sorcha is always the first to open her door when Finn or Torrin can't help a critter or when animal control isn't an option."

"Don't you like that?" Sage said. "No strangers getting in your way and hogging the food."

"It's Gaian's influence, though. And he's more of a dog fan."

We hissed at that unpleasant observation.

"I spotted some unfriendly hounds when I greeted Sorcha the other day." I lifted my booping snooter as the salty ocean scent grew stronger.

"They're annoying. Always snapping and snarling. I've been staying out of the café as much as possible. I may even consider going back to Finn's sanctuary. Even with all the honking and snorting from the beasts, it would be quieter, and I'd be less likely to get my tail bitten."

As Elijah continued to grumble, I realized he was jealous. It was understandable. Familiars must come first. Although Sorcha and Elijah weren't bonded, he'd been living with her for some time. And with Tinkerbell out of the picture, Sorcha needed someone to watch over her. A plant-munching, bike-riding environmentalist couldn't be trusted to do a proper job. At least, not until I got to know him better, and could ensure he had pure intentions.

We arrived at a chilly, dark beach. Unsurprisingly, we were the only visitors.

"This way. I'll show you the cave where I found the weird symbols," Elijah said.

I hurried along, aware of the stiff wind whipping off the sea and the pounding waves on the pebbles. I couldn't keep Smoke out in these conditions for long. He had yet to develop a downy undercoat, so would get cold quickly.

"We need to hurry. The tide is coming in." Sage yanked her harness out of a hole. "I'm not getting my wheels waterlogged for anyone."

"This won't take long," I said.

We entered a pitch-black cave, the throb of the waves echoing around us, and the thin thread of moon overhead, providing no light to assist us.

Smoke belched, and a small fireball flew from his mouth, providing a brief illumination.

"Good boy. Do that again," I said. "Belch as much as you like while we're in this cave."

"Just not in my direction," Sage said. "No singed fur for me."

Smoke loved the idea of burping as much as possible and started letting out gassy fireballs every thirty seconds, squeaking and flapping his wings every time he let rip.

"Here they are." Elijah stopped by a craggy, damp wall that smelled of seaweed and salt.

I inspected the symbols the second Smoke belched and lit the place up. "These markings are recent."

"And there's no accompanying graffiti," Sage said. "Whoever is doing this felt there was no need to conceal the symbols."

"Because no one would see them here," I said. "Where are the round marks you mentioned?"

"They're farther back in the cave," Elijah said.

I followed him and waited for Smoke to belch again, the dampness in the air fluffing my fur and making me shiver. The cave lit up and revealed dozens of slightly angular circles.

"They look like paw prints. Lots of them on top of each other." I leaned close to the markings and set a paw next to them.

"I guess they could be." Elijah's booping snooter wrinkled as he studied the marks. "You think it's an animal leaving these signs?"

"It seems odd the prints are by these symbols and not with the others in town," I said. "Could this be a base for whoever is doing this?"

"It wouldn't be a comfortable place to stay. The tide doesn't fill this cave, but if you stay here too long, you'd be wading through icy cold seawater. And you'd get frozen." Elijah lifted his chin. "I smell fish! Maybe some swam in here and got stranded. They'd be a great gift for Sorcha. Not squirrel great, but not far off. You get some big fins around here." He dashed off into the darkness.

"Fish! I should get one for Vorana." Sage trundled after him, cursing every time her harness got stuck.

"Wait! We're not here to fish. We have to figure out what the symbols mean."

"You figure it out. I've just found a shallow pool full of dead fish, and I intend to claim them." I couldn't see Elijah, but I heard the satisfaction in his voice at making such a magnificent discovery.

I grumbled to myself, wondering why I bothered with my magical misfits. Although, gifting Zandra a fish would be an unusual treat. She ate fish. She'd love one as a surprise gift.

"What's that other smell?" Sage's voice came from the darkness. "I don't like it."

"It's just the fish. They've probably been dead for a day or two. It makes them extra whiffy," Elijah said.

"No, it's something else. And I can feel something under my paws. I'm not standing on rock anymore. It's something cold and damp."

"It's seaweed. Stop freaking out because it's dark and find a fish for Vorana, or I'll take them all," Elijah said.

"I'm not freaking out! I'm telling you, there's something under my paws that stinks."

I headed toward Sage's voice. "Smoke, would you mind obliging with a burp so I can see?"

He hiccupped and a blast of flame shot out of him.

Once my eyes adjusted to the light, I discovered Sage was standing on a dead body.

Chapter 18

Man down

Sage stared at the discovery under her paws. She squeaked and slipped off the body, landing on her side, her wheels upending.

Elijah looked up, a dead fish in his mouth. He spat it out and dashed over, yanking Sage to her feet.

"Smoke, launch as many fireballs as you can, so we can see what we're doing," I said.

Smoke obliged by opening his mouth and letting loose a stream of flame. It seemed he no longer needed to burp to produce fire. Clever little phoenix.

I reached the body and studied it. It was a male, on his back, with his arms and legs splayed. He was fully clothed in dark jeans and a sweater. I inched up to the face and discovered Rabdos Morfiel's sightless, milky eyes staring at nothing.

"Do you know who it is?" Elijah said. "He's not a local."

"This is a missing Morfiel family member. Rabdos Morfiel. We've been attempting to track him down ever since his father, Erig, was murdered."

"Huh. No wonder you couldn't find him." Elijah went back to inspecting the fish.

"Told you I was standing on something gross." Sage glared at the body, her fur sticky with bits of old seaweed.

Smoke hissed and flapped his wings, not happy to see Rabdos, dead or alive.

"It's okay. He can't do anything to you," I murmured, a sharp wind whipping around us, warning us the tide was getting closer.

"How long do you think he's been here?" Sage said.

"Rabdos has been missing since he learned his father was killed," I said. "No one has seen him since then. Acer suggested he'd gone into hiding to grieve, but it appears not."

"He must have been here a few days by the smell of him." Sage backed away. "Should your little guy be seeing this? You don't want to frighten him."

Smoke nodded, his sharp glare intent on Rabdos. It seemed my feathery companion was going nowhere.

"I get the impression they weren't friends. Maybe Rabdos was unkind to Smoke, like his father," I said.

Smoke squawked and jumped up and down.

Sage shrugged. "Your call. Just don't want him to have nightmares."

I appreciated my friend's thoughtfulness. Even though Sage acted like she didn't care about much, there was a soft center to this fluffy grump.

I returned to my inspection of the body. There were no signs of obvious injury on Rabdos, although there were black marks radiating out from around his mouth.

"We can't stay here much longer." Sage's attention was on the cave opening. "The water is getting deep at the entrance, and we don't want to get trapped."

"Elijah, leave those fish and go fetch an angel," I instructed.

He groaned. "Do I have to? If I leave, you'll steal the best fish. These are mine. I found them."

"We can't leave the body here. Rabdos was a murder suspect, so he's an important clue in the investigation. And your fish are safe. I have no interest in them."

"I do! And what's the hurry with getting the angels poking about?" Sage said.

"Look at his mouth. He's been poisoned! It was the method used to end his father's life. Well, one of them."

Sage extended her neck but got only a fraction closer to the corpse. "I can solve this case for you. Rabdos poisoned his dear old dad, felt guilty, so he drank the rest of the poison himself. Case closed. Leave him here as punishment. Let the fish nibble on him, or maybe our local kraken will get a sniff and devour him."

"What if Rabdos didn't do this to himself?" I said. "What if someone poisoned him and dumped him here, hoping he'd be carried away by the sea?"

"Then whoever did this isn't from around here," Elijah said. "The locals know these caves don't flood. If you dump something heavy here, it'll only get stuck on a rock."

"Which is why we need Angel Force here. This could be a murder scene," I said.

Elijah sniffed around the fish some more then sighed. "Fine. I'll go. But I know how many are here. If any fish vanish, I know where they went." There was a flash of light, and he disappeared.

"You think Rabdos had something to do with those symbols?" Sage was already investigating the abandoned fish.

I checked Rabdos's fingers. There was no paint on them, but it could have been washed away. "I don't think so. New markings have appeared recently, and if he's been dead for days, he wouldn't have been able to make them."

A gust of warm air flooded the cave, and Cythera appeared. She landed neatly and tucked her wings away.

She looked at me, and her face puckered. "Why am I not surprised to see you here?"

"Greetings. Always a pleasure. We were out for a late-night stroll and discovered Rabdos Morfiel, your missing family member. You're welcome."

"Let me see." Cythera stared down at the body. "It is him."

"As I told you. From our inspection of the scene, he's been dead for some time. We hypothesized he could have been dumped here. And if you look at his mouth—"

"Yes, yes. I know how to do my job." Cythera looked around the cave. "There won't be any useful evidence here."

"It's a smart place to leave a body. The tide would have come in several times and washed away anything useful. But if you look at his mouth—"

"I'll get the experts to do an autopsy if you don't mind. They'll look at his mouth and use expert judgment and years of training and experience to draw suitable conclusions." Cythera glanced at the cave entrance. "I'll move him. Otherwise, we could lose him in the water."

"I was about to suggest the same thing. You take the body and then return for us."

She slid me some serious side-eye as she lifted Rabdos. "Why would I do that?"

"The tide is coming in. It's late, we're tired, and we've given you an enormous breakthrough in your investigation. Call it a gift."

"I'll send you a bouquet." Cythera shot into the air, taking Rabdos with her.

I shook my head as white feathers rained down around us. "Not even a thank you. That angel has terrible manners."

"We've still got the fish," Sage said. "If we leave them here, they'll go to waste. They're already on the turn, so they need to be eaten tonight."

I turned and looked at the symbols on the wall again. "We do deserve a treat after this evening. Smoke, can you carry a fish? It'll be nice to give Elijah a treat as a thank you for his assistance on this mission."

"He should get his own fish," Sage said. "That cat is so lazy."

Smoke clumsily flapped to the ground, grabbed the biggest fish he could see, and lifted it proudly in his beak.

"He's such a good phoenix, isn't he?" Smoke was growing on me, and I'd be sad when it was his time to leave.

"If you say so." Sage chose the second largest fish.

I sniffed around them a few times and selected a fine-looking, almost intact fish for Zandra. She'd be so excited when I deposited it on her pillow.

Sage made some muffled noises, the fish firmly clamped in her jaws. She jabbed a paw at our exit route.

Unless we wanted to swim, we'd need a little magic to get us home. "Everyone join paws and claws with me." A quick paw touch, a flash of magic, and we were back on Vorana's front porch.

I left Smoke in Sage's fairly tender loving care and dashed to Sorcha's café. I knocked on the door, dropped the fish, and ran off.

When I returned, Smoke was leaning against Sage, asleep. She'd curled her front paws underneath herself, and her eyes were half-closed.

"Wake up, you two. We have fish gifts to deliver and news to share about the murder investigation." I cat-smiled. All in all, it had been a successful evening mission.

Smoke woke and clambered onto my back, falling asleep again almost instantly. Sage gathered her fish, and we headed inside. She hauled the fish up the main staircase, its glistening tail leaving a scaly trail on the wood.

I dashed down to the basement, jumped onto the bed, and dropped my fishy gift on Zandra's face.

Her eyes shot open, she inhaled, and her nose wrinkled. She reached a hand up and patted her cheek where the fish lay. "What in the name of all things unholy is on my face?"

"I have surprises for you." I hopped from paw to paw. "This is the first one."

"Juno, whatever this stinking thing is on my cheek, get it off. You know the rules about putting dead things in the bed."

I left the fish where it was. "You always say no rodents. Nothing about fish."

"A fish! You dropped a dead fish on my face?" She snagged the fish's tail between her nails and lifted it up. Droplets of something oily and congealed landed on her lower lip. She yelped and slung the fish to the floor, where it made a soggy plop, and its guts exploded.

"It got in my mouth! I'm gonna puke." Zandra inhaled deeply. "No, that's making it worse. All I can smell is rotting fish."

"I thought it would make a change from rodent. An improvement. You eat fish."

"Not a rotting fish carcass that's been dead for days." Zandra sat and wiped the back of one hand across her cheek. "Ugh. I'm only making it worse." She rolled out of bed and her foot landed on the fish with a squelchy splat.

I winced. "Oops!"

"Juno! When I come back from the bathroom, I want that thing gone and the floor and bedding clean. I do not want to smell anything remotely fishy in here."

My ears lowered. "You don't like your gift?"

She glared at me as she hopped away.

I sighed. It had seemed like a good idea, but I shouldn't have let the others encourage my cat-like ways. I should focus my attention on getting Zandra a squirrel. One day, I'd find her a gift she appreciated.

While Zandra cleaned scales and fish guts out from between her toes and off of her cheek, I used magic to remove the fish, change the bedding, and ensure the room smelled of jasmine and lavender.

When she came out of the bathroom, I was settled on the end of the bed, Smoke asleep beside me.

Zandra's sour expression revealed her mood hadn't improved, even though she was fish free. She glared at the spot on the floor where the offending fish had been discarded. "You didn't go out so late just to get me a rotten fish, did you?"

"I was on a mission. I went out with Sage and Smoke, and we bumped into Elijah. Then we ended up on the beach in a cave, and—"

"Found a pile of rotting fish. I hope no one else is getting a fishy gift tonight."

I glanced at the ceiling. Sage would deliver her gift any second. "That's not important. When we were in the cave, we discovered Rabdos Morfiel."

Zandra's eyebrows rose as she rubbed peppermint lotion onto her feet and pulled on clean socks. "Our missing family member was hiding in a beach cave?"

"No, he wasn't hiding. He was dead."

Her sour expression was replaced by one of surprise. "No kidding. We assumed he was hiding from the family. Do you know what happened to him?"

I was glad the news about the dead body had shifted Zandra's attention from the fish. "We had little time to examine the scene. The tide was coming in, and we didn't want to get trapped. Elijah went and got Cythera, and she removed the body. But I'm certain the autopsy will reveal Rabdos was killed with poison. There were black marks around his mouth and no other injuries on his body."

"Poison? Again. That can't be a coincidence. Does Finn know?" Zandra was already reaching for her snow globe.

"Unlikely. Cythera won't tell him anything since he's not supposed to be on this case."

She made a connection, but it took several minutes of buzzing before Finn's sleepy face appeared. "Zandra? What's up?"

"Hey, sorry to wake you so late. Juno made a discovery on the beach. Rabdos Morfiel's body was found in a cave."

"Hold on a second. You might have to say that again. My still-asleep brain needs time to process." Finn scrubbed a hand up and down his face several times. "Rabdos Morfiel is dead?"

"Greetings, Finn. He is. And I believe he was murdered. Poisoned, to be exact," I said.

"That makes two dead family members," Finn said. "Give me half an hour, and I'll see what I can find out. I'll stop by as soon as I can. You at home?"

"Yep. We'll get the coffee on." Just as Zandra disconnected the call, there was a scream from upstairs. She stood, her head tilted to one side. "What's up with Vorana?"

"It's nothing." I gently stroked Smoke, hoping the scream wouldn't disturb his slumber. "Just Sage waking her with a fishy treat."

Zandra groaned and shook her head. "You two will never learn."

Footsteps stamped down the main staircase, accompanied by indistinct, high-pitched complaints from Vorana. Softer paw steps and clanking metal followed her.

Zandra hurried up the stairs to meet Vorana, and I dashed along a few steps behind her. "You got a disgusting fishy surprise, too?"

"Dropped on my hand!" Vorana extended a pink, freshly scrubbed palm. "I squeezed it, and it exploded all over the bedroom."

"I got mine on my face," Zandra said. "I'm sure I can still smell rotten fish."

"Let's have tea and wait for Finn to arrive." I hurried past them, noticing Sage hiding behind the kitchen door.

"Finn? Why is Finn coming over so late?" Vorana strode in behind me, sniffing her hand and grimacing.

"There's been a development in the murder investigation." Zandra updated Vorana about what had been discovered on the beach while she brewed hot drinks.

I settled in next to Sage and let our witches talk. "So, no more fish gifts?"

"Definitely not," Sage muttered. "Elijah has the worst ideas. I'm never listening to that dumb cat again."

There'd been logic behind the idea. Our witches just needed to be more open-minded with the gifts they received.

We only had to wait twenty minutes before Finn arrived. Vorana ushered him into the kitchen and made him a coffee.

He looked at us, his hair messy and his white shirt mis-buttoned. "I've got not great news and bad news. What do you want first?"

"Let's go with the bad news," I said. "Always brightens the day."

Finn sipped his coffee and then smacked his lips together. "Cythera has arrested Forfax Morfiel for both murders."

Chapter 19

Case closed?

We all stared at Finn in stunned surprise.

I hopped onto the table. "What evidence does Cythera have that convinced her Forfax killed Erig and Rabdos?"

"I couldn't get many details, but a buddy of mine on the inside told me she's convinced she's solved the case."

"She must have found something conclusive to show it was Forfax," Zandra said. "Cythera wouldn't want to make any mistakes with such an influential family breathing down her neck."

"From what I've been told, she's certain she's right. And you were correct about poison being used as the murder weapon, Juno. Only prelim tests have been done, but it was poison that ended Rabdos's life."

"They must have found evidence on the body that revealed who the killer was," I said. "What did Angel Force do after Rabdos's body was brought in?"

"Logically, they'd have visited the Morfiel family to inform them he'd been discovered," Finn said.

"Maybe when they were there, something was said or fingers got pointed at Forfax," Zandra said.

"Whether it was evidence found or an accusation made, it was enough to convince Cythera to make the arrest. Forfax is in custody. He's probably already been questioned."

"We should go to Angel Force and offer our assistance." I hopped off the table. "Since Cythera believes she's solved this case, I'll no longer be under suspicion. And Finn, you can get more involved because there's no longer any conflict of interest."

Zandra pulled a face. "She'll still find a reason to keep us on the outside. We have to accept that Cythera doesn't like us."

"She's warming to us," I said. "After the bakery exploded, she was almost civil to me. She didn't even dismiss my suggestions about what happened."

"Juno, I was there. She was pretty rude to you," Finn said. "But I'm game for going into work if you want to join me. But I should warn you, Cythera is even grumpier when she's had little sleep."

I checked the time. It was just past three in the morning. Prime Grumpy Cythera time.

"I can look after Smoke if you need to go," Sage said. "So long as he doesn't nip me when I'm asleep."

"He'd welcome the company," I said. "I don't like to leave him alone in the basement."

"Bring him upstairs with us." Vorana's narrowed gaze shifted to Sage. "After my naughty familiar has dealt with her revolting fish."

"What's this about fish?" Finn said.

"Just our familiars being even grosser than usual," Zandra said. "Give me five minutes to get changed, and I'll come to the office with you."

I stuck by Sage and stayed out of Zandra's way to avoid any glares or reminders never to drop a dead fish on my witch's face again.

Sage huffed and grumbled as she cleared the remains of the squished fish out of Vorana's bedroom. "If she hadn't squeezed the thing so tight, there wouldn't be all this mess. I don't think even I'd eat this." She waved a paw in the air and a broom and wet mop flew into the room and made swift work of clearing the fishy carnage.

"Fish are delicate creatures," I said. "We'll stick to rodents in the future."

"Agreed. No more fishy gifts."

I trotted down the stairs to discover Finn pacing by the front door. "How's the vandalism investigation going?"

"It's not. Not really. Someone's been prolific with the spray paint, though. Three more sites were discovered yesterday."

My ears pricked. "All with the same markings?"

"Yup. How did you get on speaking to Sorcha about Gaian's involvement?"

"Not well. Gaian overheard us talking and claimed he had nothing to do with it. And then Sorcha got defensive. She argued with Zandra."

"Was she defensive because she knows what Gaian is up to and feels bad about it?"

"Sorcha would never let anyone harm this town, no matter how fond she is of them. She's smarter than that."

"It's been a while since she's seriously dated anyone, and she's really into this guy."

"You don't approve of him?"

Finn tapped his fingers against his biceps. "I did some digging into Gaian and his gang. I wanted to learn about their reputation."

"Does a trail of graffiti follow them wherever they go?"

"It doesn't. But they're on DAPM's radar."

"What branch of law enforcement is that?"

"Department of Advanced Pernicious Magic. DAPM enforcers go after those who want to damage or alter the fabric of magic."

"By doing what?" Finn had my total attention. Gaian and his gang sounded dangerous, and I didn't want Sorcha near them if they'd cause her trouble.

"They claim they want equal rights for all, but it seems their aims have a darker undertone."

"Is it to do with mischief making?"

Finn's forehead furrowed. "It's more serious than that. They want to bring down figures of authority, including those in Angel Force. They claim we're inefficient, expensive, and provide sub-par results."

"What would they replace you with?"

Finn lifted one shoulder. "Anarchy?"

"Does Gaian have an affiliation with the gremlins?"

"Um... not that I'm aware of. Nothing like that showed up in my research. Why do you ask?"

"It's linked to the markings on the walls. They reminded me of a past encounter I had with an unpleasant force I thought had died out many years ago."

Finn cocked his head. "Back in the days when you were... different?"

I nodded. "I'd hate for trouble to be weaving its way through the town again. It's not been long since we banished a demon and herded out all those non-magicals."

Finn rocked back on his heels. "Same here. We need to keep a close eye on Gaian and his friends. So far, they haven't set a foot wrong, but I don't trust them. You think they're linked to this gremlin force?"

"I've no evidence to suggest one way or the other, but they show up and the graffiti begins. Coincidence?" I washed an ear with one paw. "Does Gaian have a record?"

"He's been cautioned for trespassing and questioned numerous times over the misuse of magic, but nothing stuck. This guy has resources behind him and can afford expensive legal defense."

"Where does he get his money from?"

"Not sure. I'll have to look into it some more, but I need to be discreet."

"You think he's a threat to Sorcha? I could always visit him with my companions, and we can administer some mild obliteration."

"Let's not go mass murdering the bikers just yet. And I don't think he's done anything bad to Sorcha. Every time I see them together, she's smiling." Finn pinched his chin between his finger and thumb. "I'd suggest we caution her about him, but from what you've said about the conversation with Zandra, it would go badly."

"Sorcha threatened to end their friendship." I paced alongside Finn. "We'll have to act carefully. We don't want Sorcha to shut down and refuse to talk to us if she learns we're investigating her beau."

"If we can link the weird symbols to Gaian, it might convince her he's not all he seems to be. You want to share more about the symbols with me?"

"Are we ready to go?" Zandra appeared, carrying a sleeping Smoke in the crook of her arm.

I nodded at Finn. I trusted this angel. We could examine the symbols together when the investigation was over. "Sage is upstairs. She'll watch over Smoke until we get back."

Zandra dashed up the stairs and returned a moment later. We said goodbye to Vorana and headed to Angel Force.

We'd just gotten through the front doors when raised voices could be heard. We hurried into the main office to discover Acer standing toe-to-toe with Cythera.

"He wouldn't do this! You haven't got enough evidence to charge him."

Cythera glanced our way. "You're not on duty, Finn. And what are they doing with you?"

"We're your greatest assets," I said. "After all, I found Rabdos's body for you."

"Lucky break," Cythera muttered.

"Zandra and Juno could be useful to the investigation," Finn said. "And I figured, since you've arrested Forfax, you won't mind me being involved. And Juno's no longer a suspect, is she?"

"How do you know Forfax is in custody?"

"Um... you know how this town loves to gossip." Finn revealed his most charming smile.

Cythera sighed. "Stay if you must. But none of you need to be here. The case is almost closed, and I'm just about to question Forfax again. He's waiting in the interview room."

"Forfax didn't murder Erig." Acer glared at Cythera. "And he'd never kill Rabdos."

"I understand why you want to defend your brother, but we found evidence to prove his guilt. Go home. You can't work this investigation, and you're in no fit state to do anything else. And in case I need to remind you, you're still suspended from duty."

"Which is no longer necessary," Finn said smoothly. "Acer can work. She can help with the vandalism cases. We've got a lot going on right now, so an extra pair of hands would be welcome."

"Acer is overly emotional and not thinking clearly," Cythera said. "She's of no use to anyone."

"Of course, I'm overly emotional. You're trying to pin two murders on my half-brother when he didn't do it. Release him." Acer jabbed a finger against Cythera's chest.

Finn moved into action, sliding between them and gently backing Acer away before she took a step too far and got fired.

I settled on a desk while Zandra leaned against it, neither of us wanting to get involved in this battle.

"Let me speak to Forfax. I'll clear this up, and you can release him," Acer said.

"He stays here," Cythera said. "My angels found poison in his things. We've already discovered it was a match for what killed your father, and I'm certain it'll match the poison that murdered Rabdos, too. I had no option but to arrest Forfax."

I glanced up at Zandra. That evidence was damning.

"Forfax wanted out of the family. He was done with them and was working up the courage to tell Erig he was leaving," Acer said.

"Which gives him even more motive for murder," Cythera said. "Forfax became desperate because your father refused his request to leave, so he killed him to get free."

"That's not true. Forfax is the least violent of my family," Acer said.

"Hardly a ringing endorsement," I whispered.

"Poison isn't a violent way to kill. It's subtle. You don't even need to be on the scene to kill someone when you use poison. You're only strengthening the case against him by remaining here," Cythera said.

"I'm remaining here until you see sense."

Cythera squeezed her eyes shut for a second, and her wings fluttered behind her. "Acer, so far, your record has been exemplary. You're hard-working and enthusiastic. I value that in my team, but you must realize you can't be here. Please, leave."

Acer remained where she was. "Forfax will need representation. I'll sit in when you interview him."

"That's not acceptable."

"Technically, if Forfax asks for Acer to represent him, she can do that," Finn said.

"You're not being helpful." Cythera glared at him. "Take Acer home."

"I'm going nowhere." Acer crossed her arms over her chest. "And I insist on seeing Forfax."

"Acer, don't cause a scene. It's unbecoming to the family." Ollia appeared in the doorway and swept into the room in a red and black catsuit, her eyes winged with heavy black liner.

"Help him!" Acer hurried over to her mother. "Forfax wouldn't do this. You know him. You know what he's like."

Ollia removed Acer's hand from her arm. "Sadly, I do know what he's like. I'm almost ashamed to say he is my son. At least I didn't birth him."

"You know something about the murders?" Cythera said.

"No, I can't tell you details about the death of my husband or one of my beloved children, but I understand their personalities. I know what makes Forfax tick, and he had a growing obsession that had taken over his life."

"You really think Forfax is the killer?" I said.

Ollia glanced at me, and irritation flickered across her face. "After the last attempt, it's very possible he committed this hideous act."

"Don't do this," Acer said. "It won't help anyone, and it won't get you what you want by putting Forfax behind bars."

"It may ease my conscience," Ollia said. "I've done everything in my power to raise you all correctly. But sometimes, you get a bad seed, and it rots from the inside out."

"Please, don't do this to him. You'll be condemning an innocent person. If Forfax gets charged with these murders, whoever did it will go free."

Ollia considered Acer's statement. "Maybe they will, but they won't for long."

I cocked my head. Their conversation had a double meaning. I couldn't figure out what it was, but there was another issue bubbling beneath the surface.

"Mrs. Morfiel, if you have any information, I need to know," Cythera said. "Did you see Forfax murder your husband and son?"

Ollia lowered her head for a second. "Maybe Acer is right, and this is a family matter. We should deal with it privately."

"It's too late for that, since this is a criminal investigation. Do you know something that will prove Forfax's guilt?"

"She doesn't. Ollia knows nothing." Acer tried to grab her mother's hand, but she stepped away from her. "Even if Forfax has been acting up recently, it doesn't mean he killed anyone."

"How has he been acting up?" Finn said.

Ollia bared her teeth. "I cannot keep this to myself any longer. My husband had been recovering from significant injuries."

"The bruising on his face and torso?" Cythera said. "I checked the hospital records, and there was no information on how he got those injuries."

"We kept the matter private," Ollia said. "On account of how it happened."

Acer had her hands gripped together, a desperate expression on her face, which Ollia ignored.

"How did Erig get those injuries?" Cythera said.

Ollia lifted her gaze, and although she gave the outward impression of someone who was sad, there was a coldness in her eyes that sent a shudder down my spine.

"Forfax tried to run his father over. I fear he's been plotting my husband's demise for some time. And on this occasion, he finally succeeded."

I held in a gasp. Had Forfax done it? He'd been so desperate to get away from his twisted family that he'd snapped?

"Come with me," Cythera said. "I need full details of the incident."

Ollia looked straight ahead, not sparing Acer a glance as she entered Cythera's office, and the door was closed.

Acer turned to us, defeat radiating off of her. "Forfax is innocent. He's being set up."

"Your mother is lying about him running Erig over?" I asked.

Acer bit her bottom lip. "No. She's telling the truth. But Forfax acted impetuously. He wanted out of the family, but Erig wouldn't let him go. He tried every route to reason with him, but Erig said I was the only experiment, and I had to prove I wouldn't disrespect the family name before anyone else could escape."

"Forfax must have resented you for getting that chance," Finn said.

"He did. And he didn't hide it well. Our bond soured after I got accepted into the Angel Force academy. He even asked me to swap places with him, but the thought of staying in that family for a second longer made my heart freeze. I told him no. He didn't talk to me for a month after that."

"Your father must have punished Forfax for trying to kill him," I said. "The first time, I mean."

"Weirdly, he didn't. Erig took a few days off and disappeared to a clinic. He wouldn't tell anyone where he was going, not even Ollia. When he came back, Forfax told me he had a creepy look in his eyes and kept saying he'd found the perfect solution to his problem family."

"Sounds disturbing. What did he mean?" I said.

"He wouldn't say. I wasn't around, so I didn't have to deal with all his weirdness, but it wasn't the first time he got sneaky. The others said he made them uncomfortable, and they kept out of his way as much as possible." Acer rubbed her arms with her hands.

"But then your family came to Crimson Cove, and Erig was murdered," I said. "And you got sucked back into the family saga."

Acer nodded. "Erig sure knew how to mess stuff up."

"What do you think Ollia is telling Cythera?" Finn said.

Acer shrugged. "The truth. There's no need for her to lie. Apparently, she witnessed Forfax driving the van."

"I understand why he may have been pushed over the edge and killed your father," I said, "but why murder Rabdos?"

"I expect Ollia will say it was because Rabdos was modeling himself on Erig," Acer said, "and Forfax couldn't stand the thought of Erig's sick legacy carrying on. None of us wanted that, though, not even Rabdos. That was why he refused to marry and have a family."

"Do you know where the poison was discovered?" I said. "Cythera mentioned it was among Forfax's belongings. Had he concealed it well?"

"The opposite. They found the bottle in a bag he'd brought with him. Just resting on the top."

"Which is odd," Zandra said. "If you use poison or any weapon to kill, you hide it or throw it somewhere it won't be found. He could have poured away what was left of the poison and then stuck the bottle in the recycling. It would never have been discovered."

"Perhaps Forfax planned on using poison again," I said. "But even if he did, he'd conceal it better than simply leaving it in a bag."

"It took the angels five minutes to find it," Acer said. "Forfax isn't stupid. He wouldn't leave a murder weapon around for anyone to pick up."

"Do you know what Forfax's response has been to the accusations?" I said.

"He's refusing to confess to either murder," Acer said.

We all looked over when Cythera's office door opened, and she came out with Ollia and then opened the door to an interview room.

"Take your time," she said.

Ollia nodded. "Thank you. I appreciate your understanding. I'll only need a minute with my son."

"What did she say to you?" Acer marched over to Cythera.

Cythera scowled at her. "You're still here?"

"And going nowhere. Don't believe her. Ollia won't tell the truth about Forfax. And why does she want to see him if he's the killer?"

"Calm yourself."

"I can't stay calm. My innocent brother is about to be charged with murder. What did she tell you?"

Cythera puffed out a breath. "Your mother's statement was logical, and the results from your father's autopsy support that he'd recently been struck with something large. Your mother didn't tell me anything I wasn't already familiar with." She glanced at the closed door. "And she wanted to reason with Forfax. Beg him to confess, so your family can have peace."

Acer snorted. "She's lying! Why won't you listen to me?"

The interview room door opened, Ollia slipped out and shut it behind her. "Thank you again for allowing me to see Forfax. Let me know when you've charged him. If you'll excuse me, I need to be with what's left of my family." She glanced at Acer then walked away.

Cythera looked over Acer's head. "Finn, I'm about to interview Forfax again. I'll need you in with me."

"You got it, boss." He smiled and gave us a discreet thumbs-up.

"Will you charge him?" Acer followed Cythera.

"That's far enough. Go home before I fire you." Cythera looked at us but made no comment as she headed into the interview room with Finn.

"She didn't say we couldn't watch the interview from the room next door," I said.

"And I'm sure, if we're quiet, she won't even realize we're in there." Zandra looked at Acer. "You okay? Do you want to join us or go spend time with your family?"

"I don't want to be anywhere near Ollia. I'm certain, whatever she told Cythera, it'll make Forfax look guilty. I'm watching this interview and stepping in if things get bad."

"You think Ollia would turn on her son?" Zandra strode toward a door next to the interview room.

"Of course! If Forfax goes down for these murders, it takes the heat off Ollia."

"Why would there be significant heat on Ollia?" I said. "Any more than there's heat on the rest of your alibi-less family?"

Acer looked at her feet. "You'll never fully understand my family unless you've lived with them."

I studied Acer as we settled into the room with the one-way mirror so we could watch the interview. She was still hiding something. There was a piece of this mystery that was missing, and no one in the Morfiel family was prepared to tell us what it was. Without that missing piece, I wasn't certain we'd ever solve these murders.

Cythera had already begun the interview by the time we got settled. She sat opposite Forfax, who kept tugging at his shirt collar and wiping his brow.

"For someone who's supposed to be innocent, he sure looks guilty," Zandra said.

"He's nervous," Acer said. "You'd be if you were up on a double murder charge."

Forfax was sweating profusely, his hairline damp and his cheeks ruddy. He looked the picture of guilt.

"Let's start by going over what happened to your father," Cythera said.

"I've already told you. I was at the rental in my bedroom on my own when I learned of his murder. I had nothing to do with his death."

"Not that occasion," Cythera said. "The time you tried to kill him by running him over."

Forfax blinked several times and swallowed. "That was supposed to stay in the family. How did you find out?"

"Things have changed. Did you intend to kill him that time?"

"I... I... yes. I was angry with him. He wouldn't listen to anything I said. All my arguments were reasonable, and he could see I was desperately unhappy. He just laughed in my face and told me to grow a pair then walked away."

"So, what did you do?"

"The keys were in my hand, and before I knew it, I was behind the wheel and driving toward him. He turned at the last second, and I hit him. He bounced off the front of the van and hit the ground."

"Did you think he was dead?" Finn said.

Forfax dabbed sweat off his upper lip. "I hoped he was. He didn't move. I should have kept going and done the job properly. Instead, I panicked. I climbed out of the van and ran."

"Then what happened?" Cythera said.

"Ollia came out of the house. She was furious with me and hit me around the head. She ran over to Erig, and I could see he was moving," Forfax said.

"Ollia dosed him with magic and put him to bed. She said he'd be fine in the morning. The next day, he announced he was leaving after breakfast. He said he had some thinking to do. It was always a terrifying sign when Erig got lost in his thoughts. He was always plotting something devious. Usually against one of us."

"He could have been plotting revenge against you," Finn said.

"Maybe. I dunno. I never figured out what made him tick. Sometimes, when one of us yelled at him, we got a reward. The next time, we got locked in a barn."

"He wanted to ensure his children were always on the alert, never sure what awaited them," I murmured. "Erig truly was a monster."

"You admit you attempted to kill your father with the vehicle?" Cythera said.

Forfax blew out a breath. "Yeah. Sure. Ollia's told you everything, I'm certain of that, so there's no use denying it. I'd do it again if I could. And I wouldn't make the mistake of leaving him alive."

Cythera settled her hands flat on the desk. "You must realize we have to consider you the prime suspect in his actual murder."

"I didn't do it. I'd thought about it plenty of times, but I didn't poison him."

"You may have assisted in his death, though," Finn said. "Hitting him with that vehicle would have weakened him. Add in the poison and the tainted ring—"

"I'll hold my hands up to running him over. But in my defense, I was half-mad and furious with him. I was done with that family, and I had to make him see how serious I was."

"You shouldn't have used a giant piece of fast-moving metal to make your point." Cythera looked at the file she'd brought in with her. "Tell us about your relationship with Rabdos."

Forfax raked his hands through his hair. "It wasn't great, but it could have been worse. We rubbed along okay most of the time."

"He's not looking good." Zandra leaned forward in her seat. "Has your brother been sick recently?"

Acer shook her head. "It must be the stress. If Ollia gets him charged with murder—"

"You'll kill her?" I tilted my head.

Acer's nostrils flared. "Don't tempt me."

"The description of your relationship with Rabdos suggests you weren't fond of each other," Cythera said.

"It's not that. We got on fine when we were younger. But Rabdos sometimes acted like Erig. It gave me the shivers. It was like looking at a younger version of our father. It made me queasy to think anything Erig stood for would be carried on."

"That was an act," Acer said. "Rabdos's way of protecting himself from the worst of Erig's fury. If Rabdos had inherited the business, he'd have used the money for better things. He'd have been able to marry, have a family, and would have finally been happy."

"When was the last time you saw Rabdos?" Cythera said to Forfax.

"It was after that cat visited the house. Erig summoned us to see the creature off, and then Rabdos went to his room. I didn't see him again."

"You didn't arrange to meet him on the beach at any time?"

"No. Is that where he was found?"

Cythera didn't answer the question. "Why did you have a vial of poison in your bag?"

"That wasn't mine. I was shocked when you found it." Forfax wiped a hand across his brow. "Although, maybe I shouldn't have been."

"What does he mean by that?" Zandra said.

"Evidence can be planted," I said. "If it wasn't Forfax who administered the poison, it would have been simple for another family member to sneak into his room and leave the evidence for the angels to find."

Acer slumped in her seat. "Even though Erig's dead, he's still controlling us. He's like an unwanted ghost in the shadows. He won't be happy until he gets what he wants."

"What does he want?" Zandra said. "Whenever we talk to any of your family, you only tell us half-truths. I can see Forfax is hiding something. He's sweating, uncomfortable, and shifty. What's the big secret you're all concealing from us?"

Acer chewed on her thumbnail then dropped her hand into her lap. "I know I can figure this out. Stop things from getting worse."

"Two members of your family are dead! And Laylah was seriously injured in an explosion," I said. "This is beyond figuring out. It's time you share your secrets. You need help to sort this."

Acer stood and looked at Forfax. "I need to check in on Laylah and Micah, make sure they're okay."

"Wait! What about Forfax? Cythera could be about to charge him with two murders," Zandra said. "Don't you want to see what happens to him?"

Acer hesitated. "I don't think she will. Not yet. Cythera's not dumb. She'll realize the evidence was too convenient. She'll keep digging."

"And what will Cythera find if she does keep digging?" I said. "Share with us. We can help."

"Let me know what Cythera does with Forfax. He'll need support if he gets charged." Acer hurried out of the room.

"This whole family is odd. We should leave them to destroy themselves and keep whatever secret they have hidden. It must be a whopper if Acer is refusing to share." Zandra lifted her hands. "And why does she suddenly need to check in on Laylah and Micah?"

"If someone is after them, and it's not Forfax, she'll want to keep them safe."

"I'm tempted to wash my hands of this mess," Zandra said. "Why should we help a family that refuses to accept support?"

I settled my paws on her shoulders. "We're not giving up on Acer. She's a friend, and she's in trouble. Once Finn is done with the interview, we can get him digging into the details and find the missing piece."

"What do we do in the meantime?" Zandra said.

"We eat breakfast, get ready for work, and I need to feed my phoenix."

Chapter 20

Tail terrors

"Watch out for this one. It's a spitter! If that stuff gets on your skin, it'll burn a hole through to the bone." Zandra crept beside me as we hunted a baby humpbacked leaping spider toad.

"It's scared. That's why it's spitting. It thinks we want to hurt it," I whispered.

"This critter has injured three people since it escaped from the Petrelli's backyard. We have to bring it in, or Barney will issue a destroy order."

"I don't disagree it needs containing, but I have an issue with the Petrellis for having such a remarkable creature. Their license permitted them ownership of one aged humpbacked leaping spider toad. And they were only allowed to keep her because she'd lost three legs and wasn't considered a danger."

"I guess they got her a companion without letting us know." Zandra scanned the shadows in the alley.

"No more humpbacked leaping spider toads for them. The fact this little one escaped proves they're incapable of looking after such a rare and striking critter."

"The paperwork shows they inherited the old one from a family member. Maybe they need lessons in humpbacked leaping spider toad care. Although there was a long list of complaints from neighbors about her. This isn't the first time animal control has had to step in."

"They don't deserve this baby. We're finding it and giving it to someone who will show it the love it deserves." I hopped over a pile of trash and slowed. Located low on the wall were more of the cult symbols.

I walked over and sniffed them. It looked like the same paint used on the other walls, but there were no graffiti daubs accompanying them to draw the eye. Whoever had painted them here must have assumed they wouldn't be noticed, since few people would willingly choose to stroll among the reeking recycling containers.

Who was leaving these symbols? Was it linked to Gaian and his gang? Or was it connected to the Morfiel family? I wasn't convinced there was a connection to Acer's family. It seemed like two mysteries were working in parallel. But I needed to keep an open mind. Magic had a way of twisting the truth.

A hocking throat sound caught my attention, just as a huge glob of something bright green and sizzling landed by my left paw.

"Juno! It's right over your head. Hide!" Zandra yelled.

I'd been so busy thinking about the symbols that I'd taken my eye off our capture mission. I ran toward the nearest recycling container, intending to squeeze underneath it and get out of the path of the gross green spittoon globules.

I was wriggling forward on my belly when there was another phlegmy cough, and a glob of something hot landed on my tail. Why was my tail being assaulted every time I went into combat?

The revolting muck burned through my perfect white fur and sizzled my skin. A blast of something icy slammed into my fluffy butt, and I was shoved underneath the container. My tail had stopped burning, although it was now numb. I attempted to inspect the damage, but it was too dark to see.

"You can come out. I've got it in a hold spell," Zandra said. "Did it get anything other than your tail?"

I heaved myself out from underneath the container and looked at my soggy, burned tail. It would take more than a little healing magic to bring it back to its former glory.

"Juno! You good?" Zandra had her hands out, moving them slowly from side to side. The baby humpbacked leaping spider toad hovered in the air above her, writhing and snarling. Patches of dark tufty fur stuck out at odd angles all over its back. The poor creature hadn't had a decent groom in weeks.

"I'll live, thanks to you." I sniffed my mangled tail and grimaced.

"Any time. What got you distracted?" She glanced along the alleyway toward the symbols.

"I'll tell you later. Let's get this baby in the van and calm it down." I looked up at the chittering, hissing capture. "Hush, little one. You're safe with us. We'll take care of you and find you a home you'll enjoy. One you won't want to escape from."

Zandra lowered the creature to the ground, and we administered gentle calming spells so it would be easier to handle. We carried the critter to the van, secured it in a pen with soft bedding and food, and then drove to animal control.

Zandra touched a finger against my damaged tail. "That'll take some work to restore. Are you in pain?"

"Totally numb, thanks to that freeze spell you used on my rump. When I regain the feeling, I'll use healing magic and cover it in a poultice. It'll be fine in a week or two."

"I didn't realize you'd stopped hunting. I was still walking along the alleyway when I heard it make that gross noise. It got too close to you. You could have been badly injured. Worse than a frazzled tail."

"It was my fault for getting distracted. Let's get this baby settled and then stop for lunch, shall we?"

Zandra nodded. "And we need to check in with Finn, see if they've made progress with Forfax. I thought Cythera would charge him at the end of her interrogation. She grilled him for over an hour."

"She was bluffing with her bad angel act to see if he'd fold. But I expect she's got all the angels searching for more evidence to make the double murder conviction stick."

"You don't think the poison discovery is enough?"

"It could be. And the way Forfax was sweating and shaking suggested he was hiding something big." As we'd watched the rest of the interview, Forfax had gotten more anxious and even jumpier. Even I'd been considering him guilty by the end.

"Let's hurry." Zandra pressed her foot down on the gas. "See what we can do to make sure an innocent person isn't charged."

Half an hour later, the baby humpbacked leaping spider toad was sleeping on its side in a large pen in the back of animal control. Zandra had filed the paperwork, and we'd headed out to grab food, stopping at the Gingerbread Bakery to see how badly it had been damaged.

Tia and Binky stood outside. Tia was in conversation with an official-looking guy in a navy suit and a white shirt, but Binky wandered over.

"Hey, how's it going?" I said.

"Tia's stressed and complaining, but I'm grateful she's unharmed. She has the luck of Vesta and Hestia. She'd been at the counter only seconds before the explosion." Binky shuddered.

"We're glad you're both safe," Zandra said. "What's that guy doing here?"

"He's from the insurance company. He's not causing Tia trouble, but I'm keeping an eye on him. He reckons the payout will come through within a month, then we can start the rebuild."

"Months without Tia's amazing food?" I groaned. "All the great places to eat are changing."

Tia swished her thick tail. "We have a plan for that. While the rebuild is going on, Tia's renting a catering truck. We can serve most of the same things from it. It'll be basic, but that way, she keeps an income and stays busy while the rebuild happens."

"Great idea," I said. "Will you sell your famous bacon and sausage baps?"

"Sure! They're a customer favorite. Mine, too. Although Tia always stops me from taste testing every batch. I don't see the harm. We need to ensure quality baps are delivered to customers."

I nodded sagely. "I'd taste test all the time if I lived in a bakery."

"We'll visit the truck once it's up and running," Zandra said.

Binky turned away. "Look forward to seeing you there. Better go. I need to make sure that guy isn't trying anything funny with Tia."

"Food now?" I asked.

"In a second." Zandra pulled out her mobile snow globe and connected with Finn. "Hey. How's it going with Forfax?"

I jumped onto her shoulder so I could hear the conversation.

"Still no confession, but Cythera believes there's enough evidence to charge him."

"What evidence has she got?" I said.

"The poison found in Forfax's bag is a match for both victims."

"That's it?"

"That's it."

"And Forfax remains resolute he didn't do it?"

"He keeps saying he's innocent. And weirdly, he's also saying they'll get him next. I reassured him he's safe. There's no safer place than an Angel Force cell. If anyone tried to get Forfax, they'd have to get past all of us, through magic wards, and a locked door."

"Does his family know what's happening to him?" Zandra said.

"Not yet. There are still a few hoops to jump through before he's charged with both murders. But Forfax said he doesn't want his family involved. Not even Acer, and she's been by twice to get updates."

"Have you found anything on the other family members?" I said. "Any reason why Forfax doesn't want to see them?"

"I've been running every background check I can think of to see what skeletons they're hiding. So far, nothing unusual. And if you were just looking at the records we have on them, you'd assume they were the perfect family."

"Which we know isn't true," I said. "What about the missing will document? Has that shown up?"

"That's proving hard to get hold of. I think the family lawyer has a copy, but he's being tricksy about sharing. I've left half a dozen messages, and he hasn't responded to any of them."

"The family probably thinks having an evasive lawyer who avoids awkward questions is a bonus," Zandra said.

"There must be a reason that addition to the will is so hard to come by," I said. "Could it be why the family is being secretive? There's something in that document that makes them a target?"

"To answer that question, I need to look at the document."

"Keep trying," Zandra said. "There must be a clue somewhere as to why they're acting strangely."

"If Forfax doesn't feel safe, it suggests he knows who's targeting them," I said. "Or at least, the family is aware someone wants them dead."

"Why haven't they been given protection by Angel Force?" Zandra said.

"They've been offered protection several times, but they've refused. Ollia, in particular, was adamant they didn't want outside interference and they could look after themselves."

"Outside interference could have saved Rabdos and Erig," I said. "I want to talk to Acer again. She seems the most likely to share whatever secret they're hiding."

"I figured the same thing, and I've been trying to reach her, but I can't get hold of her. I've left messages to let her know Forfax is about to be charged, but she hasn't responded," Finn said.

"Perhaps she's at the hospital with Laylah," Zandra said. "We could stop by now before we go back to work."

"Let me know if you find her. I know she's worried about what'll happen to Forfax."

"She was also worried about Laylah and Micah. That was why she left during Forfax's interview," I said. "We've not heard from her since then, though."

"We'll see if we can find her," Zandra said.

We said our goodbyes and hurried to the hospital. We headed to the room where we'd last seen Laylah recuperating, but it was empty, the bed stripped and the window open.

"Maybe they've moved her to a different part of the hospital," I said.

"Or she's dead." Zandra stalked around the room. "If someone is picking off this family one by one, Laylah would be an obvious target. She was weakened from being almost blown apart. The killer could have snuck in and got her in her sleep."

"Having met Laylah, she's no shrinking violet. Even in her weakened state, she'd have fought back, and there's no evidence in here of a fight."

A woman in a blue hospital uniform marched in with an armful of bedding. "May I help you?"

"We're here to visit Laylah Morfiel," Zandra said. "Has she been moved?"

The woman set down the bedding. "Let me look at the records." She pulled a chart off the end of the bed. "Says here she was discharged."

"So soon?" I said. "Laylah nearly died in an explosion. The last time we saw her, she was recovering from some serious injuries."

The woman flipped through the chart some more then looked into the corridor. "Doctor, just a moment. These visitors have questions about Laylah Morfiel."

He wandered in and smiled. "Friends or family?"

"Neither. We're working with Angel Force to investigate the explosion that injured Laylah," I said. "We were surprised to learn she's already been discharged."

"Against my advice. She still had injuries that needed several days of intensive healing magic before she was recovered." The doctor took the chart and scanned through it. "But this morning, she demanded to leave. She got unpleasant and aggressive. In the end, I decided for the safety of my staff to allow her to go. I wasn't happy about it, though."

"Why discharge herself if she had so much healing to do?" Zandra said.

"I'm uncertain, but she said she needed to see her family and find out what was going on. I assumed she'd gone home to recover under their care."

"Did Laylah have visitors this morning?" I said. "We're also looking for her sister, Acer. You may know her. She works for Angel Force."

"I do. Acer stopped by, but Laylah had already left. She asked similar questions to you about her sister and then dashed off. She looked panicked about something." He nodded at us. "If you'll excuse me, I'm halfway through my patient rounds."

The woman in the blue uniform nodded at us then got to work making the bed.

With nothing left for us to do at the hospital, we headed back to town.

"Should we try the house they're staying in?" I said. "See if Laylah went there? Acer could be with her."

"We need to get back to work," Zandra said. "And I need food. I'm starving."

My stomach grumbled in agreement. "We can try later. We have to get someone from that family talking. The secret they're keeping is killing them one by one. Erig first then, most likely, Rabdos. Laylah almost got blown to pieces. And now Forfax is saying he's not safe. They know who's after them."

"But which one of them is next on our mysterious murderer's hit list?" Zandra said.

Chapter 21

Family reunion

The rest of the workday passed uneventfully, but our evening plans proved more exhilarating.

I was lurking behind a bush with Zandra outside the Morfiel rental. We'd had a hurried dinner then raced over to see if we could locate the rest of the family and get them to open up. Although how we'd do that, we'd yet to determine. How many more needed to die before they'd reveal what was going on?

"Someone's coming." My ears swiveled as swift footsteps approached.

It was Micah, his head down as he walked to the door and opened it. He hesitated on the step for several seconds, his shoulders moving up and down as if he was working up the courage to enter. Then he walked in.

Several lights were switched on in the house, suggesting he was the first one home.

A few minutes later, Ollia arrived with Laylah beside her. Although Laylah limped and held her ribs with one hand, Ollia made no attempt to assist her.

"There's motherly love in action," I whispered.

Zandra nodded. "Acer was right about Ollia. She didn't adopt those children because she wanted a family to love. She wanted accessories to go with her impressive collection of catsuits."

A few more lights were switched on once they'd entered the house.

"Perhaps they've come together to figure out how to help Forfax," I said.

"From the way Ollia behaved at Angel Force, she's more likely to throw him under an enchanted pumpkin than get him off a double murder charge."

That was very true. "I wonder if Acer will join them."

We waited another ten minutes for any more arrivals, but Acer didn't show.

"If this get-together is about Forfax, Acer would insist on being here," Zandra said. "You can tell by the way she speaks about him that they like each other."

"She can't have been inside unless she was sitting in the dark. Micah switched on the first set of lights."

"I checked with Finn not half an hour ago, and he still hadn't seen her or had any reply to his messages. He sounded worried."

"Maybe Acer's left town. She's had enough of her family and their secretive ways. After all, she moved here to get away from them, then they followed her and continued to mess with her life."

Zandra hummed out a breath. "We need to find out what they're talking about. Let's go see if we can hear through a window."

We crept toward the house and hurried around the side of the building. We checked several windows before finding the room the family was using. They were settling around a dining table. They all had drinks, and although it was time for dinner, there was no food set out, suggesting the meeting wouldn't take long.

"None of them look happy," Zandra whispered.

"They have little to laugh about since someone wants them dead." I strained to hear the conversation, but it was too muffled through the glass. "We need to get inside."

"It's too risky to break in," Zandra said.

I froze then whipped my head around. Something was stalking us through the darkness. I growled and approached it, my hackles raised.

"Don't attack! It's Ember. Sage's new friend." The adorable black and white kitten appeared and bounced toward me.

"Hush! Stay low and make sure you're not seen. What are you doing here?" I hiss-whispered at him.

Ember crept closer in a crab-like position. "Sage said I needed to spend time with you. I had to get to know her friends to make sure I'd fit in. I followed your scent trail, so I knew where you were."

"I thought she sent you back to the Academy."

"She didn't mean that. I know it's just a test. I must prove to her I'm good enough."

"Hey, turn the volume down." Zandra pressed a finger against her lips.

"Sorry! What are you doing?" Ember whispered.

"Investigating murders," I said.

Ember's eyes grew wide. "Sage said you always do the best stuff."

I was surprised to learn this, given how much Sage grumbled every time I took her on a kitten impossible mission. "Stay quiet. We were figuring out how to get inside and hear what they're saying."

"The murderers?"

"Or they could be about to be murdered," Zandra muttered.

"I can help! I have advanced invisibility powers, so I can cover both of you in my magic. We can go inside, and you can hear everything. Then you can catch your killer. Or stop someone from being killed. Either way works."

"What do you think?" I said to Zandra.

She glanced at Ember. "You're that good?"

I nodded. "I've seen him use his invisibility magic. It works."

"You're the cat with the story." Zandra raised her eyebrows at me. "A story I've yet to learn from Juno. Why are you in town?"

"I'm here to replace—"

I clamped a paw over Ember's adorable mouth. "Another time. We can't get distracted from our mission. Shall we try to get inside?"

"If they see us, they'll be furious. And if one of them had anything to do with the murders..."

"I guarantee my magic will hold. You stay quiet, and they won't know we're in there." Ember bounced on his paws. "Can I help? I wanna. Sage will like me more if I do."

"It's worth a try," I said.

Zandra shrugged. "It seems this is our only way to hear their conversation. Let's do it."

"We'll try around the front," I said. "No one used a key to get in."

Luck was on our side, and the door opened smoothly with no hinges squeaking.

Ember fluffed his fur, and multicolored magic sparked out of him. It surrounded us, and we vanished.

"That's some skill. I can't see either of you," Zandra said. "Nice work, Ember."

"You're welcome. I got top marks in training for my invisibility power. I like it. It's fun. What do we do now?"

"We get close to the dining room and listen to their conversation," I whispered. "This family has been keeping a deadly secret, and until we know what it is, we're not able to help them."

"I forgot to say we should have held paws before I started. Juno, you find my tail, and then if Zandra touches you, we won't lose each other."

It took me a few seconds to locate Ember's invisible tail, but I soon had it clamped between my teeth. Zandra gently held my tail. Not something I enjoyed, but I'd endure it so I didn't lose my wonderful witch. Then our invisible train inched toward the dining room where voices could be heard. None of them sounded joyful.

"Which one of you did it?" Laylah said.

"That information is of no importance," Ollia said. "We'll deal with the situation together."

"Fake being a family until it's someone else's turn, you mean?" Micah sounded bitter, although his words wobbled.

"Watch your tone," Ollia said. "If your father could hear you, you'd be struck for being so rude."

"He can't hurt me anymore. He's dead."

"And we all know who killed him," Ollia said.

I spat out Ember's tail. "They know who murdered Erig."

"Who's Erig?" Ember said.

"The first victim."

"This will all be over soon," Ollia said. "We deal with the current situation, and then we part and make our own plans."

"You're insane," Micah said. "You can't believe you'll win."

"I'm still here, aren't I? And I doubt you have the stomach to do anything about it." Ollia paused. "And as you can see, Laylah discharged herself against medical advice, so she's in no position to get the upper hand."

"For now. But don't underestimate me," Laylah said. "I may have cracked ribs, burns, and a concussion, but I know who to watch out for."

"They must know who's after them and believe they can deal with them without any help," I whispered.

"If they know who it is, why not tell Angel Force? Cythera will get a troop of angels out, arrest the person, and this'll be over."

"Zandra, I can see your feet!" I looked around, but, of course, Ember was invisible. My gaze narrowed. Curtain tassels were moving on the other side of the hallway. "Ember! Focus!"

Tiny paw pads hurried back toward me, and Ember jostled against my side before more magic sparkled over us, and Zandra's feet disappeared. "Sorry, but they looked so enticing. How can you resist?"

"You resist because you're on a mission. If you're taking on a familiar role, you need to have laser focus. You can never get distracted, or your witch will be vulnerable."

"Who is Ember bonding with?" Zandra said.

"That's the story I need to tell you." I focused on the feuding family.

"Who's going to do it?" Micah said.

No one spoke for several seconds.

"We do it together." Laylah twirled a strand of hair around a finger. "Then none of us will know who succeeded, so no one is at risk of being ratted out to the angels."

"If we deal with this current problem, what'll happen to Forfax?" Micah said.

"He won't be an issue for much longer." Ollia arched an eyebrow.

Micah thumped a hand on the table. "He'll talk! If the angels charge him with Erig and Rabdos's murders, he's got nothing left to lose by telling the truth."

"Forfax wouldn't dare talk. If he did, his involvement in all of this would come out, and he'd be no better off than he is."

"He'd be alive," Micah muttered.

"For how long?"

They went quiet again but kept glaring at each other.

"If Forfax is guilty of the murders, why are they fighting?" I whispered.

"This family finds it impossible to stick together, even in tough times," Zandra said. "They hate each other."

A gentle thud over our heads caught my attention. "You hear that?"

"It could be the killer." Zandra gently tugged on my tail. "We should go see."

I felt around for Ember and grabbed his tail, then we headed toward the stairs.

"Maybe they're here to finish them off while they're together," I whispered. "Take them out in a single attack."

Zandra sucked in a breath. "There's no way we're letting that happen."

We hurried up the stairs as best we could without bumping into each other. I remembered now why group invisibility magic was so tricky.

"Let's check in each room," I said.

The first room we came to had been set up as a temporary office. There were papers and books stacked around and a box full of what looked like trophies.

"Ember, you can drop the invisibility magic while we're in here," I said. "Although we may need it at a moment's notice, so be ready."

"Just say the word." Magic fizzed in the air, and we became visible.

Ember immediately leaped on a small ball of silver foil and chased it around the carpet.

I sighed as I watched him. This adorable young cat wasn't ready for a familiar role. He was competent when he focused but had too much kitten energy to be relied upon.

Zandra pulled a trophy from a box. "Why bring these when visiting Acer?"

I hopped onto the desk. There were a dozen awards and trophies inside. "Are they hers? Maybe she asked them to bring them."

"No, not hers. And they were given out for the weirdest accolades." Zandra turned over a star-shaped trophy.

"What's so weird about them?"

"Look at this one. Ollia was awarded this for advanced magical curses. Although it doesn't say where she got those skills from or who awarded her the trophy."

"This one's not so strange. It's Micah's award for advanced botany, with a minor in baking. You use plants in cooking."

"Again, there's no school or college connected to it. And this one is plain odd." Zandra lifted a gold star. "Awarded to Rabdos Morfiel, for mind manipulation in business – expert level. No one would teach that in a college."

"And here's one for Laylah. It's for explosives," I said. "Definitely not a typical college course. And Forfax got one for combat skills."

Zandra heaved out the largest trophy. "Huh! No name on this one, but it's for the Ultimate Champion. Although it doesn't say the ultimate champion in what. There's a space for a name to be engraved."

I sniffed the gold trophy. It looked expensive. "You think Erig and Ollia got these made for their kids? They wanted them to have abilities that enhanced their own power?"

"I wouldn't put it past them to train their children to be assets. And as we've discovered, the children weren't adopted so they could be offered a loving family."

"They built themselves an army," I said. "Made themselves almost invincible by surrounding themselves with a strong, skilled, warped family. Although, since Ollia got an award, maybe Erig was the brains behind these twisted prizes."

"That's the dead guy, right?" Ember said.

I wrinkled my booping snooter at him. "As I said, he was almost invincible. But something went wrong. Erig's family couldn't save him when he needed them the most."

"Or the army turned on him," Zandra said.

There was another thud.

"That came from the room next door," I said.

We abandoned the search and hurried to the next room. The door was locked, and it took some serious jiggling with unlock magic before the mechanism opened.

"You ready for this?" Zandra looked at me and then Ember.

We nodded.

She inched open the door. There was no light in the room, and the curtains were drawn.

"Who's in here?" Zandra whispered.

There was another thud, like a foot thumping on the carpet.

I poked my head around the door to get a better look and make sure nothing lethal was about to spring at my witch. As my eyes adjusted to the gloom, I discovered Acer wrapped in magical chains and tied to a chair.

I rushed over to her, and Zandra and Ember followed.

Zandra went to touch the chains, but I pushed her back.

"Careful! We don't know what magic is on these chains. It'll be strong to hold a half-angel. It could kill you."

She arched an eyebrow but then carefully removed the gag from Acer's mouth. "Who did this to you?"

Acer drew in a deep breath, her eyes not able to focus. "Family. Trouble."

"We know someone's picking you off. We figured Laylah was next because she'd already been injured, but they got to you instead." Zandra peered into Acer's face. "Why did they leave you here?"

"No. Listen. Help." Acer's words were woozy and unclear, suggesting she'd been drugged.

I was exploring the chains as Zandra tried to get sense from Acer. The magic holding her was sticky and unpleasant, but I could undo it with a little time.

Acer drew in a ragged breath. "Forfax. In danger."

"He's in danger of being charged with a double murder because you're keeping secrets," I said sharply. "Don't worry about your brother. The angels will protect him."

"Juno's right. Forfax is fine. He's locked in a cell, so no one will get him in there," Zandra said. "Why did your attacker leave you chained up? Why not kill you? And how come no one else heard you thumping around?"

Acer groaned. "Must save Forfax. Please!"

I risked touching a piece of the chain. Magic sparked off it, but it didn't hurt me, so I rested both paws on top of a link and forced release magic through it. The power in the chains groaned but finally shattered, releasing Acer.

She slumped forward and heaved in several deep breaths.

"I need to get you to the hospital," Zandra said. "You've got a deep cut on your head."

"No time. Save Forfax."

Zandra sat back on her heels and looked at me, her eyebrows lifted. "From?"

"My family!"

I looked at the broken chain and then at Acer's distraught face. "They did this to you, didn't they?"

Acer heaved out another breath. "I... I thought I could salvage this. Please, we must go to Forfax."

"Let's get out of here. Then I'll call Finn and make sure your brother is fine. Then you have some explaining to do." Zandra looked at Ember. "Can you conceal Acer, too?"

"It would be my pleasure." Ember waited for us to catch hold of a tail or a hand and then flung out his invisibility magic.

We hurried down the stairs and out of the front door, while the remaining Morfiel family members still feuded at the dining table.

Once we were far enough from the house, Ember released us from his invisibility magic.

Zandra pulled out her mobile snow globe and connected with Finn. "Hey. No time to explain, but can you check on Forfax? Make sure he's okay."

"Err... weird timing. I was about to message you."

"Why? Did something happen?"

"You could say that. Forfax has just been found dead in his cell."

Chapter 22

To the victor, the spoils

I stood outside the open cell with Zandra, Ember, and Acer. Forfax was on his back, his sightless eyes staring at the ceiling.

"What happened to him?" Zandra said.

"No idea. The last time he was checked on, he was fine. Still seemed nervous but didn't complain about feeling unwell," Finn said. "Then Bertoli looked in on him, and he found him like this."

I stepped closer to the body and sniffed around it. "Did Forfax always wear this ring?" I asked Acer.

She approached cautiously, her eyes wide and her face pale. "No. It's too flashy for him. It looks like something Erig would have worn."

"It's similar to the ring we took off Erig's body," Finn said. "The one that concealed the tainted magic."

Acer let out a shaky sigh. "That's how they got him."

"Who got him?" Finn said. "If you know who's doing this to your family, you must tell me. We won't be able to protect you until we know the full story."

Acer stared at her feet. "It's complicated."

"It's not so complicated," I said. "I've worked it out. When I saw your family plotting together, you tied up in a room, and a box of weird trophies, it suddenly made sense."

"It did?" Zandra said.

"The Morfiel family literally wants to kill each other, don't they?" I focused on Acer.

She swallowed and licked her lips. "I've never hidden that my family is a mess. I tried hard to accept them for what they were, but it became unbearable. That's why I got out."

"You're not answering the questions," Finn said. "Who is doing this?"

"It's not one person," I said. "They're all involved. And they're all at risk of being murdered next."

"I still don't get it," Zandra said.

"We need to see the missing will appendix to be certain my theory is correct, but I'd wager a pound of finest salmon I'm right."

"You won't get that document from any of my family," Acer mumbled.

"I don't expect we will because it'll reveal they've been goaded into killing by someone who should have protected them. And as we discovered at your house, your family has skills to get rid of people in various gruesome ways."

"You mean the trophies?" Zandra said.

I nodded. "Erig was obsessed with having people prove to him they were the best. The stars everyone wore revealed this was far from a regular family."

"They were Erig's idea," Acer said. "I stopped wearing mine the second I moved out."

"We need the rest of the family here so they can explain themselves," Finn said.

"I was about to suggest you summon them. They need to see Forfax, so they know there's one less family member in the running for the prize."

Finn looked confused. "What prize?"

"Get them here, and I'll explain."

"Give me half an hour," Finn said. "I'll take reinforcements to the house in case they get difficult."

"They'll be happy to come, so they can confirm Forfax is dead," I said. "Keep things simple. Let them know they need to come and claim his body. Try not to make them think we're suspicious or they may run."

"My family is suspicious of everyone," Acer said. "One of Erig's mottoes was trust no one."

"No wonder nobody liked him," Zandra said.

"There were many reasons his family despised him," I said.

Although I had a dozen questions for Acer, I could see she was flagging under the weight of the secret she'd held onto so tightly. "Let's get a drink. This next bit won't be easy to hear."

Acer was silent as we went into the kitchen, and Zandra made herbal tea for both of them.

Ember had been silent this whole time, too, watching with wide eyes and quivering whiskers.

He nudged me. "This is exciting. Sage was right. You always do the best things."

"That's kind of you to say. If you stay alert and pay attention, you notice the little things others miss."

"And solve all the murders?"

"That's the plan. Now, hush. We have killers to uncover."

Zandra settled at the table with Acer, and I hopped onto Zandra's lap. Ember remained on the floor, watching. He was a bright little student.

"I know you think you're doing the right thing by keeping the family secret, but people can't keep dying. No secret is worth that." Zandra nudged a steaming mug toward Acer.

"I thought they'd change. Forfax and Rabdos wanted to. Micah, too. They were just struggling to take the leap. Erig had an impressive line of threats to keep them subdued."

"What about Laylah?" I said. "Did she want out?"

Acer gripped her mug. "Of course. Laylah was so full of hate, and she was always terrible at hiding her feelings. She used to hold them in, but then they'd burst out like a volcano. And she said some terrible things to Ollia and Erig, which she couldn't take back. Not that she wanted to, but it made them wary of her. They knew she'd cause trouble if she lost control."

"I still don't get it," Zandra said. "Juno, you said the family is all involved in these murders?"

"Most of them. Or attempted murder. Excluding Acer and Rabdos, that is. Go on." Acer was close to revealing the grim truth about her family, and I wanted nothing to distract her.

"I wanted what everyone else had," Acer said, "a loving, warm family. A home where I was wanted. Not a home where hugs were reserved for special occasions or public events, so it looked like we were happy."

"Everyone needs regular hugs," I said.

"I remember once throwing my arms around Erig and hugging him. He was disgusted and locked me in the barn for two days. He said displays of affection were reserved for public occasions, and there was no point in putting on an act when at home."

"You had the worst childhood," Zandra said.

"I didn't realize it was so bad at the time. I thought every family worked the same way. They acted happy around other people, but in private, they barely tolerated each other. That was what I was used to."

"No family is perfect," Zandra said. "Mine is super messed up, but we always show each other we care. That's natural."

"I didn't know that. I thought I'd landed on my feet when a rich, influential couple wanted me. And not just me, they were adopting other children, too, so I got siblings. But the dream morphed into a nightmare."

Finn strode into the kitchen. "They're all here. None of them are happy. Juno, are you ready to do this? Ollia is looking for someone to yell at."

"Just a moment. I must make a call. May I borrow a snow globe?"

"There's one on my desk. Help yourself."

I put in a call to Sage, told her what I needed, and then returned to the others. "Shall we find out what's really been going on since the Morfiels came to town?"

"I'm all ears." Cythera walked out of her office, her expression suggesting she'd just learned her favorite brand of wing whitener was being discontinued. "Did I authorize any of this?"

"You can accept the praise for a successful arrest in just a moment," I said. "I promise I won't hog the glory."

"You're so benevolent." Cythera arched an eyebrow. "Why are the remaining members of the Morfiel family all here?"

Finn looked at me. "Um... Juno solved the case."

"You don't sound too sure about that." Cythera crossed her arms over her chest. "Explain. Now!"

"I will." I trotted toward the family, Ember by my side. "And with the Morfiel family present, they'll be eager to know how many of them are going to prison."

Cythera muttered to Finn, while Zandra walked alongside Acer as we joined the family. Ollia was there, looking haughty and beautiful in a gold catsuit. Micah stood separate from the rest of the family. Laylah had eased into a chair, holding her ribs.

When they saw Acer, they looked alarmed before their blank expressions fell back into place. That initial blast of shock confirmed what I already knew.

"I'm sorry for your loss," I said to them all. "You must be saddened by what happened to Forfax."

"I need to know exactly what did happen to him." Ollia stared unblinking at Acer before looking at me. "You'd think my child would have been safe here."

I let Ollia's haughty words linger. "Why don't you tell us what happened?"

She splayed her hands, a picture of innocence. "I wish I knew."

"You were the last one to speak to Forfax before he went into his cell," I said. "How did you convince him to put on that ring tainted with a curse?"

Ollia's expression remained a frozen canvas of blankness. "I have no idea what you're talking about."

"That's what killed Forfax. Did you promise you'd get him off the murder charges if he wore it? Or did you give it to him so he had a way out if he was about to be charged?" I said.

"What my deceased son wore on his fingers was of no concern to me."

"It should be since you now have one less obstacle in your way to victory. But before we get to that point in this twisted tale, let's go back to Erig's murder. That's where this murky story began." I hopped onto a desk and found a pile of crisp paper to stand on. Ember followed, but misjudged his jump and clung to the side of the desk.

"Sorry! The surface is slippery."

I hauled him up by his scruff and settled him in a corner then turned back to the family. "Forfax, Micah, and Ollia all had a hand in killing Erig. And I suspect the others weren't far behind with their plans to get rid of him."

None of them said a word.

"No one wants to confess and make this easy on Angel Force?" I looked at each member of the Morfiel family. "Thought not. When we visited your rental, we discovered a box of unusual awards and accolades."

"You were in the house without my permission?" Ollia looked at Cythera. "None of this will stand up in court if they broke in. I know they don't work in law enforcement."

Cythera's wings flared. "They're consultants. I gave them permission to enter your home if they considered lives were at risk."

I hid my surprise. Cythera had just covered for us. "And we had a right to enter since you were holding Acer against her will."

Acer nodded, her expression tight. "You drugged me, tied me up, and planned on killing me."

Ollia tapped her painted nails against her thigh. Micah opened his mouth, but a glare from Ollia kept him quiet. This family was on the verge of breaking. It wouldn't take many more nudges before someone spilled the secrets.

"Returning to the twisted trophies," I said. "None of them were from colleges or schools. That's because Erig created them. Although I suspect you were involved, too, Ollia. Did you choose to specialize in curses? Or did Erig demand you learn that skill?"

She inspected her nails, failing to hide the rage in her eyes.

"And you trained your powerful children, so they had the skills to defeat any enemy. Erig must have been so proud of himself for coming up with the idea. Or was it your idea?"

Ollia drew in air through her teeth. "Why would I train my beloved children to become monsters?"

"To survive your family," Zandra said. "Forfax was skilled in botany and baking, and I suspect he excelled in poisonous plants. You, Ollia, were trained in curses. Rabdos was skilled in mind manipulation, so he could get Erig what he wanted from any deal. Forfax had combat skills. And Laylah had explosive talents."

Laylah touched the bruising on the side of her face. "For all the good it did me."

"They all had talents that could destroy others," I said. "Or more precisely, destroy those who got in Erig's way. He stopped at nothing to get what he desired."

"More power and money," Acer muttered. "Erig could never have enough. No matter what he got, he needed more. It became an addiction, and he'd do whatever it took to get it."

"Don't play the dummy. You got a special skill, too," Laylah said.

Acer's cheeks flushed.

"What did you learn?" I hadn't seen a trophy for Acer in the box.

"I wasn't made into a weapon. I have an enhanced ability to repel magic."

I twitched my booping snooter. "Erig used you as a shield against attack?"

She nodded. "He hit me with so many spells, I almost died. But it made me strong. I can stop almost any magic with my wings. But most people were so scared of him, they never tried to get him, so my skill wasn't so valuable. That's the main reason he let me leave."

"Erig needed an obedient army," I said. "The bullying and the cruelty broke you all, so you followed him without question. And those stars you wear were used as his status markers. Erig had a gold star, and the rest of you were given one that fitted his belief in you."

Laylah looked at the gray star on her chest. She went to take it off, but Ollia stopped her.

"You didn't mention Forfax in this fanciful explanation," Ollia said. "He tried to run Erig over. I saw him. There's no skill in that."

"He only did that because he was desperate and saw an opportunity," I said.

"He was," Acer said. "Forfax was driven half-mad by his desire to leave the family. Every time he tried, Erig blocked him, so he couldn't see a way out."

"Hold your tongue," Ollia said. "You may work for Angel Force, but you're still a part of this family."

"I choose not to be. I made that clear when I moved away. Yet, you won't leave me alone."

"We couldn't take the risk," Laylah said.

"What risk are you talking about?" Cythera said.

There was a crash in the reception area, followed by muttered curses.

"I thought you could fly! That's more like drunken leap-flapping. Get a move on. Juno is waiting." Sage's clipped tone drifted into the office.

"The missing puzzle piece is here," I said.

Smoke hop-flapped at speed into the office, Sage shuffling behind him. He carried a document in his beak that dragged on the floor, almost tripping him.

I hurried over, retrieved the document, and petted Smoke. "Good boy."

He jumped up and down, squawked several times, and bit my booping snooter.

Sage shook her head. "He keeps doing that. And making weird groaning noises. He must be constipated. I need a nap. Looking after a baby phoenix is exhausting." She found a piece of paper dropped on the carpet and curled herself onto it.

"Thanks for getting here so quickly," I said. "This document will explain everything. Where did you find it?"

Sage kept her eyes closed. "Bottom drawer of a cabinet in the rental place. One of the bedrooms. It wasn't hard to find."

Ollia took a step forward, but Finn blocked her path.

Ember leaped off the desk and landed next to Sage. "Mind if I join?"

"So long as you stay quiet." Sage shuffled over and made room for Ember on her paper.

Smoke groan-squawked. He'd better not make a mess in here, or Cythera would get mad.

"Now everyone is settled, we can continue. Smoke was always with Erig, so he learned about his devious schemes," I said. "It must have been stressful for such a magnificent creature to endure watching Erig's cruelty. Phoenixes are naturally loving birds."

"That dumb bird was lucky we took him," Ollia said. "He has a deformed wing, so nobody wanted him."

Smoke snapped his beak at Ollia and groan-burped at her.

"This beautiful bird isn't dumb." I gently settled Smoke with Ember and Sage, but he refused to leave my side. "He stayed quiet, and he listened. He learned a lot, including what Erig added to his will."

"That's a copy of the missing will appendix?" Cythera said.

I passed it to her. "Please, take your time. It'll make for fascinating reading and explain why this family is intent on killing each other."

She flipped open a page and began to read.

Ollia sucked in a breath. "We had no choice! I had to protect myself. I was scared they'd kill me."

Laylah glared at her. "You told us not to say anything."

I paced in front of the family, Smoke beside me. "After Forfax tried to murder Erig by running him over, Erig decided to teach the family he'd twisted into monsters a final lesson. He wanted to see how far you'd go. So, he left a new condition in his will."

Cythera was still reading, her eyes growing wider with every line she scanned.

"The condition was, and correct me if I'm wrong, there could only be one person who inherited Erig's fortune." I looked at their faces. Ollia, Laylah, and Micah didn't notice me. They were too busy glaring at each other. "Initially, Rabdos was to get most of the money, but Erig enjoyed making people prove their worth. What greater challenge than seeing the family, who longed to kill him, destroy each other?"

"Whoa! Erig pitted them against each other to get his money?" Finn said.

Smoke burped again. It sounded like the word *killers*.

"Erig was a monster," Acer said. "I couldn't believe it when the new condition was read out. I told everyone not to take it seriously and forget the fortune."

"But it was too late. The wheels of greed had been set in motion," I said.

"Is that why you used a cursed ring on Erig?" Laylah said to Ollia. "You knew what he had planned and wanted to stop him."

"Don't come the innocent with me," Ollia said. "You're as guilty as everyone else. Acer included. She'd have joined us, eventually. No one is stupid enough to walk away from such a fortune."

Smoke leaped and flapped. He burped again. No, not a burp. A word. He was getting his voice back!

"You admit you had a hand in murdering your husband?" Cythera said to Ollia, shooting Smoke a warning glare.

"No! Micah poisoned him with his disgusting little candies. I watched him prepare them and then give them to his father."

Everyone looked at Micah.

He gulped. "I only did what Erig taught me to do."

"You see! My ring did little to him. It was a playful warning. We did things like that to each other all the time. Erig enjoyed it." Ollia said. "Arrest Micah for the murders."

"Erig enjoyed almost dying at the hands of his wife?" Zandra shook her head.

Ollia lifted her chin. "We got our kicks where we could."

"That's some twisted kick," Sage muttered from her curled position on the floor.

"Should I arrest Micah?" Finn looked at Cythera then me.

"In a moment." I petted Smoke. "Your knowledge will be invaluable to resolve this mystery once and for all."

"Stop fooling with that creature," Cythera said. "Burp it if you must, but I don't want it fouling in here."

I nodded at Smoke. "Ignore the grumpy angel. Whenever you're ready."

"Juno!" Cythera hissed at me. "Focus. Are they all guilty?"

"Almost. Forfax hit Erig with the van, leaving him with significant injuries. He'd have recovered, but Erig knew his days were numbered. The family he'd broken and put back together so many times was turning against him."

"Erig knew he was on their hit lists?" Zandra said.

"He did. So, he set them the ultimate challenge. That trophy we found with no name engraved on it would have gone to the last family member standing." I kept an eye on Smoke as he deep breathed and mumbled to himself.

"What trophy is this?" Cythera said.

"All the evidence is waiting at their rental property," I said. "Did Erig take those trophies everywhere? Reminders of your achievements? A way to rub your noses in it when he considered one of you underperformed?"

"He loved waving those things in our faces," Laylah spat out. "Reminding us we'd be nothing without him."

"He did that to you the most," Micah said. "You could never keep your mouth shut. That's why you always got the gray star."

"I stood up for myself. You should learn from me."

"You almost got blown up because you wouldn't behave!"

"By you! Admit it. You were always watching me tinker with explosives. I know it was you. You used to snoop on us and see what we were being forced to learn."

Micah looked away.

"Micah is our killer?" Cythera moved toward him.

"One of them. Staying with Erig's murder," I said. "Erig was weakened by his injuries. Then Ollia sweetly slipped a curse onto his favorite ring, weakening him more. And to finish him off, he was given a fatal dose of slow acting poison."

"By Micah?" Cythera said.

"Of course it was him," Ollia said coldly. "He loved making us sick with his poisons."

"Because Erig forced me to poison you!" Micah threw up his hands. "Why not give him a taste of his own medicine? The rest of you failed to stop him."

There was silence. Then Smoke burped the word *stone*.

"Stone? Is that important?" I said.

"Shut that bird up!" Ollia grabbed a mug off a desk and hurled it at Smoke.

I repelled the missile, and the mug exploded in the air. "Go on, Smoke. You saw everything this family did. What about a stone?"

"The bird is simply belching," Cythera said.

"Phoenixes remember everything from their former lives. He was Erig's silent shadow and watcher. Smoke, what's special about a stone?" I said.

"Stone. Laylah. Pocket. Boom!" Smoke coughed out a tiny fireball.

Laylah huffed out a breath. "Of course. My latest project. Micah watched me build a reactive stone explosion, and he must have copied me. I touched something cold in my pocket just before the explosion in the bakery. You jerk!"

"I only did to you what you planned to do to me. I heard you plotting with Forfax. You wanted me dead."

There was another second of silence, then they turned on each other and yelled accusations back and forth.

"Silence!" Cythera shouted. "Juno, what else did Smoke witness?"

I stared at her in surprise. Cythera respected me, and it had only taken solving multiple murders for her to see my value.

"Micah's poison caused Erig's death. Poison hidden inside candies he made." I checked with Smoke, and he nodded. "But the cursed ring and the injuries from being hit by a vehicle weakened him."

"And Rabdos? Who poisoned him?"

"That wasn't me! But I know who did it. I'm not the only snoop." Micah looked at Laylah. "And I know who framed Forfax with the poison." His gaze cut to Ollia. "I'm willing to talk if you'll shorten my sentence."

"No! I'm talking!" Laylah struggled to stand. "I want to make a deal."

Smoke leaped up and down. "Candy. Curses. Secrets."

My wonderful little phoenix had found his voice, and nothing would silence him from pouring out the truth about this broken family.

Ollia sneered at the children she was supposed to love. "You're as bad as each other."

Cythera stepped forward. "And you're all under arrest."

Chapter 23

Happily ever after for now

"Solving a murder always makes me tired. And a double one, even more so. I could sleep for a week." I was stretched across Zandra's lap while she reclined in a comfy chair in Vorana's bookstore.

Twenty-four hours had passed since we'd uncovered Erig's twisted last request and how his family had acted on it. And thanks to Smoke finding his voice and revealing all, they'd been interviewed and charged with varying counts of murder or attempted murder. Only Acer had gotten away without a formal charge.

Zandra scratched her short fingernails through my fur. "It's the weirdest case I've ever dealt with."

"The weirdest family, too. I've never had a phoenix as the star witness. Smoke sure is cute. And tough. That bird went through a lot." Finn sat opposite us with Bertoli, along with Vorana and Sage, who'd sent Ember packing and seemed content to remain as her witch's familiar. Smoke was wandering around the group, flapping his wings and accepting treats. He was getting big.

"It always amazes me what people are prepared to do for money," Vorana said. "And letting one of your children poison your husband and not do anything to stop it..."

"Yep. Ollia knew all about the poisonous candy. And she knew exactly how efficient Micah could be. She waited and watched then followed Erig and stood over him while he died. Smoke saw it all." Finn puffed out a breath.

"You got lucky she didn't kill Smoke." Vorana petted the adorable bird as he waddled past.

Smoke hiss-squawked. "Tried. Hit chain with spell. Got free. Fled!"

"Brave bird," I murmured.

"And I got a look at the new will document," Finn said. "Erig made it clear that the last surviving family member got the lot. The houses, the business, all the money. And there was a lot of money up for grabs."

"There must have been a way to break that insane condition," Vorana said.

"Maybe, but without money and time wrangling in court, they'd have gotten nowhere," Finn said. "Erig had control of all the assets, so when he died, everything got frozen."

"Meaning the family had no way of funding a fight against the new will condition," Zandra said.

"And none of them, other than Acer, were prepared to walk away," I said. "Erig must have orchestrated a visit to Crimson Cove, so she'd have no choice but to be involved."

"You think he knew his family was about to turn on him? That was why he made the change?" Vorana said.

I nodded. "Erig realized they'd act against him, eventually. His endless cruelty had become extreme."

"The catalyst was when Forfax tried to kill Erig by running him over," Finn said. "It only takes one person to act before everyone else follows. Kinda like lemmings."

"Vicious, killer lemmings," Zandra muttered.

Vorana shuddered. "It's one way to leave a lasting legacy."

"A legacy that means everyone thinks you were a giant douchebag." Bertoli looked at our shocked expressions and shrugged. "I'm only saying what everyone is thinking."

Finn slapped him on the back. "Nice one. Thanks to that amazing bird, we've got eyewitness testimony for it all. Smoke saw Ollia curse Erig's ring. He watched Micah poison those candies found in Erig's jacket pocket—"

"And Smoke stopped me from eating a poisoned candy the first time we met." I still had a small scab on my booping snooter from where Smoke had scratched me, but I wore it proudly.

"He could have warned Erig about the candies," Bertoli said. "Saved his life."

"Would you have done?" Vorana said.

Bertoli twisted his mouth to the side. "Maybe. Although Erig sounded like a terrible person."

"He was the worst," Finn said. "Smoke even saw Laylah leave poisoned candies for Rabdos."

"Erig told me Rabdos had a sweet tooth," I said. "He used to make Smoke report on him if he ate something he shouldn't."

"He definitely shouldn't have eaten those particular candies," Zandra said. "Poor guy."

"Maybe not. We found a list of family members in Rabdos's bag. Those he planned to kill in order of difficulty. He was chasing the fortune, too," Finn said.

I tugged my tail out of Smoke's beak. "Until his sister snuffed him out and dumped his body."

"What happens to the money?" Zandra said. "Since everyone other than Acer is going to jail, they won't have access to the funds."

"We're figuring it out." Finn looked up as Acer walked through the doorway of the bookstore. "Hey. We were just talking about your charming family."

She grimaced, glared at Bertoli, then slumped into an empty seat. "I'm still suspended while Cythera decides what to do with me. She's not sure she can trust me after I hid the details about the will from her."

"If we'd had that information from the outset, things may not have happened the way they did," I said.

Acer tipped back her head and sighed. "I'm sorry about hiding things. I believed I could get my family to see sense. Such an idiot. I was looking for a shred of decency when I should have known better. They're all corrupt and rotten."

"It's not your fault," Finn said. "You kept hoping they'd change. You wanted them to be the family you'd dreamed of."

"I should have told you all what was going on from the start." Acer laced her fingers together and leaned forward. "It's so hard to know who to trust when you've been raised by a family like that."

"You can trust us," I said. "We're your friends. Even Bertoli."

His cheeks grew pink. "Of course. And I'm sorry for lying about our date. I never meant to get you in trouble. I'm sure Cythera will come around soon."

Acer didn't look at him. "Whatever. Maybe Angel Force isn't for me."

Smoke squawked when he noticed her sadness and dashed over. "Friend. Sad. Smile."

Acer tickled his head. "At least someone cares about me."

"We all care." I looked at Bertoli. "Everyone here cares. And none of us want to see you leave."

"We were discussing what'll happen to your family fortune." Finn nudged Bertoli and side-eyed Acer.

"I've been talking to the family lawyer. Because everyone's going to jail, he thinks it may come to me. There'll be some legal wrangling, but in a couple of years, it could be mine."

"You don't sound happy. That'll be life-changing," Vorana said. "What will you do with so much money?"

"I don't want it! That money is tainted with misery. If I bring it into my life, it'll drag me down."

"You can't let it sit in an account and do nothing," Zandra said.

Acer looked pensive. "I won't. If that fortune comes to me, I'm donating it to the Angel Foster Foundation. I want the money to help kids like me, Finn, and my siblings."

Finn's eyes glazed over. "They could do a lot with that amount of cash."

"I want angel rejects to have access to support, counseling, and opportunities to go to great colleges. I want them to have choices. Choices I never had. That lack of support meant I got forced into a messed-up environment and then stuck there." Acer gulped back tears. "We were so scared of putting a foot wrong or telling anybody things had gone bad. And this is what it led to. Everyone trying to kill each other. If I get my hands on that money, I'll ensure it does a ton of good."

"That's incredible. And you're incredible for planning to do that." Finn stood and hugged Acer.

Bertoli also stood. He held out a hand. "We're lucky to have you at Angel Force."

Acer looked at his hand. "I know."

"And... I'd like to make things up to you. Take you out again."

"Why bother?"

Bertoli lowered his hand and cleared his throat. "Should I have offered a hug, instead?"

"What you should have offered was honesty from the start. I'm done with people lying to me, telling me one thing to my face while they figure out how to mess with me."

"I'd... I'd never do that. Acer, I like you. I respect you."

"Then show it through your actions."

"Of course! How?"

"I'll think of something. Something public." A sharp look entered Acer's eyes, then her gaze softened. "Don't worry. I don't take after my family, so I won't humiliate you. I know how lousy that feels. Forget about it. I'd better go. I only dropped in to say hi. I've still got loads to sort out."

"In a way, it's good you've been suspended," Bertoli said. "It gives you time to fix your family's mess."

Finn groaned and dropped back into his seat. "Some people you just can't help."

A half-smile hovered on Acer's lips. "It's fine."

"Will you still see your family once they're in prison?" Zandra shuffled me off her lap then stood and walked Acer to the door.

I followed a short distance behind them with Smoke at my fluffy heels.

"I'm not sure. Maybe if they agree to get help and change, but I'm keeping my distance for now."

"You do what's best for you," Vorana said. "And any time you need a quiet place to sit and think or drink a mug of coffee and stare into space, there'll always be a chair in this bookstore waiting for you."

"I appreciate that."

"What about Smoke?" I said.

Smoke flapped his wings. "Friend. Acer. Kind. Stay?"

Acer looked down at Smoke, who hovered by her feet. She smiled. "If you'll have me, I'd love to keep you. My apartment is basic, though. You won't be living in the lap of luxury like you're used to."

"Smoke will have love, endless kindness, and friendship from you. Money can't buy that." I nudged the chubby bird. "What do you think?"

Smoke leaped into the air, flapping his wings as fast as he could. He squawked joyously, and a small jet of flame blasted from his beak.

"I'd take that as a yes," Zandra said.

"You'll be happy together," I said. "But if you ever need a babysitter, you know where we are."

Smoke nipped my booping snooter then zoomed up and settled on Acer's shoulder.

"Well, it looks like I'm raising a phoenix." Acer laughed as she petted Smoke, who crooned while he leaned against her hand.

After a round of goodbyes, Acer stepped outside. She turned. "Juno, have you got a minute?"

"Of course." I walked outside to join her and Smoke. "Already got a date for when you want me to babysit?"

"It's not that. I wanted to say again how sorry I am that Erig cheated you. Although I'm glad he did because it meant you got involved in this case. If it weren't for you and Zandra, I'm not sure it would have been solved."

"Those are kind words, but the angels would have figured it out."

"I'm not so sure. I enjoy my job, but there's a lot more paperwork than I thought there would be, and so many rules to follow. You had none of that holding you back. You saw a problem, and you fixed it. You figured out the mystery. I'll be forever grateful to you."

"You're welcome. Maybe next time, don't keep secrets. Then we could have solved this in a day."

She ducked her head. "Lesson learned."

I turned back to the bookstore. "Have fun with Smoke."

"Wait! There's something else. I looked into the request you made to Erig. I couldn't get your gold back, but I spoke to his researchers."

I faced her. "Oh! I didn't realize he'd kept records of our conversation."

Acer arched an eyebrow. "Erig kept records about everything. He'd say you never knew what information could be useful. What he meant was that he may be able to get some information he could exploit."

"That sounds like Erig. Your father told me he couldn't retrieve the magic I sought, though. I wasn't surprised. It was no easy task."

"He lied." Acer rolled her eyes. "Erig did that whenever he discovered a treasure that was worth a fortune."

My heart beat faster. "You mean, he found my magic?"

"He did. At least, some of it. A package arrived this morning with his name on it, and I looked inside. I don't know for certain, but I'm assuming he'd have gotten in contact with you and demanded a larger fee than you'd agreed on."

"We'd already agreed on ten percent of my assets. That's a considerable amount."

"Not to him. Erig would have demanded more to see how desperate you were to get your paws on this magic."

I wrinkled my booping snooter. "It's been said before, but your father was a monster."

"I couldn't agree more." Acer pulled a small cardboard box from her pocket. "I hope this is what you were looking for." She crouched and set it on the ground in front of me.

I stared at the box. I'd given up hope of getting anything useful from Erig, but here it was, right in front of me.

"Are you okay? Need a hand with the lid?"

"I'm perfect. Just surprised."

"Call this a thank you for helping stop my insane family from killing each other."

"That's quite some thank you. You don't know what this means to me. Would you do the honors?" I gestured at the box, my legs shaky.

Acer lifted off the lid to reveal a small purple stone. She frowned. "It doesn't look like much. Is it the wrong thing? I can always ask the researchers to keep looking. No charge."

I stepped forward and lowered my head over the stone. As soon as my booping snooter got within a few inches of it, the stone glowed, and a wave of warmth flooded over me. "This is exactly what I was looking for."

"I'm glad. I felt terrible after learning about what Erig did to you."

I looked up, tears in my eyes, and cat-smiled at Acer. "Thank you."

"Juno. Magic friend!" Smoke squawked and almost slipped off Acer's shoulder.

"I need to get this little one down for a nap." Acer gently touched my head. "Before I shut Erig's business, I wanted to do this. I hope it helps with whatever you're looking for."

"It will. It does. Thank you again." I nudged the lid onto the box, and sat with it outside the bookstore, watching Acer and Smoke walk away.

Smoke flapped a wing at me and blasted out an impressive fireball.

I couldn't have dreamed this twisted mystery would turn out any better. There were loose ends to tie up, particularly whether Gaian and his environmental bikers were everything they appeared to be. But for now, Crimson Cove felt safe. The murders were solved, and I'd acquired more of my marvelous magic.

"Juno, get in here!" Zandra called from the open door of the bookstore. "Vorana's brought out smoked salmon for you and Sage. Hurry! Or she'll eat yours."

I nodded at her then touched the box with my paw. And the day was only getting better.

About Author

K.E. O'Connor (Karen) is a mystery author living in the beautiful British countryside. She loves all things mystery, animals, and cake.

If you want to practice spells, solve a few murders, and spend time with amazing witches and their talking familiars, join her weekly newsletter.

Sign up today.

Newsletter: https://BookHip.com/GXDVFRA

Website: www.keoconnor.com/writing

Facebook: www.facebook.com/keoconnorauthor

Also By

Witch Haven: Welcome to Witch Haven, where nothing is what it seems. Meet four fabulous witches as they struggle with their destinies, deal with misfiring magic, murder, and the Magic Council.

Crypt Witches: Meet Tempest Crypt, a witch who swallows demons, and Wiggles, her mini talking hellhound, while you enjoy magical murder and intrigue.

Lorna Shadow: A cozy mystery series set in the fun world of a personal assistant who sees ghosts. Meet Lorna, her ditzy sidekick, Helen, and Flipper, the dog who senses ghosts, as they solve crimes and save the day.

Holly Holmes: An adorable cozy culinary mystery series set in the beautiful village of Audley St. Mary. Each book is full of treats, murder, and twists. Join Holly and Meatball, her clue-hunting dog, as they solve murders and eat cake.

www.ingramcontent.com/pod-product-compliance
Lightning Source LLC
Chambersburg PA
CBHW050808190726
48285CB00005B/1838